THOSE WHO DREAM

THOSE WHO DREAM

A NOVEL

BY TIM STAFFORD

Franklin Park Press

The characters, names and events as well as all places, incidents, organizations and dialog in this novel are either the products of the writer's imagination or are used fictitiously.

Visit the author's website at timstafford.wordpress.com

We were like those who dreamed.
Our mouths were filled with laughter,
our tongues with songs of joy.

— Psalm 126:1–2

1   AT THE MISSION

The mission's building was an ugly two-story, blue-gray plaster structure built right up to the sidewalk, with a neon "Jesus Saves" sign hanging under the eaves. Nothing about it would stand out to somebody driving by except the constant presence of loiterers. Right now two men sat side by side on the sidewalk, their heels pulled up and their backs against the building. Three other men stood by the parking bay, bent as though the wind and damp had warped their backs. And there was Gila, a small, silent woman with a face like an apple doll, who spent her days at or near the mission. At the moment she was walking up and down the sidewalk, acknowledging no one.

Nowhere else in Santa Rosa were you likely to see people dallying like this—not panhandling, not pursuing any business at all, but simply congregating. The lure, of course, was the restroom inside and the nightly meal and bed. But was it also the atmosphere? Kent thought so. He had certainly felt it when he first came here after his divorce. He wasn't an addict, but he was a man who had lost everything. The mission's no-questions acceptance had folded him in.

He felt it now, looking at the building from his car. A deep affection welled up in him, not only for the way he had been treated, but for the building itself—this decrepit structure dedicated to men who had nothing.

Kent sometimes thought that if the mission disappeared one night, vaporized without a trace along with the 100 or more men who took shelter there, not a soul in Santa Rosa would feel the loss. For the city government, for the local businesses, even for the churches, it would be nothing. They would shake off the memory like a dog getting out of the ocean. Nobody cared about these men; they were a problem, and their disappearance would mean one less problem. He had felt that about himself.

* * *

The mission's reception was a bare room about the size of a broom closet. Kent spoke to a man behind a glass window whose powerful arms were covered with tattoos. He asked Kent's name.

Momentarily surprised, Kent paused. "You don't know me?" Then, "No, of course you don't. We haven't met, have we? I'm Kent Spires. I'm here to see Jake."

The receptionist introduced himself as Elvis. He had a chipped tooth that left a gap in the front of his face, but even so, he was a handsome man with a fine head of hair, a bronzed face, and a jagged scar down one cheek. "Will Jake know who you are?"

Kent smiled. "Oh, yeah. He'll know."

The mission had speakers placed throughout the building. Elvis called Jake to come to the front desk to meet "Ken Spire." Kent let it go.

Of course the men in the program didn't know him. He spent all his time raising money nowadays. Or failing to raise money.

While he stood waiting in the tiny reception a bald-headed, coal-black man appeared from the inner door. He held his arms wide, flashed a toothy smile, and wrapped Kent in a bear hug. Knox Johnson had become deputy director of the New Life program last year. He had come into the program with apparent brain damage, unable to stitch two sentences together. *Now look at him*, Kent thought.

"Hey Elvis," Knox said to the tattooed receptionist when he had untangled himself from Kent. "You know who this is? This is Mr. Kent Spires. That's *Spires*, not *Spire* or whatever you said. He has been the man running this place for the longest time, way before I ever came on. He made this place. You should know Mr. Kent. He is one good man."

Elvis came out from behind the glass to shake Kent's hand. "Hey, I'm sorry I didn't recognize you," he said. "I didn't put the name together."

"Elvis here is Phase 2, aren't you, Elvis?"

"No, Knox, don't you remember that I chose to leave?"

"Chose to leave" was the phrase they used for men who violated the seven unbreakable rules: drugs, alcohol, fighting, and so on. "I'm glad you came back," Kent said. "That's a good sign."

"Where you been, Kent?" Knox wanted to know. "Jake's having a hard time."

Just at that moment Jake appeared behind Knox, who turned when he saw Kent looking over his shoulder. Knox shrank his face in embarrassment. "Hey, I apologize, Jake; I should leave it to you to tell Kent how you are."

Jake did not respond verbally; he shrugged. He was a burly man with a light-brown Viking beard, like an outsized version of Kent. Ordinarily he was a very robust character, brimming with energy. Not now, obviously. It was a shock to see him so reduced.

"Jake," Kent said, feeling suddenly shy. "It's good to see you. Can we go up to your office?" He was Jake's boss but found it hard to tell him or anybody what to do.

Ordinarily Jake would bustle along; now he walked like someone whose shoes hurt. They clambered up the dark linoleum-tile stairs to the long upstairs corridor, passing doorways where bunk beds filled up the space floor to ceiling.

Jake's office had no more atmosphere than Kent's: a Giants poster on the wall and a gaudy golden plastic softball trophy on his shelf. Kent knew vaguely that Jake had been a star athlete before he became an addict, but they had never talked about it.

Usually they discussed the men in New Life. The program was like a living thing, breathing on its own rhythm, sometimes whole and hearty, sometimes sick and gasping for air. It changed with the seasons; it changed with the wind. When Kent asked Jake about it, his face was unreadable; he showed no expression, but he looked off to his right. "I guess the house is all right."

It occurred to Kent that he had been too filled up with his own problems to really see Jake's. And vice versa. Jake probably had no idea of Kent's budget worries. Jake probably didn't know how many of the mission's supporters wanted to let him go.

"And how are you, Jake?"

Jake looked impatient with the question. "I'm not good, to be perfectly truthful. You know that Krystle went to see her mom."

That seemed innocent enough. "When does she come back?"

Jake shrugged, a gesture so eloquently despairing that words were unnecessary. Kent raised his eyebrows in an equally eloquent question. "Some of the neighbors told her I'm a rapist," Jake explained. "Their kids were ragging on Reggie. You know she's sensitive."

Kent grimaced. It didn't really surprise him. People were cruel, and Jake *had* talked too much to that reporter. This was not the time to remind him of that, however. Kent reminded himself to shed his own worries and take an interest in Jake. "She didn't say when she was coming back?"

Jake shook his head.

"Have you talked to her?"

"Yeah. We Skype every night."

"And how does that go?"

"It's not great. She doesn't really talk. She just shoves Reggie at me and tells him to talk to Daddy."

Kent wanted to sympathize. He remembered when Alice told him he had to move out so long ago.

"You see why I don't want you to talk to any more reporters?" Kent asked. As soon as he said it, he wished he could take the words back.

Once again Jake did not react. Normally he would start defending himself before Kent completed his sentence. The passivity stabbed Kent. The real Jake always talked; you couldn't shut him up.

"I've got troubles too," Kent said. "The board is upset with me. People aren't giving. Donations stopped the day the lawsuit was in the paper. And what can I do? I'm defending you, of course. I know you didn't do anything. But it's hard to prove a negative."

He was already saying too much, and it wasn't helpful. Kent plunged ahead anyway, telling Jake that he thought it was a hopeful sign that the lawyer had offered to settle; surely he had figured out by now that he wasn't going to win the case or get any money out of the mission. Jake just grunted.

Kent asked again how things were at the house. "Anybody graduating?"

The New Life program took ten months, and more dropped out or "chose to leave" than ever graduated. When a man was in his final month, they all watched him closely, as though holding their breath.

"There's Michael," Jake said. "He just has to learn his Bible verses."

To graduate, you had to recite four Scripture passages. Michael was compliant, but he said he couldn't hold anything in his memory. He was sixty years old; maybe his mind was shot from all the alcohol. If he was the best hope for a graduation, the program wasn't thriving.

Kent stood up. "Jake, somehow, with God's help, we'll get through this. The lawsuit isn't going anywhere. It's just nonsense. We have to be patient until justice is done. And pray."

It occurred to him that he sounded like the old men on the governing board. *Just pray, pray more.*

"Your wife will see the light; she will come home. Our donors will see the light too and start giving again. The only thing is, I don't know when."

Jake had also stood, but he continued looking off to one side, not at Kent. It was astonishing how bad news can weigh down a person. Kent wished he could do something to lift Jake out of his hole, but he didn't know what that would be.

Kent realized he had more that he needed to say. He reached out to touch Jake's shoulder. "Jake, I need to remind you, we have to cut down any expenses we can. Don't spend money if you can possibly help it."

That jolted Jake; you could see it run through his body. "I'm not. You told me and I'm not."

"Well, I know you're trying, but there are still some expenses coming through."

"I can't stop everything. I've made promises. Guys have made plans."

Some of the men needed help paying off fines so they could get their drivers' licenses back. Some needed help paying tuition to culinary school. They needed dental work. They needed eyeglasses. Jake ordinarily had a lot of discretion on these expenses. They had always done whatever they could to set the men on a solid foundation.

"I know," Kent said. He cringed at having to say it. "But even that. We don't have it."

"Not even if I've told them I will?"

Kent shook his head. "We can't help it, Jake. There's no money coming in. People have just stopped giving. Until that changes we can't do anything. We have to try to keep the doors open, that's all."

Jake looked like he wanted to cry; his mouth was twisted. He said nothing.

"I'm sorry, Jake. Keep your head up. It will turn around. God has his hand on this place, and he's always provided. He will again."

It sounded like a cliché coming out of his mouth. Kent wondered whether he really believed it, and if he didn't, whether he should stop saying it.

* * *

On the way out Kent stopped at Knox Johnson's office, located just behind the reception. He loved Knox. The floor of his small room was crammed with stacks of papers, cardboard boxes, new backpacks still in their plastic bags. Who knew what all that clutter was doing in there? Knox was busy talking to one of the men. He put the conversation on hold and came to the door.

"I don't mean to interrupt," Kent said. "Just wanted to say good-bye."

Knox gestured with his eyes and the tilt of his head. "He's bad, isn't he? Just like I told you?"

Kent did not agree or disagree. His impulse was to tell Knox that if Jake was bad, he was worse, but he knew he couldn't do that. "It's a hard time, Knox, for lots of reasons. I think he'll be okay."

"He told me," Knox said, "that he wished you would take up that offer and just get out of this old building. I was surprised he would say that, you know? I told myself he is pretty bad."

A developer had come by a few weeks before and made an offer to buy the building. It seemed financially appealing, but Kent had turned it down. He had a sense that this property was more than a building that you could just sell and leave behind.

Jake took a less exalted view. He had to deal with the plumbing and the leaking roof and the bedbugs infesting the walls. It came as a disappointment, however, that Jake would bring up their difference of opinion to his staff. They were supposed to keep a united front.

"Oh, well, don't worry about that," Kent said, waving his hand through the air as though harassing a fly. "He's just frustrated. I don't blame him."

Kent had expected to leave after seeing Jake, but standing in the entryway he found that he didn't want to. The house lured him to stay. "You got time for a cup of coffee?" he asked Knox.

Knox finished his business and they walked down a narrow corridor that opened into the dining room and kitchen. These appeared to have been outfitted at a garage sale. Mismatched chairs were set up around half a dozen Formica tables. Hanging lamps with woven sisal lampshades lit the room—a gift from a visiting missionary, years ago. The walls seemed to have been rubbed with an oily rag. Kent pulled out a chair for Knox and went to pour himself a cup from a massive stain-less-steel coffee urn. While he did, Michael Brown wandered into the room, looking as though he was dreaming.

"Michael," Kent said. "Want to join us?"

It seemed to take Michael a moment to focus on what was being said, and then to look at Kent and recognize him. "All right," Michael said. He was a supremely quiet man.

Michael had gone to UCLA, which made him the most educated man in the house, including staff. He looked old. His body had a stooped, worn look, though his skin was starkly white, unlike most of the sun-grilled veterans you saw at the house.

"I understand you are almost ready to graduate."

Michael leaned forward over the table as though he had been invited to inspect a rare butterfly. "Who said that?" he asked, sounding genuinely curious.

"Jake told me, just now."

A tiny smile grooved Michael's mouth. "I don't know about that," he said.

"He said all you had to do was to memorize your Scriptures."

Michael nodded his head. "True. That's true."

Michael had been stuck at this point for eight months. He claimed that his mind went blank from one day to the next. Maybe it was the alcohol he had drunk; or maybe he was just scared of the wide world that waited for him outside the door. For a 60-year-old man, that was not inconsiderable.

If it were up to Kent, he would have found a way to graduate him. A sober life didn't depend on being able to recite some verses. Jake, however, had come up through the program, and he treated its rules as having sacred power. Perhaps they did for him. Kent let Jake run the program according to his own lights.

Kent was about to ask Michael whether he had heard from his mother, who lived in a Florida nursing home. Just then a hand clapped him on the back, wrapping around his neck. Leo sat down next to him.

Leo was a short, brawny man whose receding hair was combed straight back. Leo wore lederhosen—every day. He had done it for years. "What are you doing here?" Kent asked with a smile.

"Where else would I be?" Leo said.

"Leo came into the program what, three weeks ago?" Knox said politely.

"How come everybody knows you, Leo?" Elvis asked. Unable to escape the pull of a conversation, he had followed them into the dining room, and now he took a seat.

"Leo goes way back with us; don't you, Leo?" Kent said.

"Oh, yeah; way back," Leo said and gave a guttural bark that passed for a laugh.

Elvis was looking from side to side, as though waiting for someone to explain the joke. "You been in the program before?" he asked.

Leo barked again. Knox quietly mentioned that Leo had started the program some time ago but had taken time out from it. "Now you're back to finish, aren't you, Leo?" Knox nodded and smiled as he said it.

Leo gave another bark with a look of satisfied enjoyment on his face. "First time I came in," he said, "that was '08, I was just sick. I wasn't sick and tired of being sick and tired. I was just sick, and I came in and puked my guts out and lay on my bunk sweating and itching and rolling around for three or four days, and then I felt better and began to eat again and I thought I had it all fixed. I was back on the street in a week and using in two. No good.

"I came back within the year, sick and tired of being sick and tired. You know? The detox was terrible again, and I almost didn't get through it, but I did, and then I knew I needed God. I was a terrible holy roller, wasn't I, Kent? You remember?"

"I remember," Kent said. "I really thought you had it."

"And I did, until I stopped going to chapel, stopped going to church. I lost God as quick as I had found him. This guy came in with some crystal meth, claiming it was really good stuff, and I fell back into the hole.

"After that I was on the street for about a year. I was bad. I nearly died that time. I had an OD that scared the bejeesus out of me, so I started going to AA, and I met some of the guys from the mission who were going to the same meeting. You remember them, Kent. Robert? And Ronnie? I don't know where they are now. They graduated but I don't know what became of them. They said I should join the mission again, and I did, and this time I didn't really have to detox because I was already pretty clean. Once I got here I went all in with the twelve steps, sometimes two meetings a day, and I worked them until I really felt I had yielded my life to a higher power, and I had made amends and all that. I was serious."

Kent was nodding happily. The whole cluster of men, sitting close to each other around the chipped table, seemed to lean closer. "You were," Kent said. "And you graduated, didn't you?"

"I did. I got out and got a job..."

"What kind of job?" Elvis wanted to know.

"Concrete. I'd done that since I was a kid. With my dad. That was in 2012, and within a year they had me running my own crew. So I did okay, and I went to meetings five nights a week. I had a girlfriend, and..."

"You go to church?" Elvis asked.

"No. Well, sometimes. The girlfriend didn't want to. She liked to sleep in on Sundays."

"What was her name?"

"Vera. Vera Rogin. You know her?"

Elvis shook his head.

"How long were you clean and sober, Leo?" Knox wanted to know. He had a lovely, soft way of speaking, almost caressing the words. Kent thought to himself that he could listen to Knox talk all day.

"For two years. Then I started smoking dope, because if you've ever done concrete you know what happens to your knees. I told myself I wouldn't use anything harder, but you know how that goes. In no time, I was the worst I've ever been. Girlfriend kicked me out. I lost my job."

"How long ago was that?" Elvis asked.

"About a year."

"You been on the street for a year, then?"

"Yeah. No, two years. Lived in a tent. Well, some of the time my nephew let me sleep in a little travel trailer on his property. But that got burned up. I was smoking. Lucky I got out alive. Most of the time I was living by the creek in a little pup tent. I had a terrible cough that wouldn't quit. Too much, man. Finally I just decided I had to give in, give in all the way this time. So I'm back. It's different this time. I know I need AA and I know I need God, and I've got to put them together."

"You need a good church," Knox said in a tone as soft as spun cotton. "Where they teach God's word."

"You're right," Leo said. "That's what I'm looking for."

While they were talking, one of the kitchen white coats carried in a tray of doughnuts. He set the tray on a serving table by the kitchen bay. "These are pretty fresh," he said to everybody and nobody. "Somebody from Tan's brought them in last night." Elvis got up first, ambled over, and came back with a napkin full of sticky, chocolate-iced donuts. Watching him wolf them down while leaning over the table to keep the icing off his chest, the rest of the men got up one by one to get some for themselves.

* * *

Driving home, Kent reflected on why he had found the conversation so comforting. It should be depressing to talk to a man in his fourth go-round in the program. You couldn't be confident that Leo would do any better this time. Not to mention Michael, stuck in the final phase of the program with little sign of movement. But failure was so common in the world of addicts that Kent hardly noticed it anymore. What cheered Kent was that they were still trying. What cheered Kent was that the mission gave them room to keep trying. It wasn't like the courts or the DMV, where your record always traveled with you, and your options got narrower the farther down you went. In the mission you could always start again, no matter how you had failed. Kent had designed it that way.

He had probably looked as beat as Michael when he first arrived at the mission, having lost his marriage and his kids and his calling to be a pastor, feeling so bone-sick he could barely stumble in the door. The job had been a stopgap, filling in for the director who had suffered a heart attack but would soon be back. Kent actually remembered Leo from that time. Wearing those lederhosen. Young, cocky, sure of himself. Nobody could tell Leo anything then. It never occurred to Kent to try. He had no advice for anybody.

The old director never came back; he died of congestive heart failure. Kent attended the memorial, where people shook his hand and assumed that he had taken over the job, even though he hadn't been named. The mission at the time was a shelter for bums, for derelicts, for winos. Those were the faces that came to Kent's mind when he remembered those days: men without teeth, men with yellow eyes, men in three layers of clothes, men milling aimlessly and passively until something invisible tipped and they had a bloody fight on their hands. The men got a welcome, they got food and a bed; there was one leaking, moldy shower they could use to clean up. Some of them slept all day. Enforcement of rules was sporadic. Volunteers were lenient and staff overworked. Some of the men were still using right in the dorm and hardly bothering to hide the fact. You couldn't say it was a good program when he arrived; you couldn't even honestly call it a program. It did have something, though. It treated people like they belonged. It was so different from what he had just experienced at his church.

He made up his mind that he never would lose that atmosphere. People talked about AA, how its honesty and acceptance made it so much better than church, but AA was a one-hour meeting. At the mission they had to live together, eat together, sleep together.

He had built the program by trial and error. Some of it came from his experience as a pastor, and some of it came by comparing notes with other rescue missions, but mostly he experimented. He tried to listen when the men complained. People have a deeply engrained habit of not listening to addicts because they are so quick to find fault with everybody but themselves. But sometimes they are right.

Kent was driving through six-lane traffic passing under the 101 overpass. It was late afternoon and the sun was right in his eyes, scattering off his dirty windshield. He hardly knew where he was, thinking about the mission and how it had changed. In the last five years, give or take a year, they had reached a point where the program actually ran itself, and ran well. There was discipline and also grace. Kent had moved on to administration, which needed to be done, and he didn't get to the old building often enough.

He was deathly afraid of losing the whole thing.

2   THE FACEBOOK WORLD

That evening, on semi-rural Lovejoy Lane, Kent searched Facebook for news of his children. He was not an adept in the Facebook world; he never posted or friended anyone, and he had no idea how to control the settings. Occasionally he got on to see what Andy and Suzanne had posted.

Neither of his children was married yet; their posts were of kayaking expeditions and friends' birthday parties rather than of babies and family gatherings. Most of the people on Suzanne's page were girls, people he supposed she knew from college. She had recently gone up in a hot-air balloon for somebody's graduation. He didn't recognize any of them. He saw few young men, and none whose face repeated. That was disappointing. He was of a mind to hope that marriage would change things between him and Suzanne, that she would introduce her intended to him and they would hit it off. On the other hand, Suzanne might tell her fiancé the same stories about her father that she had heard from her mother. Kent had no way to challenge those. He didn't even know what they were.

In one of Suzanne's posted pictures he could see through her adult face to the underlying little girl he had loved so helplessly. Kent stared at it for several minutes, then reached up over his desk for a three-ring binder, filled with old photos in plastic sleeves. He flipped pages until he found a photo when Suzanne and Andy were still toddlers. Both carried huge grins on their faces, as though they had done something deliciously naughty. Dear God, he had been happy then. At the time he thought Alice still loved him, and maybe she did. He didn't know exactly when Alice had turned away.

Kent remembered a scene from a later time, after the divorce. He had gone to pick the kids up on Saturday morning. He parked at the curb, because Alice never let him come in her house or even to the door. He had to wait in the car until she made up her mind to bring the kids out. This time they didn't come. For ten or fifteen minutes he waited. He thought about going to the door. He thought about honking the horn. He didn't do it because he didn't want to get into an argument in front of the kids.

Eventually, after something like half an hour, the door opened and Andy and Suzanne straggled out, carrying backpacks. As soon as they saw the car they ran toward him, jubilant, and threw themselves in. There had been plenty of love in the early years. His alternate weekends kept him alive. He didn't find it hard to adore his kids, and they sustained him when everything else in his life was difficult.

It had been okay until they turned into teenagers. Then they became busy with activities—sports, camps, overnights with friends—and Kent became more chauffeur than companion. When he went to pick them up at their mother's house, they were now the ones who stalled, dithering in their rooms while he parked at the curb and called their mother. She didn't necessarily pick up, and when she did she claimed that they didn't want to come. She said she didn't encourage them or discourage them to go with him; they were old enough to decide for themselves.

He believed her when she said they didn't want to come. He disrupted the rhythms of their lives, and perhaps he asked too many questions. He wasn't sure, however, that Alice was 100% truthful when she said she didn't discourage them from coming.

Now, fourteen years after the divorce, he was trying to get to know his kids again. Andy was perfectly cordial, but he taught high school chemistry and was busy. He often couldn't find the time to meet. Suzanne, just out of college, was pricklier. They usually connected for birthdays or holidays, but it felt like she found it a bother.

So he went to Facebook. At least it gave him something. He always felt furtive searching through his kids' timelines. The pictures they posted were of celebrations he was not invited to attend. He spied on the bright poses and brilliant smiles without their knowledge. As far as he could remember, neither one had ever once posted about him.

* * *

Kent got up from the computer to stare out of the picture window of his living room. The view across his lawn took in an apple orchard, now dressed in green, and far beyond it the dark bulk of Mt. St. Helena. It was a lovely vista, the reason he had rented this house in the first place. He still spent time most evenings looking out through this window.

Lovejoy Lane was in unincorporated Sebastopol, a fifteen-minute drive and a world apart from Santa Rosa. The wine business had changed both cities, boosting everybody's business, though in different ways. Santa Rosa, a county seat, had grown hospitals and shopping malls. The west county had become hip and organic, defiantly iconoclastic. Kent liked the west county, against his better judgment.

Books dominated the room, indeed the house. Many were stacked on tables or beside chairs, and he had covered the available walls with shelves. Books overflowed these, with some stacked horizontally on top of neat vertical rows. His bedroom, similarly, had bookshelves covering two walls. That was where he kept his Lewis collection.

He had first discovered C.S. Lewis in high school, when he stumbled on *Perelandra* in a pastor's library. Kent had read plenty of science fiction before then, but nothing remotely like *Perelandra*. Lewis' mind worked in a way completely unlike that of anybody Kent knew.

He chose to attend Westmont College partly because he saw a course on Lewis in the catalog. His senior thesis focused on Lewis' understanding of joy. Kent had every book that C.S. Lewis had ever written, and a considerable collection of books by Lewis' friends, such as Owen Barclay and J.R.R. Tolkien. He had collected less omnivorously from critical books or biographies, but he still had two broad shelves. Kent was capable of overwhelming people with his knowledge of and love for Lewis. His ex, Alice, had told him that he bored people to tears—and she included herself in that.

In his life as a pastor he had been forced to put his love for Lewis aside, because most of the people he served had no interest in it. At the mission this was even more strictly true: the men for whom he felt such kinship could not begin to understand his love for books, let alone the clear, ice-cold running water he found in Lewis' rational prose. For the most part, Kent kept his love for Lewis a secret, and as a secret it grew keener, attached to his blood supply like a slippery leech.

* * *

Scrolling down deeper on his daughter's timeline, Kent came to a post from Alice. She was standing on a sailboat in brilliant sun. It was just she, with nothing to provide clues to why or where the picture was made. Seeing her with a squinting smile, dressed in a skimpy shirt and jeans and bare feet, provoked in Kent a mélange of powerful feelings: anger, despair, nostalgia. Alice was still an attractive woman.

He had loved her, no doubt about that. Maybe he still did.

He clicked on her name and instantly entered a universe where he knew he had no business. He felt he was stalking her, but nevertheless he went from one photo to the next, always instantly finding her in a group, and then trying to identify the people she was with. A few of them he recognized; they had been his friends at one time.

People had to choose after a divorce. You couldn't really stay close to both parties. Kent had made no effort to compete. He found a new church where no one knew him. He moved out of Santa Rosa, to rural outskirts where you only saw your neighbors when you drove past them. He didn't even own a dog. His only continuity with his old life was the Saturday morning men's Bible study he continued to attend. But none of those men had been close to Alice, and she never came up in conversation.

For years they had done business over the finances of child support and the logistics of weekend visits. Now that the kids were grown, those encounters had ended. Kent steered clear of Alice's life, and she of his.

You thought that if you kept your distance it would minimize the pain. Fourteen years later he didn't know. The pain came nonetheless. You had no choice but to live through it.

Judging by her Facebook account, Alice had a full life. She painted and did ceramic sculptures, which seemed to have grown steadily more important to her. For every picture of the kids, there were ten of charity auctions and wine and cheese receptions, clusters of well-dressed people grinning at the camera. Kent also saw photos of her artwork, which he had given up on learning to like long ago. It seemed to him that there was a violent subtext in everything she did: bite marks, dissections, eviscerations. He didn't care for it, but somebody did, apparently.

Kent did his best to think charitably of Alice, but whenever he saw her photo or heard her name, the old wounds reopened. Deep in his chest there survived a lump of resentment and of self-vindication. Every divorce has two sides, of course, and he didn't deny he bore part of the responsibility for letting the two of them drift apart. But nothing, he thought, could excuse what Alice had done.

His children had no idea. And they shouldn't know. They didn't need to drink the same poison he ingested day in and day out.

It was painful to relive these feelings, which Facebook stoked, but he found himself unable to stop scrolling down, poking the wound. All these smiling people.

* * *

All right, Kent thought, *I'm lonely. I miss having a woman in my life, and that confuses everything. I know what Alice is like, and what she did to me, but when I look at her picture I still drift into dreaming of that life we had.*

Tears came into his eyes. He had been so happy then. Falsely so, but he would gladly fall back into the same illusion if he could. They'd had no money, but they had few responsibilities, either. They got in the car and went to the beach. They made chili and invited another couple over to watch a movie. They slept in on Saturday mornings and made love.

When the children came, they took turns getting up with them and changing their diapers. They held them, they rocked them, they pushed them endless miles in the stroller.

It must have been during those years that Alice began to build resentment against him and against the church. She didn't tell him about that, or at least—he had to be truthful with himself—he didn't hear her. As a young pastor he had loved his work and loved coming home to his little family. He was so happy he couldn't dream that Alice was equally unhappy, as she must have been.

Each one of Alice's Facebook photos brought pain like a badly stubbed toe, shooting into him. And yet he kept looking.

Then he came to a picture of Meg Fletcher. He had not seen her in ages, but she jumped at him. Meg was a tall, athletic woman with dark hair framing a wide and almost exaggerated face. Plush lips. Large nose and wide eyes to match. The photo seemed to have been taken in Alice's studio, for there were unframed canvases on the wall behind Meg, who had her arms stretched around Alice and a balding man he didn't know. In the picture Meg looked twice the size of Alice, though she wasn't in the least bit fat.

He had not seen Meg since the divorce, so far as he could remember. She and her then-husband Greg had been in a couples group with him and Alice at Sonoma Grace. The Fletchers' marriage had unraveled at almost the same time as Kent's and Alice's. Neither dissolution had been graceful. The Fletchers performed brutal arguments in front of the group, with tears and nasty verbal cuts that left everyone else helpless. The strife of two marriages breaking had been too much for the group, which also dissolved.

Kent clicked on Meg. Her husband had been a police officer, a prosaic, silent man who always left Kent wondering what he was thinking. Greg and Meg. Kent had liked Meg, who was talkative and friendly and eager to help. He never knew their children very well; they had three, he thought.

Had he ever felt an attraction to Meg? He might have repressed it: a married pastor would want to. And he had been so thoroughly content with Alice that he perhaps never consulted his feelings about other women.

Certainly, he felt something now as he looked at her photo. *I'm just lonely*, he reminded himself. *I don't know this woman.* But that didn't stop him from continuing to explore her timeline.

He scrolled down and saw pictures that might be of her children: a blond young man, slightly pudgy, towering over Meg; two young women staring adoringly into each other's eyes; a family photo in front of a Christmas tree featuring a woman who looked very much like Meg, with a toddler and an infant in her lap and a husband (presumably) hooking his arm around her.

Meg's bio said she was the owner of Wine Country Products. He clicked on the logo and found spa products in Sonoma County lavender and olive oil, plus oddities like cabernet flour and a variety of lavender-colored garments. He couldn't see any way to order these off the web; it looked like her business distributed to local retailers.

Meg and Alice had been friends, but he found just the one picture shared between them. They must not be close any more. It would be interesting to catch up with Meg after all these years. He wondered how she had recovered from the divorce, and what her relationship with her kids was like.

Deep within his solitude he discovered a tremendous longing. He understood that it really had little to do with Meg. Almost any woman could provoke such a feeling. Nevertheless.

He clicked to make a friend request.

3 MEG AT WORK

The Brickyard was an attractive retail space in Santa Rosa that had never really worked. Despite a parking lot across the street on one side and a parking garage across the street on the other, you drove up and didn't see any parking next to the stores. You had to *cross the street*. That extra effort was a bridge too far for the average shopper.

Meg Fletcher's Wine Country Products wasn't geared for retail, however, so the Brickyard was a good space for her: visible, tasteful, and inexpensive to rent. Meg was working there today, striding around and studying the products displayed in the 400 square feet of her shop. She had placed them as they might appear in a spa or a tasting room.

Meg liked working close to downtown Santa Rosa, near the mall, and she particularly appreciated the clean, modern appearance of the Brickyard. Now that the economy had rebounded and wine tourism was going nuts, she could probably use more space, at least for storing product. She was reluctant to move, however. The Brickyard had brought her luck.

As a young woman married right after high school, she had worked in a vet's office handling cats and dogs and dispensing scientific diet dog food. She didn't hate it; it was just work, which slid off her life like snow on a steep roof. She liked animals, and she liked the people who came to the vet because they, too, cared for an animal.

After the divorce, she needed more income, and at a friend's suggestion, got her real estate license. Only an idiot could fail to make money in that pre-2008 market, and Meg was not an idiot. She was smart and vigorous and she genuinely liked helping people. Real estate picked her up from her broken marriage and helped her mend. She kept her own schedule and had flexibility for the kids. She did not miss Greg.

That was when she acquired Wine Country Products. Alf Rostov, a friend of her ex's, had come on to her after the divorce. He was older than she by some distance. He kept asking her out, and Meg eventually accepted though she had no romantic ideas about Alf. She simply liked to be seen with a man. Over many dinners they talked about real estate and business, and he told her about his struggles with Wine Country Products, which he owned. It wasn't a good business for him. He lacked a sense of style and customer service. He had practically run it into the ground. Meg liked the business; she thought it had potential. Purely on a hunch and because she had money to invest, she bought it off him for cheap and applied her enthusiasm to making it thrive.

Her timing was great, because nobody made any money in property after the real estate market crashed in 2008. Meg pivoted into full-time involvement with Wine Country Products, which grew like a well-watered vine. She liked it better than she ever had real estate. In real estate you are a slave to the client. When you own your own company, you are truly independent. Each morning she unlocked the door to her store with pleasure. Clients came in and she could seat them in comfortable overstuffed chairs and offer them a cup of lavender-scented tea, just as if they were visiting a spa.

Meg smiled as she thought of this, patting the soft leather sofa. The only thing bothering her at the moment was her son, Brian, the lunk currently seated in a windowless space in the back room, playing video games on the expensive computer he had insisted she buy. She had thought that with his interest in computers he would be a natural to start up internet sales, but as far as she could tell he had done nothing on it.

Meg got up to stand in the doorway to the back room, watching him. She loved her son's eyes: they were soulful, she thought. But he slumped, and his clothes never seemed to fit properly. For a large person, someone with potential weight problems, clothes were critical. They had to be stylish, and most of all, they had to fit. She had tried to pass this on to Brian, but he showed no interest.

"Did you get to Osmosis?" she asked.

"Not yet," he answered without looking up, his thumbs continuing their work.

"So when are you planning to go?"

"Not sure."

She pulled up a chair alongside him and put a hand on his arm. "Brian, I pay you to make these calls."

He glanced at her. "Mom, I don't like you to micromanage me. Now quit."

"I am not micromanaging you. If you worked for anybody else you would know that. I am your boss and I deserve to know what you are doing."

"Fine," he said, continuing his game. "I'll work for somebody else."

"Who would hire you?"

"Dad said he would. He wants me to come over there. I told him I was committed to you, but if you don't want me, just say so."

She snorted. "Yeah, you would love working for your dad. I can see that."

Greg had retired from the police force and now worked at a body armor factory in Petaluma. Meg didn't know how much hiring he could do. She knew he talked big.

She left Brian and went into the display room, sitting down on one of the comfortable gray leather chairs, surrounded by shelves and tables of spa products. At the moment it didn't matter whether Brian made calls or not. Really, it was better for her to make those calls herself. What she wanted was for Brian to start up internet sales. It was a field where she was quite at sea. She could learn, of course, but she didn't want to. She wanted Brian to do it. It would be good for him.

Meg returned to the back room. "What about the internet?"

He was more slouched than ever. In the dim light he looked like a troll about to eviscerate its prey. "What about it?"

"Do you have a plan?"

"For what?"

"For internet sales."

He flashed a look of annoyance. "No, of course I don't have a plan. It's a lot of work to make a plan. You can't just roll it out and hope it works. You have to be certain."

That was different from the way Meg had built the business. In her experience, you try things and then you improvise. You go with your gut and if it doesn't work, you try something else.

However, she realized that the internet might be different. She didn't know. She stopped short of arguing.

"Okay," she said. "When will we have a plan, do you think?"

"Probably by August," he said with a shrug. "But don't bug me, okay? It's hard to know."

She recognized that she had reached the point where further conversation was useless. It was time to wrap it up for the day, anyway. She told him she was going; would he lock up? He grunted while failing to take his eyes off the screen.

Meg needed just eight minutes to get to her Fountaingrove home. She drove a Jaguar XJ, which she had given herself for her birthday just eighteen months before. It was pearl white, quiet, and powerful, giving her the sense that she was floating just above the ground. What extraordinary feelings a car could generate. It flung her up the steep curves of Fountaingrove Parkway, to the very top.

Meg recognized that she lived in a starter mansion, a graceless thing shoehorned onto a small lot, all stucco and stone facades and tree ferns. It lacked charm or the tall trees that only come to a house with years; it radiated newness, from the bright stones in the walk to the high cocoa walls in the den. Meg was not sure it was really her. Every few months she contemplated selling it.

And yet she loved coming home to it. It was cool and large. It felt like an upscale Caribbean resort that she entered like a stranger, feeling its novelty and its spaciousness every time. She was not by nature a homemaker, and she did not care for anything cozy.

People asked her if she ever felt afraid living alone. The answer was no. She never thought of danger. She loved her freedom.

Her two dogs bounded at her, barking. They were another reason she wasn't afraid. One was a Russian wolfhound named Rach and the other a Chesapeake Bay retriever she called Cheerio. They were rescue dogs that had captured her heart when she met them at the animal shelter, big dogs that fell over each other and wanted to stand up with their paws to her chest. It was too late to train them, and anyway, she liked the commotion they made every day when she came home. She hired a neighbor boy to walk them but they were still too energetic.

Meg threw herself on the sofa and let them climb up and over her, whining. She held their muzzles and shook their heads, she pushed hard to knock them back. Cheerio's yellow eyes, looking straight into hers, made her laugh. The dog must weigh 90 pounds now.

The cat, Muscles, appeared and spat at Rach when he pranced over to greet her. Muscles had also been rescued: nobody knew her history but she had come with patches of fur missing from her face. Now she arched her back and expanded her fur. While Rach skittered backwards, Muscles advanced toward Meg with great dignity, rubbing against her and purring. The dogs kept their distance, excited and wary.

Meg got up and went into the high-ceilinged kitchen. She poured herself a glass of chardonnay and went back to the sofa, telling the dogs to lie down. They obeyed and sat watching her, Rach's long elegant face and Cheerio's blunt muzzle oriented toward her like compass needles. She laughed and called them over, tussled with them a little, then pushed them away and told them to sit down. She got her phone out of her purse and looked at her Facebook account. When she saw Kent's friend request, she could not think who he was. After a moment she placed him—Alice's ex, and at one time a pastor at their church. Of course she knew who he was. They had been in a Bible study together.

She felt dismayed. It brought back an unhappy time. She didn't want to think about those days.

She remembered him clearly now. Greg had never cared for him, but then Greg didn't care for a lot of people. Greg was super-macho and Kent wasn't.

Meg couldn't actually remember talking to Kent one-on-one. She recalled him saying wise things in group discussions. Naturally he would, since he was a pastor. Alice had complained a lot about him in private, and Meg, on the edge of her own divorce, had listened sympathetically. She and Greg had led the way toward dissolution; and she had not been surprised when Alice and Kent followed suit. What had Alice complained about? She couldn't exactly remember. She had a vague memory that Alice had felt tied down by the church. She hadn't wanted to be a pastor's wife.

Meg had not seen or heard from Kent since that time, but she did keep slightly in touch with Alice. A couple of years ago she had dropped by her studio for Art Trailways. Meg had been the only visitor at the time, so they talked. Later she had been invited to a gallery opening. She had seen Alice to air-kiss, but at that crowded event they had no chance for conversation. They hadn't seen each other since.

Meg was big on Facebook, and ordinarily she accepted any friend request. What was the harm in it? She felt curious about Kent. He was nice-looking, she thought—not her type, but she wouldn't mind being in touch. What had caused him to think of her? That piqued her curiosity. It must have been, what, fifteen years?

She was about to accept when she felt a hesitation, something like a shadow glimpsed from the corner of her eye. She put down her phone.

Meg remembered what it was. Alice had told her she was fooling around with a kid who was staying with them after his parents kicked him out of the house. It had been a silly crush—the kid was half her age—but Meg had never said so to Alice. At the time she had felt very drawn to Alice—excited to trade confidences, eager to gain independence from men who seemed so heavy and dull. She admired Alice's cool and opaque style. Alice was small and blond. Meg had never quite recovered from being the tallest girl in junior high.

Kent wouldn't know about that relationship, she didn't think. Or maybe he did know, and that had helped push them into divorce. What if, these years later, Kent asked her about it? It was possible. Men always seemed to want to tell you about their divorce. In retrospect Meg was embarrassed to think that she had known what Alice was plotting, even while they gathered with the group to talk about the Bible and to pray. She regretted that. It wasn't her best self.

It would be better not to answer the request, she decided. You didn't have to say yes or no; you could just ignore it.

4 GOSPEL MISSION BOARD

Kent Spires paced miserably around his Sonoma Gospel Mission office, past the desk of his gum-chewing secretary, Marci, who paid him no mind. She had seen him this way before, forever.

"Did you get the minutes done?" he asked with polite anxiety. She gave him a condescending smile and said they were laid out on the conference table.

"And there's water?" He wanted the soon-to-arrive board members to feel that he had provided everything they needed. Even though he wished they would all come down with the flu and phone in their regrets.

Marci didn't even honor that question with a smile. She was a fixture who had preceded Kent at the mission by years. No doubt she had aged, but to Kent she seemed comfortably timeless. Her hairdo of tight blond curls had not changed.

The Berger Street office was a soulless space in an industrial area north of town. It housed the mission's administrative offices as well as a large thrift store. Kent sometimes thought the mission had a personality split between this workaday structure and the original run-down two-story gray stucco building downtown. He still saw that place as the organization's soul. Men came there to conquer their addictions. Anybody could get a meal and a shower and a bed. That was a Rescue Mission. This was an office. He knew on which side of the split he belonged.

Eight years ago, it had made perfect sense for the mission to move operations out of that crowded downtown space. Kent had led the move. But now he felt what had been lost. Berger Street might pass for the offices of a small independent insurance agency. Its desks were plastic wood laminate; the floors were gray linoleum tile; the ceiling's white acoustic squares were filled with hundreds of tiny holes.

* * *

Kent felt some pride as he entered the boardroom. He had asked Marci to look into its decor two years ago, and she had found a gigantic oak table with matching armchairs that somebody's church was getting rid of. There was a soft red carpet underfoot, and on one wall a large framed black-and-white photograph of Yosemite Falls.

Members were beginning to straggle in, making small talk, touching each other on the elbow. Kent circulated, shaking hands. He had worn a tie, but the board's apparel ran the gamut: sun-withered old men in roomy suits; fireplug men in shorts and Keen sandals; everything. This was California. Sonoma County, in fact.

Most of the fifteen members were businessmen. Kent appreciated their dedication to the mission, and he recognized that they understood finances better than he did. He was well aware that financial steward-ship was extremely important. It also seemed utterly dismal to him. This board held Kent responsible not for the number of men who had gained sobriety, nor even for the number of beds filled and meals served, but for a balanced budget. Kent knew that without a balanced budget they would not be able to continue their work. Yet sometimes you had to spend money that you hadn't planned on because a flesh-and-blood sit-uation stood before you. The board didn't understand that. At bottom they seemed to think of it as unnecessary.

Kent knew he would be reprimanded if he couldn't raise more money. This made him act defensive, which only aroused suspicion that he was hiding something or resisting the board's authority. No wonder board meetings felt tense.

It had been nine days since the *Press Democrat* published a story headlined HOMELESS SHELTER SUED FOR SEXUAL ASSAULT. Since then Kent had been fielding telephone calls nonstop, mostly from alarmed donors. Why were people so quick to think the worst? Why did they put no trust in you? After a flurry of emergency phone calls, the board chairman had called this meeting.

* * *

His name was Michael Tilden, and he stood with his hands clasped together in front of him, as though about to pray. "God is on the throne, brothers," he said in a mournful baritone. "We are facing a trial. But let us not lose confidence." He gestured toward Kent with one hand. "Our brother Kent will give us a briefing."

There was something unreal about the atmosphere, for which Kent had only himself to blame. He was the executive director, a title he always felt should rightfully belong to somebody else. Nevertheless, he had suggested most of these men for the board, largely based on their giving history or their capacity to give.

"I guess I should start by telling you what I know," Kent said, getting slowly to his feet. "When the newspaper story came out, I was as surprised as anybody. I'd heard nothing about the incident. Of course I talked to Jake right away. Also Knox Johnson, one of our staff, because he was there for most of it. And Daniel, one of the men in New Life, whose arm got broken."

There were some indisputable facts, Kent explained. Daniel's arm was broken, and so was the window for the reception desk. There were records from the ER regarding Daniel's injury, and they had repair bills for the window.

"Beyond that," Kent said, "It gets a little murky. As we all know from the newspaper, Kasha Gold says that Jake molested her. According to Jake—and Knox supports him—Kasha was banging away with this metal stick..."

"What do you mean, metal stick?" David Stearns asked. He was a retired oil company executive with a brush of gray hair. Though he was in his sixties, he belonged to the younger, pragmatic group on the board. "What on earth is a metal stick?"

Kent stammered. "I am not really sure, David. Maybe something like a metal cane? I never saw it."

David flexed his mouth but said nothing.

Broadly speaking, there were two factions on the board: older men whose memories went back to the founding of the mission, and younger pragmatists. These younger men watched the budget and asked for data about the effectiveness of the programs. Whenever such matters were raised, the older men became inert, like woodland creatures drifting into hibernation.

The older men were rarely critical. Their answer to questions—whether to the mission's effectiveness or to the state of the budget—was always to put on bright, gentle faces and say that there was not enough prayer. This was hard to disagree with, since prayer was always a good, but Kent sometimes thought that these men, as the Titanic plowed toward an iceberg, would recommend more prayer.

"Anyway, Kasha," Kent said. "They all say that Kasha is a different kind of woman. She considers herself the spokesman for the homeless. Kasha is slamming at the glass with this stick, or cane, and she breaks the glass. So Jake tells her to leave and he calls the police. They come but Kasha has disappeared by the time they arrive. A few minutes after they leave, Kasha comes back, and this time she breaks Daniel's arm."

"What was Daniel doing?" This came from an auto mechanic, who wore his hair long, over his collar.

"From what I understand, Daniel was the receptionist. He told her he didn't have any applications..."

"Applications for what?"

"Kasha apparently thought she could apply for a job as a counselor. Daniel told her that we don't have any counselors and he didn't have any applications, and she got upset and out of control. Apparently. That's when Jake came out—he was right there because they were drug testing in the office behind the reception—and grabbed on to her. He says he put her in a bear hug, and she slid down on the ground. She stayed there until the police came."

"When does she claim he molested her?"

Kent hated that word. He was embarrassed at the mere mention of molestation. "I don't think I know the answer to that, but I have to assume it's when he grabbed her to stop her hitting Daniel."

A long pause followed. Around the table most of the men looked down; one or two stared into the reaches of space. Kent looked at the photograph of Yosemite. He tried to imagine the waterfall in motion.

* * *

The word "molestation" transported Kent back to the days after he learned of Alice's infidelity, after he was removed from his home, after the children were taken away from him. Not that the situations were parallel. It was only that the word carried the same feelings of violation and helplessness. Standing before the board today, he felt nearly the same emotions he had felt facing the church's board of deacons then. He remembered being unable to think clearly, unable to complete sentences, unable to look anyone in the eye.

While his life was in chaos he stayed in a hotel, a chain that offered businessmen rooms by the week. The long, featureless hallways, the silent elevator and its chime, even the breakfast room with its weak coffee and pastries in plastic were psychedelic to him. He didn't sleep and couldn't concentrate to read. It was a relief to escape the hotel in the morning and begin his regular duties at church: staff meetings, committees, sermon preparation. For a few hours he could almost forget what was happening to him.

As the weeks went by, though, he got more people asking about how he was doing, and whether he and Alice were in counseling, and did he think it would be wise to take some time off. He noticed people studying him.

He was preaching through the Gospel of John and came to the story of Doubting Thomas. That was obviously relevant to his life. As he prepared, he was torn with an urge to describe what he was going through. Surely that wasn't purely self-indulgent.

Doubt was intellectual—that was how he had always encountered it—but now he learned how much suffering it could entail. In his sermon he tried to capture that without making it too personal. He talked about the age of the earth and students' doubts about whether God really created everything in seven 24-hour days. He discussed the uncertainty that Christians can feel when they are out of step with the surrounding culture—when young people are living together, when nephews and nieces are coming out gay, when Christian leaders we admire get exposed for moral failure. Kent could still vividly remember looking out at the congregation and seeing the puzzlement on their faces. It wasn't going well, but he didn't know how to pull it back.

He called Ross that afternoon. They weren't particularly close then. Kent admired Ross, whom he had met as a seminary intern and who was now a pastor in Anaheim. Ross was talented and charming, funny and articulate. Kent always made a point of finding Ross at church conventions and saying hello, and Ross, even if surrounded by fans, made a point to talk to him.

Now Kent sat on his hotel bed, legs splayed forward, and told Ross almost everything. He told about Alice's asking him to leave, and taking the children, and he described how it had affected him. Then he told Ross about the morning's sermon.

"Oh, no," Ross said.

"Oh, no, what?"

"You basically told the congregation you're not sure about a seven-day creation and you have doubts about what the Bible teaches about sex."

"I wasn't talking about me. I was sharing what a lot of people feel. You know they do."

Ross let out a deep breath. "Sure, but they count on the pastor to have it figured out. It sounds like you just told them you don't. At a time when you're getting a divorce and they have all kinds of questions about you."

"I guess I should have stuck to easier topics."

Ross didn't immediately answer. When he did, it was to change the subject. "Look, Kent, I'm going to help you as much as I can. Can you give me the phone number of your chairman?"

He did help. It hadn't even occurred to Kent that he would have to resign, but Ross saw it immediately and worked to make it as easy as possible. He negotiated a way for Kent to move on.

*　*　*

"Thank you for that report," the board chairman said. "Are there any more questions for Kent?"

"Do you know this woman?" one of the younger members asked.

"I don't," Kent replied. "Apparently she's been coming around to the mission for the last few years, but I don't think I've ever seen her. Jake knows her. He says that she's a little off."

"What does that mean?" David asked. His tone of voice startled Kent; it sounded hostile.

"I'm not sure exactly what he means," Kent said. "I think he's saying that she's unstable."

"And Jake is qualified to make that judgment?"

Kent realized that he was looking down at the table. He had been told that when he did that, he looked uncertain and shifty. He lifted his glance in the direction of David and saw an expression that frightened him: hard, suspicious.

"Look," David said. "The whole town believes that we have a sex offender running the mission. All he has to say for himself is that the woman accusing him is 'a little off.' That's not going to fly. This lawsuit has the potential to destroy the mission, and we have got to do something about it now, before it's too late."

All Kent could think was how mean David's tone of voice sounded. His words seemed designed to rip and tear.

In his seamless voice, Michael Tilden asked whether anyone else had a reaction. Nobody spoke.

"Apparently we haven't even suspended this Jake," David continued. "Have we done anything at all? People are asking. We have got to have an answer."

"Kent?" Michael asked.

Kent knew he was no good at thinking on his feet, especially when he was under scrutiny. "We did do something," he managed to say. "I looked into it. And I believe Jake. I don't think there was any assault, except Kasha's assault on Daniel."

Kent could feel the doubts circling in the air, spirit vultures. Once again, nobody wanted to say anything.

Finally Don Markens, who ran Redwood Credit, spoke up. Don was business-oriented, but he sometimes fit the profile of the older men, keeping the spiritual purposes of the mission uppermost in his mind. "I think we have to give Jake the benefit of the doubt," Don said. "If Kent thinks he's telling the truth, we should stick up for him. But I'm worried that if this thing goes to trial, it's going to be in the newspaper again and again, and we are swinging in the wind, aren't we? I think what we need to do is put Jake on leave for the time being. I don't think it's right to fire him, unless more comes out, but I don't see how we can just do nothing."

Kent felt the air in him expand until he was ready to burst. "If Jake isn't there, who runs the program?" he asked.

"Why can't you run it?" Don asked. "You used to do that, didn't you?"

"Yes, but if I'm doing that, who does my job? Right now I'm spending all day answering phone calls from our supporters. I can't stop talking to them, can I?"

"Isn't there somebody else who can do Jake's job?" David asked. "I don't even know what he does."

"He runs the New Life program," Kent said. "He oversees thirty men who have a lot of very deep problems. No, I don't think it's so easy to replace him."

John Brown, one of the older men, challenged them all to pray about the situation. In a melodious and sorrowful voice he raised the question of whether they had even prayed for Jake, who was a brother.

David pressed the point that Jake should be suspended or let go, but Kent resisted and the rest of the board seemed reluctant to overrule him. Two more of the older board members challenged them all to pray about it. The meeting concluded with an agreement to do that, which left them all in an unsettled mood.

After Michael, the board chairman, said a prayer and adjourned the meeting, nobody wanted to leave the room. Eventually, the old men stood slowly, carefully moving their chairs out of their way. The board gradually drifted out the door.

With all his heart Kent wanted to leave too, but instead he approached David and offered his hand. David took it, but his eyes were burning black circles. "You better hope you are right," he said. "I don't know how we get through this."

"I don't know either," Kent said. "It's terrible."

He didn't say what he thought, that they should do what was right, not what was expedient. It would be insulting to say that to David.

"You realize what this does to the mission," David said.

"I don't know exactly. I think it's hard to predict. Believe me, though, I'm the one taking calls from people who are upset."

"And you're still happy to cruise ahead."

Kent started to say something but the words, whatever they were— he did not even know—caught in his throat. The silence was awkward. He made himself keep his gaze on David.

David straightened up, pulling away. "It's on you, then. Whatever comes, it's on you. I've done my job. I've warned you." His eyes had traveled away from Kent's face, but Kent saw that they were dark as holes in the ground. David jerked his body around and stalked quickly out the door.

Three of the older men were still finding their way out. They must have heard the interaction, but they said nothing. Kent remembered again how he hated these board meetings. It must have showed on his face, because Charley Imwalle came over and clapped him on the shoulder. "Don't worry, Kent," he said. "God works everything for good. It will all be all right if we just pray."

Kent nodded, said, "Amen," shook Charley's hand, and escaped as quickly as he could. He went into his private office and closed the door, hoping nobody would follow to talk to him. At his desk he shuffled papers, lifting one up and putting it down, moving one across the desk, stacking, all this utterly mindlessly, without even knowing what he did. He could scream, but that would do no good at all. He thought about doing it anyway.

He was glad he had not caved in, but he also knew that David Stearns was right: it could be a very difficult time for the mission, and everything just might fall apart. It would surely be considered his fault.

He told himself he was overreacting. But then, swooping over him like a death star, came the memory of those days when he was helplessly stripped of his children, his church, his life. He had come so far from that. He had rebuilt. But he did not know whether he could do it all again.

He trusted Jake. Jake was a good man, and if he said he did nothing, then he did nothing. They couldn't sacrifice him just for the sake of appearances.

David would calm down, he hoped. He had seen David get excited before, and generally it didn't last too long.

Outside the door, everything sounded quiet. Nobody had pursued him into his office. Kent didn't know whether that was good or bad, but he was grateful for a few minutes. He hated the board.

His thoughts wandered to Meg. He looked at his phone. He had no messages. Maybe Meg had not seen his request yet. Some people don't look at Facebook very often.

The more anxious he became, the more he wanted to hear from Meg.

5   ALICE'S STUDIO

Meg had never before seen Alice's studio, which stood behind her house on a dead-end street. The lot sloped upward toward the back so that the studio, a large single room with a deck, seemed to float detached above the landscape. It gave a marvelous view toward the brown and camo-green hills, which were steep enough to qualify almost as mountains. The studio seemed splendidly isolated, almost startlingly so considering its situation on an ordinary suburban street.

Meg remembered visiting Alice when she and Kent were still married and living in a tract home on the west side of town. This was something completely different—very relaxed, very charming, very Sonoma County. Meg turned a pirouette to catch the 360-degree view while telling Alice that it was absolutely perfect.

The two women sat together on the deck now, as different as could be. Alice was small, cool, and blond, with her hair cut short. Meg was warm-blooded, with a tendency to talk. It often got her into trouble, but she had few regrets. She felt that it was in her nature to stir things.

Alice's art and Meg's products were both selling in the same winery on Westside Road. Since she was going there this afternoon, Meg had texted Alice to see whether she could help her out by transporting anything. It was more of an excuse for interaction than a real offer, but Alice surprised her by saying yes. And Meg was glad. She liked helping people.

It was hot on the deck, with the sun drilling through the clear air. Alice had poured them both a glass of white wine. The air was perfectly still and the song of a mockingbird could be heard, rapping through its repertoire. Meg closed her eyes for a moment. "Thanks a lot," she murmured to herself, as a sort of prayer. She asked Alice how her work was going, and Alice took her time answering. "Good, I'm working on a new series."

"And you're excited?" Meg urged.

"I am. I'll show them to you. They're ceramics of horses and men. Nothing like anything I've ever done before."

She didn't have the sound of excitement in her voice, Meg thought. If she, Meg, were an artist, everybody would know how much she cared about her work. She would be so proud.

"Yeah, I'd love to see them," Meg said. "You're amazing. A successful artist. Who would have dreamed it when we were starting out? I remember you talking about that as a goal. I don't know exactly how you put it but I remember you said something about being an artist. And I was like stunned. With kids, with the house, with everything we were doing, how could anybody think about being an artist? You might as well talk about flying to the moon."

"It's what I always wanted," Alice said. "And I knew I could do it. I just had to get out of that life." She made a grimace.

"That's just like me. I never dreamed about owning my own business. You remember I worked for Doctor Palmer at the vet clinic? I thought I was going to spend the rest of my life lifting dogs onto the examining table. That was the full extent of my career ambitions." She laughed. "I love having my own business. It's so creative. Very challenging and very fun."

Alice did not bother to respond. They sat in silence for a few minutes, feeling the sun on their skin, looking up at the hills. Meg felt embarrassed. How could she even think of comparing spa products with Alice's paintings? Alice probably thought that what she did now wasn't so different from lifting dogs onto the examining table.

Meg wanted to reboot the conversation, to talk about kids or plumbers or cherries from Oliver's Market. Something. Instead, she decided to go for what she was really interested in.

"Do you stay in touch with Kent? Your ex?"

Meg felt uneasy asking. You never know what people go through when they divorce. But Alice seemed unperturbed. "No. Not since the kids are grown. We don't run in the same circles."

Meg smiled. "I guess not. Isn't he working at Sonoma Gospel Mission?"

"He was the last I heard."

"Don't the kids tell you about him?"

"I don't know how much they see him either. He's kinda isolated himself is what I hear. Lives out in Sebastopol and doesn't see anybody."

Alice got out of her chair and stood, stretching. Meg thought it was a signal for her to go, but then Alice sat back down again. "I feel kind of sorry for him," Alice said. "I mean, he's not a bad person. I just had to get out of that life."

"Whereas," Meg said, "he's gone in even deeper, hasn't he? Working for the mission?"

Alice shook her head, not to disagree but as though to say she had nothing to do with it. "I should have realized before I married him. Or maybe he should have realized it about me. I wasn't going to ever love his church life. I was really young, you know. I just grew. Our trajectories were in different directions. We might have started out in the same place, but the farther we went, the farther apart we got.

"When the kids were growing up, he wanted them to go to church every Sunday. Regardless. Even after we were separated and it was none of his business what I did with them. If they had other activities, he wanted them to cancel those and go to Sunday school. I put my foot down. Let the kids decide for themselves. That was a big source of friction."

Meg reflected on her own marriage. "I wish I could say that Greg and I grew apart, but we were oil and water from the honeymoon. I don't know how we stayed together as long as we did. I remember seeing him popping all these pills in Maui. I asked him, 'What are you doing? We're in Hawaii; what do you need pills for?' All he would do is grunt and take some more, and if I kept after him he would threaten me."

"Did he hit you?"

"No, but he would have sooner or later if I'd stayed. I feel sure about that. What about Kent—did he hurt you?"

Alice shook her head and smiled. "No, Kent would never hurt anybody."

"It's funny," Meg mused. "I like a man who is really a man. But it always turns out that they're scary. Greg had a dark side. I have to admit that fascinated me. But when we were married, I didn't like it anymore."

This time it was Meg who stood up. She never felt at ease when women started complaining about their husbands. And here she was now, doing it herself.

Sometimes she wondered whether they had really needed to get a divorce. Greg wasn't unfaithful, as far as she knew, and he wasn't violent. Scary sometimes, but he never hit her. He did pop a lot of pills, but some women would probably have put up with him.

Meg could wonder about that, but eventually she got back to remembering what it was like being with him. There was no way she could regret getting out of that. And look what it led to. Life was a lot better.

She switched subjects by saying what she had really come to say. "I heard from Kent yesterday. It had been years since we had contact. He friended me on Facebook. I didn't respond, and today he messaged me."

"Aren't you going to accept?" Alice asked.

"Well, I might. I usually don't even think about it; I just friend anybody. You can always unfriend them later if you change your mind. But with Kent, I wasn't sure. It just seemed strange, since you're my real friend."

Alice raised her eyebrows and formed a sort of Cheshire cat smile. "Don't mind me. I really don't care. If anything, I'd be curious what you learn about him."

"So you are really over it?"

"Way over it." She stood up and gave a little shimmy to her shoulders. Meg noticed, again, how small she was.

"Let me show you my stuff," Alice said, and opened the door to the studio.

Inside the light was muted and full. There was a faint smell of paint and an agreeable clutter of canvases and tools. Alice led her to gray metal shelving, where she displayed at least fifty small busts of horse heads and human heads. The humans were androgynous, with enlarged noses and eyes. All the busts were glazed in multiple layers of brilliant colors. Their most memorable aspect, whether horse or human, was the violence that had been done them: in some, a wedge had been chopped out, as though by an axe; some had multiple crude gouges; some had been lacerated so as to distort their shape.

In addition to the small sculptures, Alice had displayed two life-sized busts on a battered dining room table, one a gorgeously articulated horse's head with part of its eye sliced off and hanging at a strange angle; the other of a human with outsized eyes and a chop mark deep into its skull.

Meg required some minutes to take them in. Then she said, "This is amazing." A few moments later she asked, "Does it mean something?"

"Does what mean something?"

Was this a game that artists played? Pretending not to understand your question? "The destruction. The violence."

"I don't know. Or I should say, I do know, but I can't say."

Meg decided not to ask what she meant by that. "Whatever they mean, they're beautiful. Or striking. Are you displaying them at the gallery?"

"Yes," Alice responded. "Could you take a boxful up there? I want to display all of them together, and I'm making even more, but I can't get them all into my car. If you would take a box, I could get the rest."

Meg said she would be honored. They needed the next twenty minutes to pack busts into a sturdy wooden box, wrapping each head in newspaper. They were able to fit twenty, packed tightly. The filled box was heavy, and when Meg tried to carry it to her car, she staggered before she even got to the door. She hurriedly set the box on a large, silver metal cube with dials and switches. "What's this thing?" Meg asked. It looked like it might be a time machine for squirrels.

"It's my kiln. Where I bake them. That little thing gets over three thousand degrees."

Meg looked it over with more curiosity. "Must warm up the room, too."

"It does. I try to use it on cold days. If not, then at night."

"How much does a kiln like that cost?"

"That one was over two thousand dollars. You can get them cheaper, but I wanted one that was pretty big."

Alice helped her lift the box. It was an awkward job to carry it together, one of them backing up, feeling for steps that she could not see.

Just as Meg had expected, Alice noticed the car. "Are you sure you want to put these in there? I don't want to mess up your car."

Meg waved it away. "I use this for everything. I've got two hundred lavender sachets and a bunch of other junk in the back seat. No problem. I'll get Roy to help me carry it." Roy was the gallery owner. He would have been an interesting topic of discussion.

Alice thanked her. "Feel free to contact Kent," she added. "Or not. Who knows? You might get along."

Later, while she was on the freeway driving north, Meg wondered about Alice's laissez-faire. Could a woman be so neutral about somebody she had lived with for years, had slept with and borne children with? It wasn't so for her with Greg. For a few years he had been with somebody ten years younger, and it had made her crazy. Now he was alone again, and she thought he deserved it.

Meg tried to remember Kent more clearly, but she drew a blank. That could be the problem. Maybe Alice reacted so blandly because Kent was the type that barely left a ripple. Yet Meg had a feeling of intrigue. Call it curiosity. She decided that she would friend him. It couldn't hurt.

6   PETER ANDERSON

He appeared at the reception window well dressed, in slacks and penny loafers and a tailored short-sleeve shirt. He was blond and slender, probably in his thirties or early forties. He politely introduced himself as Peter Anderson. Elvis was at the front desk and asked who he wanted to see.

"I don't know," Peter said. "Nobody mentioned a specific person."

"Did you want to make a donation?" Elvis asked.

A smile played over Peter's face. "That's not how I would put it. I'm here to join the program."

Elvis looked at him sideways. "Somebody offered you a job?"

"No." Peter blinked, confused by the question.

"You can't just join. Somebody has to invite you."

"The judge? Judge Clark. She told me to come here."

Elvis did not immediately understand. He grinned idiotically, stretched. "Wait," he said. "You're court ordered."

"I'm court ordered."

Elvis threw a high-pitched laugh, like a yelp, out of his throat. "Well, excuse me. You don't really look like you belong here, do you?"

"Maybe I don't belong here," Peter said.

Elvis leaned forward to put his head next to the glass. "What did you do? Rob a bank?" He suddenly found himself extremely curious about this well-dressed man.

"Assault," Peter said.

"Really."

"Really."

"You better talk to Jake," Elvis said, and he picked up the phone to summon him. "Wait. This is a program for substance abuse. Drugs and alcohol. You sure you are in the right place?"

"Yeah," Peter said. "Assault while intoxicated."

After a silent moment, he added, "It was this or jail."

"How long?"

"Six months, she said."

"This is a ten-month program."

Peter gave a little shrug.

Jake came down and invited Peter up to his office for the intake. It made for a standoff: Jake was in a stupor, talking in single words and short sentences, because his wife was still gone and his life was falling down. Peter had the listless resistance that came from being at the mission against his will. Jake failed to get any information out of Peter, except this:

"I like to drink," Peter said. "It can be a problem."

"Okay," Jake said with a sigh, and launched into the summary. "This is a program for sobriety. It's Christ-centered. You have to go to three recovery meetings a week. You have to go to chapel. You have to go to class for three hours every afternoon. And you also have to do a work assignment. The guys in the program take care of the guests who come here overnight. There's a lot to do and we don't have a maid. We cook the meals, wash the dishes, clean the facility, wash the linens, and take care of the guests' needs, whatever we can. In the New Life program you are busy just about all the time. You have very little freedom. You okay with that?"

Peter lifted his shoulders.

"And you have to memorize Scripture verses to move ahead. No exceptions."

Peter just stared.

"And go to church."

"Any church?" Peter asked.

"No. There are five approved churches. If you want to go to another one, you have to get clearance."

"Okay," Peter said.

"The guys in the program can be a little rough."

"I'm a little rough myself."

Jake arose from his stupor just enough to twist his mouth skeptically. "You don't look it."

"Looks can be deceiving."

"That's true," Jake said. After a moment's consideration, he decided that this mysterious man could be allowed into the program. He gave him a sheaf of papers to fill out.

Jake had doubts about anyone court ordered. They almost never really committed to the program; they just saw it as easier than jail. You could expect them to begin complaining about the rules in no time, or the food, or the beds. Their attitude dragged everybody else down. Jake believed New Life would be stronger if there were no court ordered. However, the program existed for anybody, and sometimes it happened that the worst characters caught on mid-stream and turned into men on fire. He had seen it.

Jake studied Peter as he leaned over his desk, trying to print his way in a hurry through the paperwork, muttering to himself as he did it. Suddenly he threw the pencil down and looked at Jake with an expression of disgust. "Why don't you do this online? It would be a lot more efficient."

It wasn't a question Jake had been asked before. He said, "Most of the guys don't know how to use a computer."

"Don't you think they should learn? You know job applications are all online these days."

Jake didn't respond, and after a few minutes Peter picked up his pencil and got back to work. He was probably right, Jake thought, but how were they going to fill out the application before they got computer lessons? Also, if the guys were online, they got into porn and they ordered stuff and ran up bills. It could only be a headache.

Peter finished, then shuffled through his papers again before handing them over to Jake. Jake took his time going through them. Peter had answered in only the most cursory way. Inquiries into drug history, family, reasons for joining the program were either skipped or given skimpy answers.

"You really want to be in this program?"

"Why do you ask?"

"From your answers."

"It's a stupid questionnaire and I expect you'll just stick it in a file and never look at it again."

"Well, actually, we refer to the entry forms pretty often. Not that it's necessarily your business what we do with it. I'll ask you again: do you want to be in this program?"

"I don't have much of a choice, do I?"

"Yeah, you do. You might find it easier in jail. They don't make you fill out forms there."

Peter just sat looking at him, so Jake picked up the phone and called for Knox to come upstairs. Knox knew the drill and asked no questions; he escorted Peter into the bathroom to pee in a cup.

"How could I have anything in my system? I've been in jail for two weeks," Peter complained upon emerging, but Jake just stared him down. As though nobody could get drugs in the county lock-up.

Knox took him down the hall to show him his room, which was the 12-man. Bunk beds were lined up like library shelves. Peter was shown a cubby, a two-foot cube in which to put his clothes and other gear. He was hauling everything he had in a black garbage bag, which he just jammed into the space. "You want to fold stuff and put it away?" Knox asked. "I've got the time." But Peter said no, it didn't matter.

"Which bed?" he asked.

Knox pointed out that only one bed had no sheets and blankets on it, an upper bunk in the back of the room. "That's a good one," he said. "Farthest from the bedbugs."

"You're kidding," said Peter.

"No; I wish I was kidding. They are in the walls and we can't get them out. We've had exterminators and they charge you a thousand dollars and spray around and even sometimes they drill holes in the walls—that costs more—and those little bugs hide out for a while but pretty soon they are back. Nothing we can do about it."

Peter told Knox they were stupid using poisons, which didn't work and could kill them all besides. "Diatomaceous earth," he said. "You put some of that out and I guarantee you they will be gone for good."

"What is that?" Knox asked. "I never heard of that."

"It's a kind of clay. You just need a little. The bugs get it in their system and the particles are so small, they jam in their crevices and the bugs die. You could eat a pound of it and it wouldn't hurt you, but the bugs die."

"I can't believe I never heard of that," Knox said, his voice regretful but accepting of his fate.

"It doesn't say much for the people running this place," Peter said. "It's common knowledge."

Knox offered to take him around and introduce him to some of the men, but Peter demurred. He didn't seem interested in anything about the house.

"Okay, then," Knox said. "You probably want to get a little nap. The guys are in class and they'll be coming up in an hour or so. Then we have dinner at six. You want to go to a meeting tonight?"

Peter shrugged as if to say, *Why would I do that?*

"Well, I know Rob goes to a meeting tonight. There'll probably be three or four guys walking over there on Ninth Street. I can introduce you at dinner, if you want."

Peter didn't say anything; he stood with his arms at his sides, his face lacking expression.

"Okay, then." Knox left him and stopped by Jake's office, knocking before he went in. "I don't know about that one," he said. "He's not happy."

"Somebody is going to clock him if he keeps that up," Jake growled.

"You're right," Knox said.

"Might be me."

Knox smiled. "Oh, no, you don't mean that."

7 THE FLYING GOAT

The Flying Goat was crowded with youngish people, alone with their coffee, hunched over their phones. Kent was early to meet Meg and nervous. He looked through both rooms to make sure that she had not already arrived. Just to be certain, he walked around to the very back of the east room so he could glimpse the face of a woman whom he saw from behind, bent over her phone. It turned out she didn't look remotely like Meg.

He had never done this. He knew people who had tried online dating, but it had always seemed impossible to him. Should he get coffee now and take a table? Or should he hover by the door until she came? Both options seemed awkward, but he decided for the second: to stand just outside the entrance.

The coffee shop was on a leafy corner only 200 yards from the mission, in a neighborhood where the grit of homelessness blended into the funky stores and restaurants of Railroad Square. The day was going to be hot. The sun had come up without any morning fog, and the sky was a flawless blue. Even now the shade from the trees—sycamores with their stippled bark and dusty leaves—was welcome. Kent warned himself not to talk about the weather, unless Meg brought it up. It was just so hackneyed a topic. Not that he would or could be anybody but himself, but he didn't have to present his most dreary side.

He had tried to think about topics. Not the past, or their former mutual friends: that was loaded with landmines. Maybe their children. He didn't know anything about hers. If he had to tell about his own, should he act like everything was as it should be? Or should he admit that he was trying to rebuild a relationship? He would be glad for some sympathy, but not at a first meeting.

It doesn't matter, he told himself. It's just coffee. She is an old friend.

Kent saw her coming from down the street, which gave him a chance to study her before she saw him. She was taller than he remembered. In his mind she had been more petite, more manageable. Was she wearing high heels? She was. How was it that he knew her by her stride before he could even make out her face? There was more in his memory of her than he had thought.

Meg smiled when she saw him, and when she reached him, he took both of her hands and she leaned forward to kiss him on the cheek. That captivated him more than he would have dreamed. Her scent was soft and fragrant. Kent couldn't think when he had been close enough to a woman to notice such things.

Meg launched into an apology for being late and described to him how one of her dogs had chased a neighbor's cat and then ran away. "I was on my way to the gym when she got out, and I spent the next hour traipsing around the neighborhood asking people had they seen a Chesapeake Lab. Finally she turns up at my front door—I still have no idea where she was—and she's just bouncing along like, 'Wassup?'" Meg laughed. "I love that dog."

After they ordered their coffee—Kent had a regular, black, but Meg got an elaborate concoction with frothed milk and honey and Indian spices—they took a table in the back of the east room, the same table where the woman had sat whom Kent circled. The room had plain white walls and oak tables and chairs, with a few abstract paintings on the walls. Kent told Meg that he had a dog when he was a kid, but never since. "I think I'd like a dog. Alice didn't want any pets and I went along with that."

"But that was years ago. Why not since?"

He shrugged. "I don't have a good explanation for that. Looking back, I should have. I bet my kids would have liked a dog."

"They are great companions," Meg said. "Greg and I always had dogs, and when he left I kept them. You're right; the kids loved them, and after the kids moved out I didn't have to come home to an empty house. I can live without people, but not without dogs."

"Cats don't give you as much affection, do they?"

"I have a cat too." She described Muscles' domination of the two dogs. The subject amused her so much she started laughing and found it hard to stop.

"Sounds lively," Kent said. "You're making me jealous. You talk about coming home to an empty house—that's me. But I do have a beautiful view."

He shyly told her about Lovejoy Lane, with its vista across the orchards toward Mt. St. Helena. His favorite time, he volunteered, was in March or April when the apples blossomed and the orchard shimmered white. "Sometimes it's unearthly, especially at dusk when you can see the last light on the mountain and the orchard is dark but the blossoms glow like little moons." Kent glanced at Meg and was glad to find that she was not laughing at him.

"That sounds beautiful," she said.

"Yes," he said, and thought with pleasure and surprise that it was going well, almost effortlessly, not awkward at all. They had both mentioned their exes by name in the first five minutes, with no complaining and no bitterness. Meg's face, when he looked at it, was a thing in motion that made him feel happy. Of course she was not what you would call beautiful; they were too old for that. She was lovely and full of life.

"I wasn't sure you would want to talk to me," he said. "I know you are friends with Alice."

"I stay in touch with her," Meg admitted. "I wouldn't say we are close. Why should that matter?"

"Dunno," he said, looking down.

"Do you still have feelings for her?"

His head jerked up. His serious brown eyes were looking into hers, perhaps for the first time. "No. I mean, it's over. The divorce almost killed me, but I'm not replaying that. I do still think of her. I guess I'm over her but not over the divorce. I have serious regrets about what went wrong."

Meg thought of asking what his regrets were, but almost immediately decided that should wait for some other time. She changed the subject to Alice's art, telling him that she had a new series of ceramic sculptures that she was selling at the Healdsburg gallery. He showed no interest in this at all.

"I lost you," she said. "You're not interested?"

"Do you like what she's doing?" Kent asked.

"It holds my attention," Meg allowed. "I wouldn't say 'like.'"

Kent muttered, "No, 'like' isn't the word."

"You don't care for it?"

"No," he said. "But who cares what I think?"

Meg took a sip of her drink and realized that she did. In her world, women and men mostly lived parallel lives, the women huddling to talk about their marriages and their children and their television shows and the men talking sports or looking at gadgets. That was how it had always been with Greg.

"What about your kids?" she asked.

He hesitated before telling her that he believed his kids were doing well. Andy was a teacher in Healdsburg; Suzanne worked in an insurance office in Novato.

"Neither one is married?"

He shook his head with a bemused smile. "No. I keep hoping. I have this idea that if Suzanne gets engaged, her fiancé might want to get to know me."

"Why wouldn't he?"

Until then he had seemed cheery and sardonic, slyly humorous. "Meg, the truth is that I'm not as close with my kids as I want to be. I'm not sure what Alice told them about me, but they seem very reluctant to have a relationship. It was always tense with Alice, you know, negotiating weekends and things like that."

Horrified that she had accidentally opened Pandora's box, Meg wished she could pull the subject back. She and Greg had rarely quarreled about the kids. Once he left, he showed very little interest in them. It was only recently that he had shown some concern for Brian—and still none at all for the girls.

It set her to remembering what Alice had told her when their marriages were coming apart. Had she accused Kent of anything? Meg didn't think so. She thought it was more a complaint about being married to a pastor, who was so serious, who cared so much about the opinions of ridiculous people in the church. Alice had been sick of the whole church package, as Meg remembered. And there was the kid who had been staying with them, college-age though not in college.

"What about your kids?" Kent asked. Meg was a moment in registering the question, and as she thought about how to answer, she looked into Kent's face. It was soft, pale, hesitant. You could see that he was really trying hard, that he was gentle, that he was kind. He seemed a little lost.

Meg was glad to shift to her kids. They were hardly perfect, but the subject wasn't a big downer. "My oldest daughter, Bridget, is married. She lives down in Del Mar."

"Nice place."

"Yeah, but it's hard to get down there. I probably see her once a year. Or maybe twice. She never comes north. She has two little ones. My other daughter, Eve, has a female partner. She lives out at the River and she's great. Busy, like everybody that age." While she was speaking, she waited to feel whether a chill came over the conversation. She hadn't expected to put it out there so soon, but since Kent had admitted he felt distant from his kids, it seemed okay. If he couldn't handle a lesbian, then that would be a signal to Meg. You couldn't always predict these days what people would say. Given that he was a pastor, she didn't know.

"What about your son?"

"Brian. He lives in town and he works for me. Or at least, he gets paid by me. I'm not so sure that he's working. He's supposed to make calls and he's supposed to get my business into the internet, but all I can see so far is that he spends time playing games on the expensive computer he made me buy for him."

Kent smiled. "Sounds like he is still a kid."

"Yeah, well, he's a good kid. I'm not going to trade him in for somebody else."

"How old is he?"

"He's twenty-three."

"College?"

"Yeah, he graduated. On time. With pretty good grades. He's the only one in our family who finished. But he majored in political science and since that's not employable, he seems to think that he has a ticket to spend the rest of his life on the family dole."

"I used to spend a lot of my life helping people find work. For the mission. Maybe I could help," Kent offered with some hesitation; he was used to people who resented the offer of help.

"He already has a job."

"Yeah, I understand. I just meant that I have a lot of experience with men who need help figuring out the work world."

"He's not an alcoholic."

"I'm not suggesting that he is. I think job issues are mostly the same, whether you are addicted to substances or not. Anyway, if he were interested."

"I can't imagine him showing an interest in anything that's good for him."

Kent smiled, a beautiful smile. "You sound like his mom."

Meg smiled back. "So you said that you used to do that. What do you do now?" She had noticed a couple seated near them, a girl with snake tattoos wrapped around her arms, a guy with a little porkpie hat on his head. They were leaning in to each other and she wondered what they could be talking about.

Kent drew in a deep breath and blew it out. "Right now I feel like I'm a glorified clerk. It's all administration and fundraising. I don't get to interact with the men in the program like I used to. A few days ago I went by the downtown mission and the guys didn't even know my name. I've lost touch with all that. Mostly I keep track of money."

"So why don't you go back to what you used to do? You're in charge, aren't you?"

He smiled at that, and then, as it struck his funny bone, he actually laughed. Meg was embarrassed; she didn't know whether he was laughing at her. Quickly he sobered and told her that he wished he could, but it wasn't so simple. "If I could, I would. I actually love working with the men."

"You do?" Meg wondered at that. "What about it do you love?" The guy with the hat was drawing pictures in the air with a finger. Watching him was like watching a movie.

"I guess you mean, how can I love working with addicts and homeless men? When you get to know them, you don't see them that way. I don't, anyway. They are just regular people, dealing with addictions. It's amazing to see their lives change, some of them."

"But that still goes on in your new job, doesn't it? You still see it, don't you?" Kent noticed that she was dabbling on the edge of conversation, barely pretending to be interested. He tried to think what he had done to lose her.

"Only from a distance. I'm in a different building, miles away, out on Berger." He paused and mused on that for a minute.

"So how does the mission help those men? I thought it was just like a homeless shelter."

He shook his head vigorously. "That's what it used to be. And I guess you could say it's still half that. The other half is the New Life program. Those men commit to drug and alcohol rehab for at least ten months. They work really hard at serving the ones who come in for a meal or a bed without any commitment. We call those guests. The New Life men really run the shelter. That's part of their recovery."

"When I think of rescue missions, I always remember when I was a kid driving by the one in Oakland," Meg said. " I would see the men standing around. We called them winos."

He shrugged. "Today they're more likely to be addicted to meth or heroin. Though there is still plenty of alcohol."

Meg was not very interested in the gospel mission's programs with addicts, though she didn't want to say so. The fact that he liked mixing with the addicts more than running the organization was not really in his favor.

"So you're not very happy with your work, and you don't have that much to do with your kids. What do you do in your spare time?" Meg could hear the mean subtext in her question, which she half regretted.

"I like to read," he said, as though apologizing.

Actually, it interested her. She didn't know many men who liked to read. Some of her women friends were in book clubs, but not men. "What do you read?"

"I read lots of different things," he said. "I like reading history. Some Christian books, of course." He sighed, looked her over, and decided to plunge ahead. He might as well. "I read C.S. Lewis a lot," Kent said. "I'm a little fanatical about him. At least, that's what other people have told me."

He didn't get an immediate response, so he asked, "Have you read him?"

Meg nodded. "The Narnia Tales, with my kids. And I read Basic Christianity a long time ago."

"Mere Christianity," Kent couldn't help correcting. "Did you like that?"

Her shoulders gave a quick shrug. "I can't remember. It was a long time ago. I think it was really heavy. Am I remembering right? Very intellectual? Why do you like him?"

"He's such a good writer," he said. "Very clear. It all makes so much sense, the way he writes it. It flows out so beautifully, so logically."

Meg asked him to give her an example, and rather eagerly he did so, using a point he had reread recently from *The Problem of Pain*. He didn't find it easy—he wasn't the most articulate man in the world—but he became engrossed as he explained. Meg kept her eyes on him, and he wasn't quick to realize that she had passed over from interest to amusement. When he saw it, he was horrified—not with her, but with himself. He should know better. He had been told. Nobody was as interested in C.S. Lewis as he was.

This is over, Meg thought suddenly. We've had our coffee. Time to go. Meg took up a white leather bag and slung it over her shoulder before standing. Kent seemed momentarily surprised, but he took the cue and stood also.

Now what did he do? Meg settled the question by putting out her hand. It was a strong, almost masculine gesture. They shook, and he held it for just an extra second. That was on impulse, and as they walked to the door he wondered if this abrupt ending was normal, or if he had put her off. Outside, on the sidewalk lined with cars, they shook again and she covered their hands with her left. An ambiguous gesture, but as he watched her walk away and noticed her shape and, again, how tall she was, Kent took it for all he could imagine. He couldn't help himself.

Driving slowly back to the office, he tried to reason with his feelings. It was just coffee. And what exactly had she said or done that would set her apart from others? Maybe he had not been around a woman for too long. She was definitely a woman.

On his way up Marlow Street he passed Monroe School, and on impulse, turned into the driveway. In back of the school was the Little League field where Andy had played. As soon as he passed the school buildings he saw that there must be a game on, for the long, narrow gravel drive was lined with cars, barely leaving room to pass.

Kent was immediately seized by embarrassment—he had no child here, no business—and he would have turned around, but that was impossible. There was no room to turn. He proceeded down the familiar strip, raising a thin dust trail, until he reached the parking lot. It was full, of course, but someone was leaving. He waited for the car to clear its spot and then took it.

He had spent so many hours here—not necessarily happy hours, since Andy was never very good at baseball. But if it had sometimes been miserable watching Andy on the field, it had been a period of life much happier than the present.

He got out and walked toward the diamond. Nothing had changed: not the cyclone fencing, not the ping of the baseball against a metal bat. The snack shack, he had forgotten all about the snack shack. He supposed the hot dogs and pretzels and gummy worms were the identical items once so prized by Andy and Suzanne.

When he reached the backstop, though, and slipped into one of the bleachers, he realized that the players were much, much smaller than they had been. When Andy was playing, they had looked like smaller versions of the players you saw on TV. These were children, small children, and their voices were high and piping, like seabirds. The field was tiny, too: just toy-sized.

Memories could freeze but people move on, children grow up.

He recognized that some mad hope had arisen in him, and he asked himself what he had liked so much about Meg.

After thinking for some time, he could say simply this: she was alive. He felt barely alive himself, faded, tortuously evasive, not even sure of his own heartbeat. But Meg was a living creature, and he wanted that life.

8   PRESSURE COOKER

Kent had no idea how David Stearns, his board member, got his landline. Kent gave it to nobody, since he rarely answered it. The calls on that line were inevitably from political campaigns or solar companies. He answered today because he kept thinking about Meg. Quite irrationally he harbored a hope that she might be attracted to him. It was only a small extension of that fantasy to think she might call. And as long as he was indulging fantastic possibilities, it was not impossible that she might somehow have his landline. So he answered and was surprised to find David on the line.

David was all business, making no small talk but informing Kent that he wanted to meet with him.

"Okay," Kent said. "You want to come by the office tomorrow? I'm available all morning."

"I was thinking now," David said.

"Now? Where?"

"I can come there," David said, and when Kent reluctantly agreed, David got the address and said he could be there in 30 minutes.

Kent tried to tidy the living room, stacking papers and magazines where they had been casually tossed. David was a stickler for detail and sometimes acted quite difficult at board meetings, usually over some aspect of the financial report, which was hardly Kent's strong point.

What would be the point of coming to his home? Kent could not make any sense of that.

When he heard David's car coming up the drive, he went out on the porch to meet him. The sun had set and the light was already dim. A coastal breeze had come up, stirring the apple orchard, where golf-ball-sized fruit was forming. The air was cool, almost cold, and for just a moment, as he stood waiting, Kent experienced a level of calm. The world was still beautiful.

"Hello, David," he said as a tall, straight figure came up the path. It was too dark to see the expression on David's face, but the scene was like something in a movie. Kent felt fearful of what might be coming next. Why should he feel that? He had nothing to be ashamed of.

As David stepped into the light of the porch, his face was illuminated, serious and stern. Kent ushered them inside, gesturing David into a chair and asking whether he wanted anything to drink.

"No," David said, as though the question caught him off guard. "No."

"Okay," Kent said. "What's on your mind, David?"

"I've been thinking," David said in that sober tone. "Ever since our board meeting, I can't stop thinking about this lawsuit and what it's doing to the mission. You seem to think it will all blow over, but I've seen these scandals in the corporate world and they don't blow over; they just get worse until you deal with them."

David had worked for British Petroleum and watched with alarm and horror as the Deepwater Horizon oil spill played out. He had been CFO for Oman at the time, far from the Gulf, but he knew many of the BP players and identified with their plight.

"David, believe me, I get that. I know how devastating this is. Who do you think is talking to our donors? It's me. I'm experiencing it every day. They call me."

David didn't seem to hear. "We talked about the problems at the board meeting, but I didn't hear one single word about how we would respond. It was all just wait and see, hope and pray. I'm telling you, Kent, if we wait and see, hope and pray, we are going to see the mission coming unglued. And do you know who will be held responsible?" He tapped his chest. "Me. Me and all the board members, because it's our job to protect the mission from these kinds of failure."

"They might hold me responsible too," Kent said quietly, but again David didn't seem to hear.

"I want to put it to you that we have got to do something decisive."

"What do you have in mind?" Kent asked, even though he had a sinking feeling that he already knew.

"You know perfectly well what I have in mind. You're shielding Jake. He's the one in the spotlight, and he has to be suspended, put on unpaid leave, severed from all connection to the house. That's the only way we can salvage this mess, and I'm not even sure that is enough."

Kent had been thinking since the board meeting, so he knew his own mind. "Jake didn't do anything," he said.

"You don't know that!"

"Maybe not, but I believe it."

"How can you know that? You weren't there. It's his word against hers, and a woman is going to be believed every time. People are going to say there is no way she would make up a thing like that."

"She might imagine it. People do, you know."

"How are you going to sell that in the papers? That the woman is a liar, because she imagined that she was sexually assaulted in broad daylight? The best you'll ever do is to create uncertainty, and that's not going to help us. So long as there is uncertainty, we are cooked."

With that rush of words, David seemed to have evacuated his mind. There was a pause, during which Kent realized how dark the room had become. He stood up to turn on a light.

He wanted to be sure that David was done before he spoke. "David," he said, "you may be right about that. I respect what you say, and it may be true that uncertainty is the best we can expect to get in the public eye. For me, though, that doesn't change anything. I know Jake, I've known him for many years, and I don't have any uncertainty at all. I can't suspend a man who is innocent just because somebody made a false accusation."

"That's ridiculous," David said immediately. "Nobody elected you judge and jury. Your job is to oversee the Sonoma Gospel Mission, to make sure it does its job and to raise money for its support. Nothing about deciding who is innocent. You can have your opinion, you are welcome to it, but the courts will decide about Jake, not you."

Kent felt desperately that the conversation was veering out of control. "So if somebody accuses you of something terrible, I'm supposed to act as though it might be true? When I know it isn't?"

"Why are you bringing me into this? Nobody is accusing me of anything."

"Please, David, it's a hypothetical."

They went around like this, David as solid and linear as a locomotive, while Kent tried to get him thinking like flesh and blood. Kent started out feeling strong and sturdy despite David's aggressiveness. As time went on, however, half an hour, 45 minutes, an hour, he found himself wearing down. His responses grew shorter and finally he stopped saying anything at all. That seemed to stimulate David to talk more, crashing through his thoughts like water from a ruptured dam. Now he was blaming all the dysfunction of the men on the failures of the program; there must be something wrong, he said, because they saw nothing but relapses, all day long. Relapse, relapse, relapse, and nobody seemed to know how to put a stop to it.

Kent wondered how it could be that somebody on the board didn't understand the ways of addiction. But then: how would David know any better? Kent had invited him to join the board, and he'd surely never asked him what he understood or didn't. That depressed him more than David's rants against Jake, for Kent recognized his own responsibility.

The stalemate between them might have eventually run down to a standstill if not for an accidental revelation. Kent was defending the New Life program, which meant defending himself, which required explaining that he didn't have time to engage personally with every one of the thirty men. They relied on volunteers, and volunteers weren't perfect, but years ago they had tried hiring qualified counselors and that hadn't worked out so well either. The New Life program was an opportunity for men who were motivated. It would take a lot more effort and a lot more money if they were going to reach the ones who weren't motivated, or whose troubles went too deep. That was when he mentioned the developer, a man named Buddy Grace, who had offered—at least superficially—more money than they had ever seen, just for moving to a new and possibly better location.

It took a few sputtering moments for David to realize what Kent was saying, and then he became really apoplectic.

"You turned that down?" David asked. "And who told you that it was your decision? That's a board decision. Did you consult the board?"

It was a hard thing to defend, because Kent knew David was right. Unlike his defense of Jake, Kent had acted not on some certainty but on a very hard-to-explain conviction that the time for moving hadn't come, that God's plans for the mission wouldn't allow them to move out of the building where his Spirit had been so much present. Call it a hunch, call it a spiritual instinct: he wasn't willing to admit that he had made a mistake, but his reasoning was nonexistent.

Reason was David's whole universe. His role as a board member had been usurped, and a huge windfall cast away for no good reason. There was nothing Kent could say to appease him so he miserably didn't try. But he didn't apologize, either, or admit that he should have done it differently. He glumly stuck to his guns.

"I could have you fired," David said.

And then, "This is the craziest thing I've ever heard of."

And then, "Are you well? Do you need help?" which was, for Kent, the most threatening remark. He remembered his divorce and the people who claimed to want to help him. Those who expressed concern for his well-being were the most deadly.

9   A CHANGED LIFE

Peter Anderson had been at the mission just over a week, long enough for others to observe his finicky devotion to cleanliness and his aloofness, neither of which were common traits in the New Life program. He set himself apart from the rest of them, so it was a surprise to see him stand up before the Sonoma Grace church as a member of the softball team.

Peter could play softball. At the plate, he showed a smooth stroke that squared up the ball and regularly lofted it over the shortstop's head. In center field he was graceful and quick. When he scored, his teammates wanted to slap hands with him, but Peter walked right past them, appearing not to notice.

Elvis Sebastiano also stood before the assembly that Sunday, his muscular, tattooed arms folded across his T-shirt. The mission had assigned him to act as Peter's big brother, an informal mentoring role. When he told Peter, he had reacted as though Elvis were offering to share a lice-infested hairbrush. "Why would anybody think I want that?" he asked.

A year earlier Elvis would have used his fists to make Peter sorry for the way he spoke. Now, though, he only shrugged. He was not going to let an idiot spoil his program.

Forget the big brother. He kept his distance from Peter while still watching him closely, because you don't turn your back on such a man any more than you forget that there is a rattlesnake under the back seat in your car.

Like all the program members, Peter and Elvis ate meals in the mission's squalid little cafeteria. They went to morning chapel together and attended Phase and Praise once a week. Elvis saw that Peter never spoke to anyone if he didn't have to. His face didn't vary from its single graphic of impatience. On the other hand, Elvis noticed, Peter followed the program scrupulously, did his bookwork, went to meetings, and didn't engage in innuendo and gossip.

Elvis didn't like Peter, but he almost wanted to imitate him. Elvis got distracted so easily. He always messed up. Without planning it, he moved closer to Peter: sitting at the same table over lunch; finding a seat behind his in chapel. It was like studying a starfish in the tide pools.

* * *

Early in July, the New Life program was shaken by the departure of five men, all in their third phase and not far from graduation. Two failed a routine drug test; they had been smoking weed provided by some of the guests. The other three left in sympathy. All five walked out together, with rude comments to the staff. Elvis learned of it later than everybody else; he had night desk duty from 11:00 p.m. to 6:00 in the morning, whereupon he went to bed and managed to sleep through the constant commotion of the 12-man room.

He was awakened just before lunchtime by a terrific shouting match over who would clean the shower. After he wandered into the bathroom, he learned the reason for the argument: the loss of five men left the cleaning crew badly short-handed.

It always upset the house when men left, and not just because of lost manpower. Most of the New Life members had been through programs before and relapsed; they knew what it was like to fall victim to your impulses, and it was no secret to them that most people fail to kick their addictions. When somebody quit, it brought their insecurities to the surface.

Elvis would soon be lifted into a happier mood, however, when Jake called him out of afternoon class and said he could move into the four-man room.

"The executive suite!" Elvis said.

Jake had other things on his mind and looked up with a puzzled half-smile.

"That's what we call it," Elvis said. Men in the New Life program usually started in the 12-man room, jam-packed with bunk beds. There was an eight-man, a six-man and the pinnacle of luxury, a four-man room. The Executive Suite.

The four-man rightly belonged to men in their last phase of the program, but Elvis got it because Jake wanted to shake up some of cliques. Elvis in the four-man, he hoped, would interrupt a toxic circle.

Elvis took what was offered without probing very deeply. When he hauled his gear into the room, he found two men sleeping on the bottom bunks.

"Hey, you guys sick?" Elvis asked. It was the afternoon and everyone in the program was supposed to be in class.

"Yeah, I'm sick," Manolo said, and laughed. "I'm sick most afternoons." Richard, who was also resting, laughed too.

"Well, okay," Elvis said. "I got assigned to be in here with you guys. Is this my bed?" He indicated the bunk that had no sheets or blankets. They said yes, but they weren't very friendly, Elvis noticed, and they didn't offer to help him make the bed.

He tried to kid around with them at dinner, but they stared at him. "What's with you guys?" he asked them.

Manolo was court-ordered for meth. He was a short, barrel-chested man with a baked complexion and tattoos circling his neck and forearms. He had been selected for the leadership committee that handled internal disciplinary matters. Maybe that had been unbridled optimism, a hope that he would rise to the responsibility. Manolo had two months to go in the program and had accumulated a stash of food, mostly snacks like nuts and beef jerky, that he kept in a cardboard box under his bed. He ate from it every evening before bed, and never offered to share it with anyone else. You weren't allowed to hoard food from the kitchen, but nobody called Manolo on it, because as a member of the leadership committee he could make you sorry for interfering.

Richard acted as his sidekick. He was a skinny white guy with a small gold ring in his nose but no tattoos. He wore the same tight black Giants T-shirt every day. Nobody seemed to know anything about how Richard got into the mission, whether he was court-ordered or not, whether he had family or friends on the outside, any job skills, what sort of addiction tormented him—though by the way he looked, people assumed he did meth. He had an irritating way of putting people down. Every chance he got, he said something demeaning to one of the guests.

The fourth man in the room was an older Mexican named José, who said very little and spent most of his time reading a Spanish Bible.

Elvis never suffered in silence. From the day he was assigned to the four-man, he badgered Manolo and Richard, trying to get them to upgrade their act. He questioned their afternoon naps, Manolo's stash of food, and the leadership they provided the house. His way was direct but glancing. He wasn't the kind who would try to sit down for a serious conversation. He would make comments in passing. He never got anywhere with this approach, but it wasn't in his nature to give it up. He said what he was thinking.

They warned him to shut up and mind his own business. That was not the way to get Elvis to shut up.

When Elvis was upset, everybody knew it. He was working mornings at the thrift store, hauling boxes and sorting donations. It wasn't a job that required you to talk to people. Nevertheless Elvis stomped around and muttered and managed to get in a tiff with some of the other workers, including his supervisor. When he was called on it, he felt the unfairness that *he* was singled out while Manolo and Richard got away with anything. He let his unhappiness be known.

Friday night he came in from an AA meeting, threw open the door to the four-man, and smelled the foul odor of men who had been eating beef jerky and farting.

"Could you guys leave the door open so some air gets in here?" he asked. "It smells like somebody died."

"Well, fuck you," Manolo said. "Move into the 12-man, if you don't like it."

"How can you use that language and still be on the Leadership Committee?" Elvis asked. "That sucks. You should do a self-evaluation for that."

"Fuck you," Manolo said. "That's why I'm on the LC, so I can make guys like you do self-evals. Don't you understand how that works?"

There was some shouting before Elvis had the wisdom to leave. He went into the upstairs lounge and pretended to read a book he found there until it was time for lights out.

The next morning, after breakfast but before Elvis left for work at the thrift store, he got a message to go to Jake's office. When he knocked on the door and entered, he found Manolo and Richard with Jake and Knox, Jake's assistant. There weren't chairs for everybody so Jake and Richard were standing. They had saved a seat for Elvis.

"Okay," Jake said. He was a large, husky man with dark, intense eyes. "I'm glad you're all here. Elvis, Manolo and Richard tell me that you threatened them last night. To be specific, they say you told them that if they didn't stop talking you would kick their butts, and you even moved toward them like you were ready to fight. Threatening violence is never okay here, and as you know, it's zero tolerance. According to the rules you have chosen to leave."

He said all this while looking directly at Elvis, but the rest of the men in the room kept their eyes on the floor.

"So if that's how it is, what are we doing here?" Elvis asked. "It's already decided. I just can pack my stuff and leave."

"No," Jake said. "It's not quite that simple. I want to hear from you to see whether there was some misunderstanding."

"There was no misunderstanding. I never said any of that. These two skunks are making it up completely. This is a setup."

Manolo smirked. Richard made a "phhht" sound with his lips.

"You never said anything they might have interpreted as threatening?" Jake asked.

"No," Elvis said. "Manolo used the F word and I called him on it. I told him he should do a self-evaluation."

Jake turned to Richard. "Did Manolo use the F word?"

Richard pursed his lips and shook his head, No.

"He's just trying to change the subject," Manolo said. "From his own threatening behavior."

Though Elvis was not a particularly big man, he had huge arms and shoulders. He worked out rigorously and regularly. Before coming to the mission, Elvis had a history of fighting. Guests at the mission sometimes left unexpectedly, afraid for what he might do to them because of some old grudge. Jake knew about his reputation. So did Knox; everybody did. It was quite possible that Elvis might have threatened somebody.

However, Jake had been living with addicts long enough to have developed an excellent nose for scumbags. He doubted that Richard and Manolo were telling the truth.

"You know, Elvis, that if two witnesses establish a choose-to-leave offense, I don't have any choice. My hands are tied. And you're not really making it any easier for me. Don't you have anything to say for yourself?"

"What do you want me to say? You want me to lie? You want me to say I said some stuff but I didn't really mean it? That I'm really sorry I scared them, I didn't mean to? That's bullshit. I never said anything except the truth. Those two are liars and assholes."

* * *

Elvis was so furious that he didn't even begin gathering his possessions. He sat in the yard and tried to calm his mind. Charles and Trayvon were lifting weights just a few feet away, making comfortable grunts, but he hardly noticed.

He had really wanted to graduate, so he could show his daughter that her dad could do it, and so he could feel like someone who finished what he set out to do. He always talked a good game, but he had never actually completed anything.

He couldn't think of a single place to go. He had come back to the mission because Angel had kicked him out of his own house. He couldn't go back there.

His outrage kept flaring up. He had done nothing wrong. After all the times he had been caught in real crimes, that particularly offended him.

He wondered whether this whole new life thing was a fraud. Whether it was just a big bunch of talk, words that didn't deliver anything real. If that was how it was, why would he want to stay here? He was better off outside, even if he had to scrounge to make it. Okay, he might relapse. That had always been the case anyway. He had lived through it before, and he would again.

Elvis sat there for thirty minutes before Jake appeared. He called to him from the house entrance, about 30 feet away. "Hey, Elvis. There's been a change. We're going to meet with Kent. I called him. Stay put until he can get here."

"What if I don't want to stay put?" Elvis asked. They were both shouting across the courtyard.

"What?" Jake asked.

"I don't feel like repeating myself," Elvis said. "You want to talk to me, come down here."

Jake walked out to stand in conversational range. "Elvis, I know you're mad but believe me, I'm trying my best for you."

Elvis liked Jake. In his heart of hearts he knew Jake was in a tough position.

"Those guys are assholes. You know that, Jake?"

"Look, I'm trying, Elvis," Jake said.

* * *

Jake had gone through the program himself; he understood how addicts cut corners. He knew the house would quickly deteriorate if he let the rules slide.

A small starburst of panic cut across his heart when he considered this. The rules were the rules. If he ignored them, the news would rocket through the house and he would find himself without a weapon the next time trouble arose. It was possible that Elvis had threatened Manolo and Richard. Elvis had a hot temper and a mouthy way. Jake could easily state the case for asking Elvis to leave. Yet for the last half hour he had been grinding on extreme dissatisfaction with his decision to kick Elvis out. His instincts rebelled against it.

He had called Kent, hoping to be bailed out. He expected Kent to say that we can't run the house without sticking to the rules. They are good rules, they have stood the test of time.

Instead Kent listened silently as Jake described his misgivings. He didn't even ask a question, he just let Jake talk. Then he offered to come down and meet with them.

"When can you come?" Jake asked.

Jake found Richard and Manolo sitting in the dining room while food prep for lunch went on all around them. They were stubbornly incredulous about what he said. They complained that he was going to let the little creep off.

"I'm not doing anything," Jake said. "Mr. Kent Spires wants to come and talk to you."

* * *

Kent went around the room and shook everybody's hand: Jake, Knox, Manolo, Richard, and Elvis. He had met Elvis but he didn't remember Manolo and Richard. He asked them where they were in the program and where they came from. Manolo was from Mendota, Richard from Antioch. They said they had met at the house. "You make some great friends in this New Life," Manolo said. "It's life-changing."

Elvis rolled his eyes. "This is such bullshit," he said. "These guys break the rules every day, and nobody says anything. Now I'm getting kicked out for nothing."

Kent had each of them describe what had happened. Manolo and Richard stuck close to their story. Elvis described criticizing Manolo and Richard for hoarding food and skipping class in the afternoon and swearing.

Kent looked warily around, trying to catch the eye of every man in the room. "This is a self-governing house," he said slowly. "We don't have staff whose job is to catch people breaking the rules. That's not Jake's or Knox's job. It's the job for you men who are in the program."

"There's no self-governing going on with these two," Elvis said. "I tried that. I gave them a self-eval and you know what they said? They said that's why they're on the Leadership Council, so they can make other people do self-evals, not themselves. I'm not complaining about the staff. I'm just telling you what's going on."

"Well, then," Kent said. "We have a couple of different stories. Who am I supposed to believe?"

"It's two against one," Richard said. "Two witnesses."

Kent nodded. "That's true. But is there another witness?"

They all looked at him blankly. Jake shook his head. "No, I asked about that. It was just these three in their room. Nobody else was there."

A hint of a smile budded on Kent's lips. "I'd like to hear from that stash of food," he said. "If we can. Elvis, can you show us where it is?"

Elvis looked suspicious but said he could.

"Let's go see," Kent said, and stood up from his chair. Manolo started to say something and then stopped. Richard stood up and then sat down again. "That's got nothing to do with anything," he protested. "He threatened us."

"Sure," Kent said. "But now we're just trying to get the full picture. Look, Richard, I can't come running down here every time there's a problem. I want to deal with everything right now."

He led the way down the hall, with the rest following. He paused in front of the four-man door. "Richard, you want to let us in? This is your room. I don't want to violate anybody's privacy."

Richard came forward and opened the door. The room was not neat: clothing and paper clotted the floor and under the beds. The beds were not made.

"So where is this stash?" Kent asked.

"Under the bed," Elvis said. He was beginning to feel better about his prospects.

"Can you find it?" Kent asked.

"I don't want you rooting around in my stuff," Manolo said.

"Isn't your stuff supposed to be in your locker?" Kent said. "Under the bed, there really shouldn't be anything."

At Kent's request, Elvis got down on his hands and knees and reached under the bed. He was feeling blind and at first didn't turn up anything; then they saw his shoulders bunch and he dragged out a large, full cardboard box.

"Let's have a look," Kent said. Nobody said anything as he dug through pounds of candy bars, mints, gummy worms, beef jerky, pepperoni rolls, snack packs. "This is a lot of stuff. All from donations?" he asked, turning his head to look at Manolo with a half-smile.

Manolo didn't say anything.

"Let's go back in Jake's office," Kent said, and he led them back down the hall. They sat down, unspeaking, in the same chairs they had left. There was a long pause in which Richard kept looking at Manolo, trying to get him to look back.

"Jake, I hope you don't mind if I give my impression." Kent waited until Jake could gather his wits and nod.

"It seems to me that we are in a very bad situation," Kent said. "We have two witnesses to someone threatening them. That's grounds for automatic removal." He let that sink in and then went on. "And we have two witnesses that one of those first witnesses was stealing from the program, taking food and hoarding it. Quite a lot of food that was donated to the Sonoma Gospel Mission."

"What two witnesses?" Richard asked.

"There's Elvis, and there's what we might call the material witness, the box of candy. I count that as two."

After another pause, a small smile actually gained ground over Kent's face. "As we all know, stealing is also a zero-tolerance offense." He glanced at all four faces. "So what we have is that two of you, according to two witnesses, have chosen to leave the program. I don't think Jake has any alternative but to agree with your choice and make sure that you leave promptly." Again he cast his gaze around. "Unless..." he began. "Unless somebody realizes they were mistaken."

He stood up and walked over to Manolo. Kent was not an imposing figure, but he was fairly tall. He stood looking down into Manolo's face. "Manolo, I'm wondering if you are quite sure that Elvis threatened you?"

10   HIKE IN POMO CANYON

Kent had texted Meg immediately after they had coffee, thanking her for the time. Then he could not make up his mind on the next move. He understood that a woman would take for rejection anything less than an immediate request for a date. Intending to call Meg on the weekend, he lost momentum when David Stearns, his board member, showed up at his home and tried to bully him into firing Jake. Kent was in no state of mind to think about anything after that. Not until Wednesday the following week had he cleared his head enough to text Meg and ask whether she would like to go on a hike on Saturday.

He knew that he should call rather than text. Truthfully, he couldn't bear to expose himself so directly. He dithered over that until finally texting. Her response came the next day, also a text: "Sure, what time?" No hint of how she felt about it.

He felt ridiculous, at his age, asking for a date and worrying about the answer. But he could not deny the truth: in the two days since getting her text, he had not stopped thinking about it. Yesterday he bought cheese and salami and a bottle of wine, plus olives and marinated mushrooms from an expensive grocery store where he almost never shopped. He worried over his old and stained backpack, finally giving up and going to REI to buy a new one, more expensive than he had dreamed a backpack could be. This morning, very early, he had gone out to buy fresh bread, adding a bottle of sparkling water on a last-minute impulse.

Now, on his way, Kent stopped at the Starbucks on Hopyard Avenue to pick up two coffees, managing to exactly replicate Meg's order at the Flying Goat. Her concoction with honey and Indian spices had seemed so fussy to him he couldn't forget it. He knew he shouldn't tell her that.

He was too early. He had said he would come at nine, and when he had the coffees it was twenty till. If he waited, the coffee would be cold. But how could he arrive early?

He decided to abandon caution. He called, and she answered immediately. "Meg," he said, "I just picked up some coffee and realized I'm early. Can I come and give it to you and then sit in my car until you're ready?"

She laughed. She said no, but he could sit in her kitchen. As he started up the car, tears came to his eyes. That was embarrassing, but also a sweet relief. For once he had not overthought, he had just done the obvious. He would be all right, he thought.

His Cortina strained to make it up Fountaingrove, a steep road that he rarely traveled. Meg's house, he realized, was in a very different zip code from his, and that meant her life was too. He mentally scanned the route they would follow on the way to the Pomo Canyon hike: would the Cortina have any steep hills to climb? Only when he brought her home, and it probably wouldn't matter; she would already like him or dislike him by that point.

Thinking of that, he got nervous all over again. When he parked in her driveway and stood on the front porch, jogging up and down on the balls of his feet, he felt almost panic-stricken. Then she opened the door, the dogs rushed him, and immediately he felt better.

He had forgotten again how tall she was. Why he found this comforting he could not say. It had something to do with a sense of solidity. She wasn't delicate; she could stand up. He watched her push the dogs out of the way as she leaned in to brush his cheek.

She was talking from the moment she opened the door. While she steered him into her kitchen, she thanked him warmly for the coffee, though he noticed she didn't sip at it but put the cup down on the island. "Have a seat," she said. "I'm almost ready. Where are we going? Do I need boots?"

He told her he wanted to go to Pomo Canyon, a name she didn't seem to recognize. She didn't need boots, Kent said, but walking shoes would be good. "Or boots, if you would rather." Meg disappeared, leaving him to the dogs, who competed with each other to squirm over him.

"What else do I need?" Meg asked when she returned, putting her hands out and twirling, like a girl. She had on jeans and a fitted, two-tone blue T-shirt, plus walking shoes that looked brand new.

"You should bring a jacket," he said. "We'll be out at the coast. I brought food for a picnic."

"Wonderful!" she said. "Do I need a backpack?"

He hesitated. "I have one," he said.

"One for me, too?"

He said no. She went down the hall again and came back with an old school backpack that must have been one of her kids'. When he saw it he wished he hadn't spent money on a new one.

"You look pained," she said. "What's wrong?"

He fumbled for words and then, after a moment of hesitation, decided it was too complicated to explain.

* * *

They swept down Fountaingrove, Meg chatting all the way about her business and the things that kept her busy. As she talked, she twisted toward him so that she could keep eye contact. When he glanced in her direction she looked beautiful to him, lively, animated.

Soon they were passing through vineyards along River Road, following long, swinging arcs along the path of the Russian River. Kent could make out clusters of purple or green grapes under the vines. He would have pointed them out but he didn't want to interrupt Meg; she had begun to talk about her son.

"He doesn't like to talk to his mom. Gets irritated if I want a report on what he's done. More like what you'd expect from a fourteen-year-old who hasn't finished his homework than a grown man."

"How old is he? You told me but I've forgotten."

"He's twenty-three."

"They grow up at their own rate," Kent said. "You can't really put them on a schedule."

"You can," Meg said, "but it doesn't do much good." Kent glanced and saw her grin. "Well, I can't help it; I love him. It would be easier if I didn't."

"It's tricky when they work for you," Kent said. "A lot of our staff at the mission graduated from the program and they're almost like family. We like hiring them because they understand what we are doing. Plus, they need a job. But naturally we are heavily invested in having them do well, and that doesn't always work out. We aren't as tough as we should be."

"They get lazy, don't they?" Meg said. "They don't believe you would ever fire them, and they're probably right. I'm not going to fire Brian, and he knows it."

"He certainly knows it."

"So how do you deal with that?" she asked. "It doesn't do any good to nag."

"We focus on success," Kent said. "We have measurements for everything, and they get rewards based on their performance. We keep it positive, but we make it very precise, too.

"And what if they don't do what you want?"

"Well, first, no rewards. We talk it over with them, and they know they aren't going anywhere unless their performance changes. But we try to stay positive." He paused. "This is probably really different than your son, but our guys are so down on themselves. You probably wouldn't know it if you met them, but they fall apart at any little thing. Somebody looks at them funny and they go on a tear. So we build them up, but only when they do something good."

Meg shook her head as though trying to dislodge something. "So far I haven't seen Brian do much I want to encourage."

Kent asked about Brian's job description. Initially Meg seemed happy to talk about it, but when he began to suggest ways to give Brian incentives, she shut down.

There was silence between them as they passed slowly through the town of Guerneville. The town looked impromptu and blowsy, full of summer. Kent braked to a complete stop for a family of four, crossing the street carrying beach toys. Guerneville had started out as a sawmill town—Stumpville, they called it—and later become a summer vacation spot. Now it was something in between, not quite dedicated to tourism, and not quite focused on the people who lived year round in weatherized summer cabins. It was a place where ex-hippies and gays and retirees and cellar rats mixed. Kent liked it. He wondered whether Meg would, but he didn't know how to ask.

He could feel the silence from her end. He couldn't figure out what he had done wrong until he reviewed their conversation. Then felt the burn of embarrassment.

"Sorry," Kent said to Meg as he started the car moving again. "I was forgetting that's your son we're talking about."

She nodded and didn't say anything.

"I'm jealous, really. You seem close to him, even if you don't always see eye to eye. My kids are keeping their distance."

She glanced at him, a sober look. "You said that when we had coffee. You think it's because of the divorce?"

He shrugged. "Maybe. I don't know. We got divorced so long ago, when they were little kids. I never felt any problem with them then. I think I lost them when they were teenagers."

"'Lost' is kind of strong. They are probably just busy. Do they have kids?"

"No, neither one is married yet."

"That's right. I forgot," Meg said. "Well, when they do get married and have kids, it's even harder to connect. My daughter Bridget has no time at all."

The conversation stalled again as they proceeded on a winding road through the redwoods west of town. To Kent the silence seemed oppressive, and he wondered if Meg felt the same way. It could be a very long day if it went on like this.

"I love this part of the road," he said, looking up at a hillside where cattle were grazing. "This is where you can begin to feel the sea, I always think."

"I've never been here," Meg said. "It's beautiful."

"You've never been here?" he asked, surprised but not wanting to seem so. "How do you go to the coast?"

"We would usually go to Dillon Beach. But we never went very much. It's too cold. We would go up to Lake Mendocino, where you can swim. We had a boat."

Not only different zip codes, Kent thought, but different worlds. He loved Sonoma County's rugged coastline. Cold, yes, much of the time. It occurred to him that he might have chosen the wrong hike.

He was relieved, then, when they found no fog at the mouth of the river. Steep hills dropped down to the sea, and combs of white surf ran in lines parallel to the beach. The sky was pure and cold and silvery, like the skin of a snake; far off on the horizon crouched a fog bank. The beauty moved Kent, though he said nothing.

* * *

Meg liked creature comforts; she liked warm beaches, not these foggy, frigid stretches of rock and pebbly sand, and she liked men who talked to her and made her feel special. Meg would fill in blank spaces in a conversation, but nevertheless she felt that everybody had a duty to contribute. She got edgy when others didn't do their part, and that edginess could turn to irritation. She was on the border of that when they turned off Highway 1 on Willow Road and began bouncing through the potholes.

She wasn't a woman who ordinarily attracted men. She wasn't small, she wasn't blond, and she probably scared some of them away by saying exactly what she thought. Since men were a scarce item in her life, her default position was: give them a chance. She was doing exactly that with Kent. She had known him for a long time and though they had never been close, she knew that he was a decent human being. He wasn't bad-looking, he wasn't dumb, he had a job, even if it was a job that might put some people off. Give him a chance. Their coffee date hadn't thrilled her, but it hadn't thrown up a stop sign, either.

She didn't like him trying to give her advice about Brian, though. His car didn't thrill her either, but she wouldn't hold it against him. She didn't want to be picky. However, his lack of conversational skills was a problem. When they pulled up at the campground, she was relieved to get out of the car. The silence had become too loud for her.

The campground splayed up a hill, sheltered by redwoods and bracketed by ferns. The road had reached it by a meadow that spread out behind them, deep in rank grasses. The air was warm here, sheltered from the sea, and Meg leaned against the little car and took it in with deep breaths. Kent opened the trunk, and out of politeness she followed to offer help as he filled out the two backpacks.

She liked the look of the food he pulled out. Kent obviously had planned with care. "You should have told me to bring something," she said. "We could have done this together."

Kent smiled. "Next time," he said. "I enjoyed doing it."

"What's the wine?" she asked as he put it into his backpack. He held it out to her so she could see it was a Russian River pinot noir, one she did not know.

"I hope it's good," he said.

"I'm sure it will be," she answered. "I love pinot."

They threw on their backpacks and moved immediately into the depth of the trees. Morning chill still pooled there, and the dim light had no source: it seemed to leak upward from the ferns and hover in the air like a mist. They were in second-growth forest, trees that grew from stumps less than 100 years ago, when the saws slashed and leveled everything. As forests go it was not so old, but the trees were immensely tall and straight, and the trunks glowed a rust color in the half-light. Meg did not speak as they padded on the soft duff underfoot; she only looked upward. They were alone in the woods. It felt vast.

After half a mile the trail started upward, leaving the redwoods for a more open forest of gnarled Douglas firs and bays, some of them uncut since the world began. There was enough light here for grasses and flowers to grow. The pathway turned into a steep climb, and Meg began to puff. She had deliberately followed Kent, thinking that he had a desk job and would be a slow walker. He looked soft. She was surprised, then, to find herself working to stay with him. When the hill grew even steeper, she had to ask for a break. She stood panting and red-faced.

Kent apologized for going too fast. She waved that off. "You're quite a hiker," she said.

"Well, I like to hike," he said quietly. She asked him about that: where did he go, who did he hike with. He told her that he went backpacking every summer, though so far this year he had not gotten away. "I'm hoping for at least a few days in Yosemite."

"You go alone?"

"No. I usually go with guys from my Bible study. It's been hard to get the time, with the lawsuit. I spend all my time listening to complaints or else calling donors to beg for gifts."

"Sounds horrible."

He grimaced. "I love my job. But you're right; this part is horrible." He shrugged. "It won't go on forever." He tried a smile.

Meg didn't really want to go into Kent's job. In her experience, men liked to talk about their careers as though they were Galahad searching for the Holy Grail. She hoped Kent wasn't starting in to that.

"I don't want you to think I look down on our donors," he said. "People are generous. They want to help. They don't really understand the problems that homeless people face. They have good intentions, though."

Kent seemed to be waiting for a response, so Meg nodded.

"I don't think I'm suited to fund-raising," he said. "It has to be done, though. Somebody has to do it, and I've been elected."

"I'm okay now," she said. "Can we go?"

"Sure," Kent said, and hesitated before going on. "The best thing is to call people, and I tend to put it off and put it off. I don't want to bother them. You get answering machines, and you leave a message but you don't know if anybody listens to it. And when you do reach people, they're doing something and you can tell they want to get off the phone. Sometimes people hang up on me. Christian people, who have supported the mission."

"That's terrible," Meg said, and began walking.

After a mile or more, the trail emerged from the woods. They could now see all around: high, dry-grass hills on their left, and a valley cutting toward the sea straight ahead. A breeze came through the cut, lifting Meg's hair. It tasted of the chilly ocean. It would have been uncomfortably cold if she were not heated from the hike.

"Where are we going to eat?" she asked.

He pointed up the hill. "I thought we could eat at the top. It's a fabulous view."

"We are climbing that?"

"Is that okay? It is steep, but it's not that far."

"I'm fine," Meg said. "But I'm afraid it might be cold on top."

Kent scanned the sky. The fog bank, which had been far offshore, was sending tendrils their way. "It might," he said. He did not mind—he liked weather—but he saw with dread that he had chosen wrong for Meg. "We could eat now. Are you hungry?"

She shook her head curtly. "I'm fine," she said.

"If it's too cold, we can just come back down." He spoke hesitantly, realizing that there might not be a good scenario, given the weather. You could never count on the coast. The fog was unpredictable.

"So let's just see," Meg said, and on her own began again, taking the lead.

The hill looked soft, padded with soil and tawny grass, but its appearance was deceptive. A steep trail passed through a small grove of old-growth redwoods and then assaulted a slope head-on. Only at the last moment did it veer to the left and wind around to the top. Kent led to the western side of the hill, where they could sit across from each other with their feet in a cleft. Below, the coastline stretched out for miles. Light glistened on the flat reaches of the river mouth, the town of Jenner appearing like a toy model. To the south, they could see Pt. Reyes like a triangular paper cut-out. It was, to Kent's eyes, so wild and beautiful. He waited to hear how Meg would respond.

She didn't say a thing. Had something irritated her? He couldn't tell if she was taken by the view or not. Kent didn't feel he could ask, so he began to set out food. He had brought a red-and-white-checked tablecloth, which he spread on the higher ground behind them with difficulty, as a persistent breeze flipped it. He put a bottle of olives and a plastic container of marinated mushrooms on the near corners to hold them down, spreading the cheese and bread on a plastic cutting board. "Eat up," he said to Meg, while he opened the bottle of wine and poured two plastic glasses. Handing one to Meg, he touched his to hers and said, "Clink! Cheers." She smiled at him and took a sip.

"Can I cut you some bread and cheese?" he asked.

"Absolutely," she said. "I'm starving."

"Do you want to put on your jacket?"

Without responding, she got it from her backpack. He offered bread and cheese to her; she took it and began to eat. At the moment of her first bite, the light blinked out; the first strand of fog came between them and the sun. Without the sun, the scene turned bleak and gray. The tawny grass lost its life.

Kent offered some olives; she declined.

"You look miserable," Kent said.

"Miserable is a bit strong," she said.

"Do you want to stay?"

Meg said nothing. She had her arms wrapped around her.

"Shall we go down?" The picnic that he had planned so carefully was going all wrong.

To her credit, she didn't lie. "I'd say so. This is a beautiful place but today is just too cold."

He packed up, wretchedly wishing that he had made some other plan. She must have grown up in Southern California, he thought, but he didn't say it. The coast had been a foolish idea. You could never count on the weather here. Of course, it wouldn't have mattered to him.

When he had put everything back into his backpack, he tried to fold the tablecloth. Meg saw him struggling in the breeze and reached out to help. It was a kind gesture, which he appreciated.

* * *

At the bottom of the hill, at the trailhead, they spread out lunch on a picnic table. It was warm again: the meadow was sheltered from the fog by the high hills. Meg seemed to cheer up as she ate, but she didn't have much to say.

Feeling that the day was slipping away from him, Kent broke the silence. "Meg," he said, "do you mind talking about our divorces?"

She looked at him as though he had proposed taking off their clothes.

"Not exactly our divorces, actually," Kent continued, trying to tamp down her alarm. "Post-divorce, I guess." He took in a deep breath and let it out again. "I don't ever talk about it, because I don't have anybody who will understand. But it's been hard for me. I keep thinking that it has to get better but it doesn't." Kent felt his emotions getting the upper hand, and he stopped there. "I was wondering whether you could relate."

Meg looked at him warily. She thought talking about divorce made women seem sad. She was too proud for that.

Kent thought he could interpret that look. "It's okay," he said. "I'm sorry to be such a drip. Let's talk about something else."

"Like what?" she asked, her expression turning to amusement. She shook her head. "Look, I understand. I kept waiting to get over it. I went out with girlfriends, I went out with men, I traveled. I even watched late-night movies to make myself cry. I also stuck pins in dolls that looked like Greg. I still felt horrible, a loser, a failure, and it went on and on. Oh, and I prayed. I asked God to take it away, to make up for what I lost, to forgive me." She stopped the list, exasperated. "Nothing. Not a peep out of God."

This burst of candor startled Kent. Judging by the energy she put into her words, she wasn't going to feel sorry for him.

"Did you feel guilty?" he asked. He knew it was a treacherous question, but he thought that he had already entered a danger zone.

"Did you?" she asked in return.

"Not exactly guilty," he said. "Not at first, anyway. Alice was the one who wanted out, and she didn't give me much choice. But I have spent a lot of time wondering about my responsibility in getting us to that point. I was way too wrapped up in my work, and she must have felt neglected. We married when we were pretty young, you know. She was especially young."

"Everybody is young," Meg said. "Even if you were sixty, I doubt it would guarantee anything. I mean, marriage is hard, isn't it?"

Kent smiled ruefully at Meg. "Sure, it is. Anyway, my point is that I have to take some responsibility. Which doesn't make me feel any better."

"But when Alice wanted out, by that time it was beyond your control."

"Yes. I guess so."

Meg took her time pairing bread and cheese and salami. "My situation was different. Maybe I could have stopped it. I thought about that a lot, especially when I felt like such a loser and was asking God to take away my misery. I wondered if I had done the unforgiveable sin."

"Divorce is not the unforgiveable sin," Kent said.

Meg smiled at the staunchness in his voice. It was the pastor in him. "I know. But when I was down I thought it might be.

"And then my father got Alzheimer's," she continued. "He lived in Ventura, and I have three brothers down there, and do you think any of them could help him? I was flying back and forth, and they said, 'What can I do? What can I do?' I would tell them, and they acted like I was asking them to walk a tightrope across the Grand Canyon. They said I wasn't working, which wasn't true; I was still doing real estate and I had started my business, but in their minds showing houses and selling lavender products was like selling Girl Scout cookies. Anyway, it got to the point where my dad couldn't function and had to go into a memory place. I went down to help him make the move. By that time he couldn't say my name. He was sweet; he never got mean like some people do, but he was just vacant. So I got together with my brothers and we all agreed on a place. We went together to sign the contract.

"Well, the place said they wanted us not to visit him for a month. We were horrified, because he might be vacant but we couldn't imagine just dumping him in a strange place with strange people and not trying to visit him. We knew he would feel abandoned.

"So we compromised, we stayed away for a week. When I went to visit, he was crying. He didn't want to be there, he didn't understand why we had deserted him there, and he clung to me like I was his stuffed dog. I couldn't get away. I had to trick him to escape. It felt awful. And it was the same every time I visited. As soon as he saw me, he was like an upside-down Sleeping Beauty; he awoke to who he was and the nightmare he was in. He cried. Every time. And my dad had never cried, never. Even though he didn't know my name, he knew he was in misery and I could rescue him from it.

"It just seemed so cruel. And then he got really depressed. He wouldn't look up when I came in. I thought he was dying. He didn't eat, and he got terribly thin, like he would blow away in the wind. I thought, *What have we done to him? We're killing him.* I wracked my brain for an alternative, and there wasn't one. He needed 24-hour care. I couldn't give it and my brothers couldn't give it."

Meg suddenly smiled. "Then, you know what? He forgot. He began to depend on the kindness of the staff—and some of them really were kind to him, even when he fought them. He got into the routine of the place. Like, he began to look forward to the meals, and he would automatically start heading toward the cafeteria when it was time to eat. Sometimes I would go on a visit and find him sitting there at his table while the workers were still setting up. He would be an hour early, and he was just fine with that.

"Basically, he forgot about his old home, the place he'd lived for fifty years. The memory place became his home. He wasn't unhappy anymore, as far as I could tell. He didn't seem to know who I was or who my brothers were, except that I think he knew we were familiar, so he would be pleasant with us, like we were people he met at a high school reunion and knew he should remember even though he didn't. But we weren't so important any more, and we didn't upset him when we came. Or when we left, for that matter. He had a new home, and that was his comfort zone until he died."

Meg leaned forward and touched Kent's hand, as though to gather him in to her remembrances. "You know, that experience affected me a lot. I realized that the memory place had been right. We should have stayed away for a month, or maybe even longer. By visiting him we just prolonged the agony of forgetting. He had to forget his old life and begin a new life, and it was no kindness to keep reminding him of what he had lost—even though we meant it kindly.

"Now here is the interesting part, Kent—at least, it's interesting to me. I came to believe that was what God was doing to me. When he didn't answer my prayers, didn't give a peep, he was just staying away so I would forget my old life. Not just my old life but everything that went with it: dreams about family and romantic trips and a happy home. Everything that I had lost when Greg and I got divorced. I think God was kind by being cruel. I had to forget all those dreams so that I could find a new life without them. And I did. I discovered this business, which I love, and which I never would have thought of when I was a mom and a wife. I discovered this life of complete freedom as a single person." Meg beamed at Kent as she announced this.

To Kent it was a point of view out of nowhere, and faintly alarming. It seemed too neat to him, too tightly packaged, and yet he didn't want to cast aspersions on it. He didn't know Meg very well, and he wasn't ready to disagree.

"You don't miss it?" he asked. "You don't miss...?"

"Miss what?" she said. "I don't miss Greg. I do miss other things, of course, mostly my dreams of what my life was supposed to be. I had to lose all those. I had to forget them."

"You're saying that God made you go cold turkey. Like we do with addicts when they come into the program. That he refused to give you any comfort so that you'd be able to dump all those memories."

"Dump all those memories and start a new life," Meg said.

"Wow," Kent said. "That's putting a lot on God."

She shrugged. "I think he can take it."

"It seems like a stark version of life," he said.

She shrugged again. "Maybe so. I don't think I would have come to it except through watching my dad and his Alzheimer's."

"The disease is cruel," Kent said.

"You can say that again."

On the drive back to Santa Rosa, conversation came easier as they talked of other, easier things: of their churches, of old friends they had not seen. Silently, however, Kent pondered furiously what Meg had said. He was naturally conservative but he liked to believe he kept an open mind. Working with addicts made you more flexible, he thought, more willing to leave hard questions open. He kept at bay all attempts to make the mission reflect one particular theology. Truly, though, he was surprised by Meg. In their small group 15 years ago, they had certainly talked about all kinds of issues, but he did not remember her as a deep thinker.

Meg, for her part, was also silently sizing up Kent. The hike had been a bust. She gave him points for trying hard, but he should have asked some questions before making all those plans. Maybe it was trivial that he liked cold, foggy, windy conditions, but she knew from her years with Greg that those sorts of differences set the stage for everything else.

She liked that he listened, though. It was unusual. He hadn't gone on and on about his job. He really hadn't talked much about himself at all. True, he didn't know how to keep a conversation going. That was annoying. He did listen, though. When she had gone into her long soliloquy about her dad, he seemed genuinely interested. That was why she felt safe to go into all that. He was unusually sensitive for a man, but he didn't come off like a total wimp. She had been impressed by what a hiker he was.

She wasn't sure what she thought of him. When Kent dropped her off at home, she made no effort to invite him in, nor was there a kiss—not even an air kiss. She grasped his hand firmly and said a warm thank-you, but she gave Kent the feeling she meant to remain just a friend.

He texted a thank-you that night, but it came out awkwardly, like a formula. He didn't feel sincere. She answered back almost immediately, *It was great, thanks for a wonderful time.* This sounded transparently insincere. Kent doubted there would be another date.

11   SOMETHING HAPPENS TO PETER

Jake called a house meeting Monday morning. They met in the chapel, a bare-bones room with horrible donated carpeting that never really got clean however they shampooed it, white walls that showed the taped seams of the drywall, and banks of fluorescent lights hanging from the ceiling on chains. The only real decoration was a large plywood cross screwed to the wall behind the platform and two felt banners with Scripture verses in plump, purple, cut-out lettering. It seemed normal to Elvis, similar to the churches he had attended in Ft. Bragg—those few times in his growing-up years he had gone to church, usually because of a girl.

Elvis took a seat as far as possible from Manolo and Richard. They had not spoken since meeting with Kent. Manolo glowered at Elvis as he passed, and Elvis grinned back.

Jake had been looking sunk of late, Elvis thought, but he looked particularly forlorn now, standing in front of the meeting to address the house. He was a massive, bearded man who might be mistaken for a logger or a movie Viking, but he seemed to have lost weight. His eyes were sad. Elvis was not sure what could be bothering him; it couldn't be Richard and Manolo, could it?

Without any opening greeting or prayer or song, Jake launched into a speech addressing the state of the house. Apparently he was bothered that so many men had left the program recently. He said it was disappointing when men left, but everybody should be clear that it didn't really affect them. What they accomplished at New Life was up to them, and nobody else. People were always asking him about the success rate of the New Life program. In his opinion, that was the wrong question. The New Life program wasn't a fix-it, and it didn't work by some formula. If anybody was waiting to see if the New Life was going to change them, they weren't really understanding the program. What New Life offered was an opportunity. New Life gave them a roof over their heads, three meals a day, and plenty of time to work the steps. They got to live in a Christ-honoring atmosphere, with classes about the Bible and the basics of the Christian life. The key word was "opportunity." Who in this world gets ten months to rethink and relearn?

Elvis thought it was a good speech, but since he had heard it before, it didn't make a huge impression. He was on his way out the door when he happened to notice that Peter had stayed seated. Elvis paused at the door and let the other men crowd past him.

Even after everyone else had filed out, and the chapel was empty, Peter remained in his seat.

* * *

Peter Anderson was not given to philosophical reflection. He thought of himself as mentally superior, but he had grown up in a well-off household more impressed by manners than ideas. He attended a small private college for two years but dropped out long before deciding on a major. Since then, he had held a series of jobs in marketing and sales, with stints managing restaurants. He never stayed anywhere for long.

Peter's father still lived in Healdsburg, but they managed to avoid each other almost completely. He had stopped funding when Peter dropped out of college, and after a quarrel, Peter had never found any other use for their relationship.

Even though Peter had agreed to the rehab program, he was not convinced that he had a problem with alcohol. When he was at college, a psychiatrist had labeled him manic depressive and prescribed lithium. Peter didn't like how lithium made him feel, and he found that alcohol worked as a decent substitute. He liked to drink, and it went with the lifestyle and work he had chosen. It was true that he left jobs after alcohol-fueled conflict—sometimes offense he gave with his words, and sometimes an actual physical brawl. He had a short fuse. Until now, though, he had managed to survive with his reputation more or less intact. He interviewed well, and Sonoma County, with its many wineries and restaurants, offered an inexhaustible set of opportunities in marketing and sales and low-level management. Lots of people knew

Peter vaguely. By selectively managing his resume, he found new work whenever he needed it.

None of these jobs paid terribly well. Peter skated by, keeping up appearances with good clothes and a nice car but living in rented rooms or, as often as possible, with a woman who paid the bills. In early June he had reached a small crisis when an art teacher at St. Rose High School changed the locks on her house. He had not seen it coming. Being between jobs at the time, he found himself confounded as to where to go. He had no money for even the most menial Craigslist shared room. A few relations lived in the area, but if he tried to crash with them, word was sure to get back to his mother, something he wanted to avoid. (She lived in Santa Barbara with her second husband.)

His solution was to go to an expensive wine bar downtown, planning to drink on a tab and hoping to latch on to a female who would pay the bill and take him home. It was more hope than strategy, but Peter had great trust in himself. By about eight o'clock, he thought his plan was working: he was talking down the bar to a 40-something with hennaed hair.

Peter had been edging toward the woman and making her laugh for at least 45 minutes when her boyfriend appeared. The boyfriend had three days' growth and a torso like a drum of fuel oil. He hooked his arm around the woman and ordered a drink. Peter kept talking; he wasn't 100% sure that the woman preferred this man to him, and his competitive instincts were aroused. Some witticisms were thrown around. For a few minutes the boyfriend acted willing to participate in a three-way contest. Then, without warning, he flicked his wrist at Peter as though shooing off a fly. "Go take your act somewhere else," he said.

Peter would have done just that if he had his wits about him. There was no point in putting up a fight, since he apparently wasn't going to get anywhere with the woman. But Peter didn't have his wits about him. He was drunk. He ended up hitting the guy and breaking the skin just over his cheek, whereupon the bartender called the police, and Peter was arrested and charged. He spent two weeks in jail and then, given a choice by the judge, he entered the New Life program.

In many ways Peter made a good program member, just as Elvis had noticed. He did his chores. He went to the mandated classes every afternoon, first a Bible study, then a class on recovery, and finally a Life Skills class. Guys were always getting in arguments with each other in class or debating with the teachers, but Peter never opened his mouth except to answer a very specific question. If he thought the classes were ridiculous, he didn't say so. Nobody knew what he thought.

Peter, however, was very clear: he was just biding time. The New Life program worked for him not because of its content but because of its cost: it was free. He got a bed and three meals a day instead of a jail cell. He would come out with a clean record.

Much of what the New Life program taught about life in relation to God was as unknown to him as the practices of Australian aborigines. He had gone to a Catholic high school that read Camus in its religion class. He had no history of going to church and had never found religion interesting. He didn't argue with the teachers at the mission because he really didn't care what they believed.

Peter had spent his life resisting attempts to put him on a better path. The first of the Twelve Steps, "We admitted that we were powerless over alcohol—that our lives had become unmanageable"—involved far more contrition than he would contemplate.

However, that morning Peter was struck by Jake's talk, with its emphasis on opportunity. Peter could admit that he needed to do something different. He thought that might take some practical form—going back to school, moving to a new city, starting a new line of work. But maybe because of the flood of spiritual talk all around him every day at the mission, he suddenly grasped what Jake was saying: opportunity meant personal transformation.

He was not going to engage in genuine introspection. That would go against too many long-standing habits. Yet he felt an internal note of panic, which made him stay in his seat when the house meeting was done. He did not understand why Jake's words had ruffled him, but he did not want to have anybody look at him and ask what was the matter. Control was everything to Peter, and at the moment it was in doubt. He had to keep a sense of control until this moment passed.

Eventually he glanced over his shoulder and saw Elvis at the door, smiling at him. Peter did not smile back, but Elvis took his glance as an invitation and sidled up to him and sat down.

Peter bristled. He was ready to push Elvis or anybody away, if they tried to insinuate themselves into his life. Elvis kept his peace, however. Eventually Peter realized that Elvis didn't intend to speak. For some reason this was calming to Peter, like a hand on the flank of a horse. For several minutes they sat beside each other, looking straight ahead at the plywood cross and the purple banners, saying nothing.

"I'm thinking about this program as an opportunity," Peter said at length. "I never thought of it that way before."

"How did you think of it?" Elvis asked.

"Better than jail," he said.

"You can leave anytime," Elvis said. "I did, a month ago. I was sure I was going to be fine. I knew I had it under control, and I didn't need the program any more. I ended up thinking more about where to get a hit than I did about my daughter and my lady, who I was living with. That wasn't taking me anywhere, so I came back."

"Just like that, you came back. Nobody made you."

Elvis gave a small chortle. "My lady told me to get out. But I had a choice where to go."

"I can't walk away. I'm court-ordered," Peter said.

Elvis took a pause to think about that. "You still have a choice," he said. "You choose how to respond. I notice you go to class, you don't argue, you do your bookwork."

Peter shrugged. He had lost interest in the conversation. "The path of least resistance until the day I can walk out of here."

"Where are you going to go? I mean, you got some kind of work?"

"I can get a job." Peter stood up and sidled out of the room without another word.

Yet Peter thought about the question. Where could he go? He pondered it while he worked on the cleaning crew, pushing a broom down the upstairs corridor. Then he got the vacuum cleaner and went to work on the chapel, which was empty at this time of day. It made a horrible sound, the vacuum cleaner. The noise would put off anybody who wandered in.

He had another four months to go before he cleared his obligation with the judge. He could get another job, but where could he eat and sleep until he got a paycheck? Peter loathed the thought of sleeping in the open and eating at soup kitchens. It would be late fall, near the rainy season. He detested being wet.

The mission's program was structured so that you could work during your third phase, saving your money. When you graduated you should have the wherewithal to rent a room or move into a Sober Living Environment, the halfway houses that they called SLEs.

He didn't have any interest in staying that long. Six months was already too long to live packed in with 29 other men.

Lunchtime came and the men in the program lined up to eat. The dining room was only just big enough to seat them all at particle-board tables and folding chairs. Peter got in line behind a big man with a scraggly beard, who nodded at him. Peter didn't know his name. He knew hardly anybody's name, because learning the names of people he didn't want to know seemed to be a complete waste of time. The food was laid out on a table in front of the open portal to the kitchen: the inevitable fruit salad, swimming in juice because the fruit was three days past ripe; a hot dish identified as Mexican Tortilla Casserole; green salad with a choice of bottled dressing; plenty of day-old bread and day-old pastries donated by Safeway. Peter had never felt great interest in food—there was a reason he was so lithe—but even he noticed the sameness of the diet. What did you expect? The food came from grocery stores and restaurants that were ready to throw it out.

On a wall just past the food line, where drinks were stacked in plastic bins, a whiteboard showed today's menu in red marker, along with a verse of the day in black. Peter had looked at the menu his first few days, until he discovered that whatever the food was called, it tasted the same. He had never really noticed the verse. Today he read it. "Come to me, all you who are weary and burdened, and I will give you rest. Take my yoke upon you and learn from me, for I am gentle and humble in heart, and you will find rest for your souls. For my yoke is easy and my burden is light."

Peter was unfamiliar with this saying. It caught his attention partly because he found it virtually incomprehensible. After taking his seat, he looked up at the board. He read the saying through again and tried to work out its meaning. Elvis sat down next to him with his tray piled high. Had Elvis been behind him in line? Peter had not been aware of that. He didn't like the idea of Elvis following him around.

Peter directed Elvis's attention to the board. "Whose quote is that?" he asked.

Elvis read it silently, moving his lips. "It's from the Bible," he said.

"Yeah, but who said it?"

"That's Jesus, I think." Elvis squinted at the board, trying to remember. "No, definitely, it's Jesus. It's one of the memory verses for second phase."

Peter said no more but lowered his gaze toward his meal and began to eat. There was something very odd about that quote. You could almost imagine people listening warily, wondering what to do with this man. Really a strange quote, not at all what you would think the Son of God would say. You would expect him to make some wooey-wooey spiritual observation. This was more like recruitment. At the same time, how arrogant, to call yourself humble and then ask people to yoke themselves to you.

"Doesn't that seem weird to you?" Peter asked Elvis.

The question confused Elvis. "Weird? What do you mean? I don't think so."

After lunch they had a short interval before classes began. Peter went out on the front sidewalk, just to escape the house for a few minutes. Technically men in the program could not leave the building without a pass, but nobody minded if you stayed near the door. The sun was downright hot. Peter leaned against the wall and shut his eyes. The light flared through his eyelids. He was not a reflective man, but many thoughts were jamming into his brain. He didn't know what to do for a job and a place to live, his mind was arrested by the idea that the mission offered him an opportunity for transformation, and that quote mixed up with all of it. Peter had never felt weary and burdened. Why had somebody put that, of all things, on the board? Surely Jesus had said better things.

The sun baked his forehead, and he could feel it penetrating his thin hair and massaging his scalp. Warmth scalded his eyelids. Then something happened to him, almost a blow to the back of his head. He fell suddenly to his knees, the concrete sidewalk smacking into his kneecaps and sending pain shooting up his spine. His whole body loosened and slumped; he felt like a tomato grub, rocking onto the pavement, curling into a fetal position. He could feel grit and little pebbles digging into his cheek. The sun was still strangely warm on his face, though he raised his hands involuntarily to shield himself. Despite pain and discomfort he felt strangely content, like a toddler in the arms of his mother.

Elvis did not actually see Peter go down, nor did he hear any cry, but one of the other men in the program barked sharply and Elvis turned his head to find Peter on the ground. In a moment he was huddled over him, talking to him but getting no verbal response. Elvis tugged on Peter's arms and got him to sit up. When Elvis asked if he was okay, Peter didn't immediately answer. Elvis looked in his eyes and saw that they were of a normal size and color; he could hear his ordinary breathing. He could not understand the smile.

"Let's get inside," Elvis said, and pulled up on Peter's arm like a football player helping to raise a teammate. Peter reacted to that easily, lightly, getting to his feet without a hint of a wobble. Just to be sure, Elvis kept a hand on Peter while he guided him in the door. He was startled when Peter put his left hand across his body to grasp Elvis's hand. "You're good, man," Elvis said, and gave a squeeze.

He steered Peter down the narrow hallway and into the dining area. A dozen or so men remained there from lunch, eating and talking. Some of them stopped what they were doing to watch. Peter took a chair at the nearest table, then looked around and realized that he was the center of attention. He gave a little smile and a little wave. "I'm fine," he said. "No problem." This friendly response surprised Elvis so much that he jerked his head to scrutinize Peter again. Then he pulled up a chair to sit next to him.

"What's happening?" he asked.

"I don't know," Peter said. "I really don't know."

"You seem happy."

"Yes. I am."

"I've never seen you like this."

Peter hesitated, looking straight ahead of him into space, as though trying to make out dim shapes. "I've never been like this."

"What happened?"

"I don't know. The sun was in my eyes, I closed them, and the light got brighter, and then I was on the ground."

Elvis remembered a woman at his church who came up for prayer over some kind of cancer and had fallen down like a stone. The pastor acted like it was just normal. In fact, it seemed to excite him.

"You weren't praying, were you?"

Peter shook his head.

"Maybe I should pray for you now." He said it without conviction. Elvis had prayed plenty of times for God to help him, to fix him, to get him out of trouble. But he had never prayed for anybody else in a public way. He thought of calling for Jake. Jake would know what to do.

Elvis's nature, however, resisted asking for help. Prayer was for everybody; wasn't that true? "Peter, I don't know what is going on, but I think I'm gonna pray for you. It can't do any harm. You okay with that?"

Elvis already had his hand stretched out, reaching for Peter's shoulder, but he held off and repeated his question. "Peter, you okay if I pray?"

Peter didn't even bother to answer. He was not worried. His attention was pointed inward, where he detected a gauzy, hazy golden shape, like the spinning of a caterpillar.

Elvis saw that there were other program members watching, and he signaled with his left hand for them to join him. He planted his right hand firmly on Peter's shoulder while half a dozen men gathered around, huddling together and adding the weight of their hands. Elvis did not know what he prayed. Sincere words came out, but he was not sure of their object. It was simple to ask God to keep you from doing something stupid or destructive, but how do you pray into a future for someone like Peter?

Afterward Elvis stood hovering over Peter, as did the other men who had joined the prayer. "Did you feel anything?"

"I feel happy," Peter said.

"I felt warmth in my hand where it was touching you," Elvis said.

"I didn't feel that," Peter said.

When he later tried to recapture what had happened, Elvis could not be sure that it was more than his imagination. The warmth reminded him of the feeling of an electric blanket, almost weightless, so subtle that at first you were not sure you detected it.

* * *

Five minutes after Elvis's prayer, Peter went to his two o'clock class, a study on the New Testament book of Hebrews taught by a pastor from the Nazarene church. Twelve of them met in the classroom just off the courtyard, a room cluttered with too many tables jammed into too little space, and six outdated computers facing the windowless wall. The pastor held forth from behind a small wooden podium. Peter had been in the class daily for two weeks and nothing had made any sense to him. He took no interest in what seemed like religious gibberish, such as "entering God's rest" and the layout of the true Temple in heaven.

Now, inexplicably, he found that the words in his Bible were intensely interesting, almost as though they were illuminated. When it came time for classroom discussion—there was always discussion at the mission, though Peter had never participated—he engaged the other students as though they were as interested as he. At the end of the one-hour class he remained as mystified by Hebrews as ever, but now he felt hopeful that, with study, he could grasp those mysteries.

It felt like an awkward fit, a new dance step, but this feeling remained. Some of the material taught in his classes was bewildering to him, now that he actually paid it attention. They were talking about sexuality in his Life Skills class, and neither he nor any of the other program men could see the point of staying out of bed with women who came on to you. Their questions, sincere though they were, kept flustering the teacher, who acted almost embarrassed. Previously Peter would have dropped out of this discussion before it began, seeing it as beyond pointless, but now he found himself joining in, trying to arrive at some sort of clarity.

At dinner, he looked around his table and wanted to engage. The men in the program didn't expect Peter to talk, because he never had. They gobbled their food and moved on. Yet for the first time in his memory, Peter found people interesting.

Monday chapel proved the most surprising of all. Program members were required to attend three services a week. On any given day, New Life men were outnumbered by guests, who piled in because chapel was the price they paid for dinner. They wouldn't have chosen to come and were generally not very interested. No matter how hard the volunteer musicians and the volunteer preachers tried, they rarely raised much of a response.

The band that day was from the Way Out, a local church, and they played loud rock. It wasn't music that Peter found attractive—he preferred jazz and sometimes Frank Sinatra—but he found himself spellbound by the words, which he had never heard: "Hallelujah, Jesus died for me. Hallelujah, I am free." For the first time in his life he wanted to sing, and did, in a tuneless mumble.

After chapel, while guests filed into the dining room, he went upstairs and found Elvis in the twelve-man, lying on his bed. Peter sat on the floor and tried to explain to Elvis what he was experiencing. He told Elvis how he had felt in class, and during dinner, and while they were singing praise songs in chapel.

"That's the Holy Spirit," Elvis interrupted. He had no doubt about it, even though he had never experienced it himself.

"What does that mean?" Peter asked.

"Well, it's God. The Spirit can take people and turn them inside out. Sometimes a whole room of people. Sometimes people fall down and start laughing. Or barking. It's pretty weird. It's usually more like what's happening to you, I think. Just a different feeling. Kinda like suddenly you love everybody."

"I don't love everybody," Peter said.

"That's just what people have told me," Elvis said. "They say everything changes."

Peter wondered what expression Elvis wore on his face. Was he smiling? Maybe he was laughing. The concern for others' opinion was unfamiliar to Peter.

He could not see that Elvis's face was alive with happiness.

For Elvis, as for all the men in New Life, hope was the flimsiest rope to hold. The program was all about opportunity, but men who had failed repeatedly knew themselves too well to believe in the possibility of doing anything new, even with the help of programs and workbooks and classes. In the back of everyone's mind was doubt that New Life would prove to be anything more than a kind of pep talk. It would get old. It would not last. Yet here was something Elvis could only call a miracle. A nasty piece of work named Peter had been taken over by something like love.

12   YOU KIDDING?

Meg's women's group met Tuesday evening at another Fountain-grove house, this one belonging to her friend Patricia. It was a truly extravagant house, with gigantic stressed-iron chandeliers hung on heavy chains, and stuffed furniture big enough to accommodate monsters. This was simply Patricia: she sold real estate and told gaudy stories about her clients. She sometimes wore hats; she always dressed in showy, gypsy clothes. Meg had known and loved Patricia for 20 years. They first met when the group was a Bible study for mothers of young children. Those children were now grown. The group had survived all the changes life threw at them, including Meg's divorce. They were her best friends.

She felt such comfort as they filtered into Patricia's living room, trading air kisses and gentle hugs, buzzing with talk. There was Suzette, with long silver hair, floor-length dresses and the manner of a lamb; Michelle, a happy, sloppy, voluminous woman with a screeching laugh; Janice, a no-nonsense therapist with a sensitive trigger and a tendency to offer snap advice; and Linda, prone to hoarding and depression, who lived on disability and some ill-defined inheritance. Linda drew the group together through the vigilance she required—regular texts and phone calls watching out for her.

It amazed Meg that no one else in the group was divorced. Surely by the law of averages there should be others. This had left her miserable immediately after she and Greg split. Now she was glad to be the only one. She felt oddly distinguished by it.

Meg's friends were part of the story she had told Kent on their hike. Within months of her divorce they had begun matchmaking, perhaps because she was so willing to let them. She wanted a man and they wanted a man for her. They had urged her on with Alf, who could have been her father. They treated it like a game, and it was a subject of constant commentary. Meg had always been very easy to tease, but after a while she didn't like it. She told them to stop, but instead it got worse until suddenly, one day, it didn't matter. She realized that she didn't care. In fact, she would miss it if they quit.

Meg wondered whether she would say anything about Kent. Her friends would want to know. Some probably were acquainted with him. To mention him, though, would be to suggest that she was interested in him. They would certainly take it that way.

The trouble was if they learned about it from another source. Somebody might have seen them together. Kent might mention their outing and word would get around.

As she listened to her friend Michelle tell a long story about her 23-year-old son's birthday party, Meg considered why she was so skittish. Was she perhaps more interested in Kent than she was admitting to herself?

She thought not. Kent was solid, thoughtful, caring. He listened. He was intelligent but didn't feel a need to impress you with it. She appreciated that he was trim and stayed in shape. Really, he was an attractive man. However, to have any kind of relationship required giving up something of yourself. And what part of her life was she willing to sacrifice? None.

* * *

Everyone found seats in the monster furniture, Meg sharing a corduroy sofa big enough for four. They always began with an inspirational moment, usually a reading, sometimes a song, occasionally a photograph or a piece of art. It was up to whoever was next in line. Today was Suzette's turn. In a small voice that sometimes faltered, she read something from Oswald Chambers, a famous inspirational writer. Meg never could quite understand what Chambers was trying to say. He was very spiritual in a complicated way. Meg tried to concentrate, but Suzette's soft voice distracted her. How could anyone talk so quietly? When Suzette completed the reading she kept her head lowered, as though in reverent prayer, and the others maintained the quiet. There were some sighing noises.

Patricia roused them and asked who wanted to start checking in. Over the years this had been the most meaningful part of their time together. They carried each other through crises, cried together, laughed together, sometimes contended with each other when they disagreed.

At first nobody volunteered, which wasn't really awkward for this group. They were comfortable waiting. Eventually Suzette said she would go first. She was worried about her husband, Ernst, who had sustained a concussion three weeks ago when he was putting up their camping trailer. The top had collapsed and hit him on the head; ever since, he had suffered from dizziness and headaches. "It sounds funny, but it's not a joke," she said.

She also wanted to mention her fifth-grader grandson Byron, who had been acting rebellious and had gotten himself in trouble doing things on the internet. She didn't know precisely what he had done.

They had some discussion of the internet and the temptations young people faced. It reminded Meg of Brian and the time he spent in the back room of the store. She didn't think he was doing anything wrong, other than wasting time.

Meg was still pondering whether to tell the group about her day with Kent.

"I had a little disaster on Saturday," she said as an opener. "A man. Don't get too excited." There were some titters. "Kent Spires. Do any of you know him? He's the head of the Sonoma Gospel Mission. We knew each other a long time ago, when we both were married. He Facebook friended me and we had coffee. He's a nice man, and I was curious since we hadn't seen each other in so many years. Then he asked if I would go on a hike, and I said sure. It was just awful, though. He wanted to give me advice, which I didn't ask for, and he took me out to this hike at the coast where it was freezing. He had packed a picnic. We hauled it to the top of a mountain, and when we got there we couldn't eat it. It was so cold up there. He had it all unpacked and laid out on a tablecloth, and we had to put it all back and carry it to the bottom of the mountain. It was awkward with a capital A.

"So...I'm swearing off Facebook. If anybody wants to set me up with a man, I want a full resume, a glossy photo, and references."

She could tell that her humor fell flat before it came out of her mouth, so she ate her laughter with a chuckle.

Suzette spoke in her small voice to say that she knew Kent; he was a very nice man. "I'm sorry it wasn't a good time, Meg. I think he probably just miscalculated. It's tricky to know what the temperature is going to be at the coast. It all depends on the fog."

Meg wagged her head. "You're right. I don't hold it against him."

It occurred to her to wonder why, then, she brought it up. Kent really hadn't done anything so objectionable. The point was, she wasn't interested in him.

They proceeded to the Bible study. Currently they were using a video series from a woman named Harriet Small, who had a way of opening her eyes very wide and shouting in a manner that was meant to be humorous. Meg didn't much care for her. After they watched, Patricia led a discussion based on the workbooks that went with the DVD. They had all been reading the Bible for practically their whole lives, but Meg often had the feeling that they were talking about matters that floated far offshore.

Often the best part of the gathering came afterward, when they sat and drank wine and laughed and talked. It was a warm night and they walked out on Patricia's deck, with its stunning view of the Santa Rosa plain. Twilight had fallen and Venus shone as big as a flashlight. You could trace cars moving on the freeway, little nubbins of light gliding swiftly and silently. Meg sipped at her glass of zin and thought of her comments about Kent. She felt wrong about them. Trying to be funny and light, she had sounded mean.

Hopefully her friends had other things on their minds. Thinking about it made Meg feel ugly, however. Feelings welled up like the early days after her divorce, when she thought everybody was looking down on her.

Suzette approached clutching a glass of iced tea. Suzette didn't drink. She was a gentle woman who sometimes seemed likely to wilt in the sharp company of this group. Somehow she always bobbed to the surface. Meg had come to admire her serenity.

"Meg, I didn't mean to second guess what you were saying about Kent. It sounds like it was very awkward."

Meg shook her head. "You didn't say anything wrong. I was trying to joke about it, and I think I gave the wrong impression. I just wanted to let you all know I'd seen him, before you heard it from somewhere else."

"Oh," Suzette said. "I can appreciate you don't want us bringing him up all the time."

"Or at all," Meg added, still smiling. "There's nothing going on."

Janice had appeared. In the dark Meg couldn't see her expression, but she knew who it was and braced herself. "Oh, come on, Meg," Janice said. "Why don't you give the guy a chance?"

"I did give him a chance. I went on a hike with him."

"And you were put off because the fog came in? How is that his fault?"

"It wasn't the fog. I just didn't feel anything for him."

"He annoyed you by giving you advice."

"Yeah, a little."

"I know Kent," Janice said. "He's not an advice giver. Not at all. He's a gentleman."

"I'm sure," Meg said. "Janice, all I know is, there's no magic. None at all."

"Come on, Meg. You want magic, go to Las Vegas."

13   DINNER AT HOME

When Meg tried to make sense of her motives, she found them hard to disentangle. Why had she agreed to go on a hike with Kent in the first place? Presumably because she was attracted, or at least curious. But then why had she put him up against an impossible standard? She had told Kent about her frustrations with her son Brian, and then held it against him when he offered suggestions. She had expected him to be a mind reader, to know that she didn't like the coast, and then furthermore to be a magician, controlling the weather. It was unreasonable; she couldn't help seeing that. That's what her friend Janice had said.

And yet she remained angry at him. She had said goodbye brusquely, had given him no encouragement at all, and indeed, he seemingly had taken none, for she had not heard from him, not a peep. This too she felt as a violation of sorts, as though he owed it to her to overlook her plain message. By Wednesday Meg realized he was not going to do that.

What, was he too proud? Or was he wounded? Either possibility suggested hostile interpretations of his character.

Meg considered herself sensible and logical, and the obvious conflicts roaming her brain were not welcome. She tried to replace them with work. Meg loved her business. She loved swooping into the parking lot in her Jag, she loved contemplating product to include in her line, she delighted in visits to spas and wine-country venues where she met people who understood glamour as a business proposition. This combination of make-believe and money-making, the union of artistic license with cold-eyed calculation reminded her, strangely, of dress-up when she was a little girl. It made her happy.

She arranged more sales calls, got in her car and paid visits to business contacts, perused online catalogs. However, she did not succeed at eliminating Kent from her mind. She looked up his Facebook page and saw that he never posted anything. Literally, never. That did suggest something unattractive, that he was a lonely, isolated man approaching middle age. This possibility raised a further unattractive thought, that she herself was a lonely, isolated woman approaching middle age. But that wasn't really the case. She had a circle of friends. Her Bible study cared for her, and so did her bunko group. Her daughters, too. No doubt Brian would claim to care for her, though right now he was not about to show it.

Maybe the truth was that she still missed having a man. After telling Kent that she had gone beyond the pain of her divorce, she found that an unwelcome thought.

Nevertheless, it persisted. She knew what her friends would say. Essentially, her Bible study had said it on Tuesday night: why don't you give him a chance? They had not taken her seriously when she told them she had no interest in Kent.

Her bunko group would be even less sympathetic. They were a jokey bunch. They would hound her if she brought it up.

Seeking distraction, she went online to look at merchandise. Sometimes she scanned through Amazon, just looking for ideas. She tended toward clothing. Hours went by while she scanned fashions that would never have any possible place in her line of product. She did all right with a few items in the lavender colors, and with a small manufacturer that named its shirts and jackets according to wine grapes—cabernet, pinot, etc. But clothes were a tough market. The markups were much better on specialty product, like lavender sachets and bubble bath. Looking at that kind of product bored her, however, and she found herself stopping in the midst of her search to think about Kent.

Rather impulsively, she decided to call him. She used his cell phone number, which he didn't answer. Instead of leaving a message, she called his office. A woman answered, and when Meg asked for Kent, wanted to know her reason for calling.

"It's personal," Meg said.

"He's very busy," the woman answered. "Can I ask your name?"

Reluctantly Meg gave it, and a moment later Kent came on the phone. "Hi," she said. "It's Meg. I was wondering whether you could come over for dinner on Friday."

"You want me to come to dinner?" Kent asked, taken aback.

She felt her adrenaline thrumming. "Yes, on Friday. Does that work? I know it's short notice. I haven't even thought about what I can cook. What do you like? Do you like fish?"

"I don't know," he stammered. "I mean, sure, of course. I just don't usually cook it myself." He stopped and started. "But I like fish. It's great."

"Wonderful. Maybe we'll have fish. Are you free on Friday?"

He said he was, and thanked her. "What can I bring?" he asked.

Meg suggested a bottle of wine would be nice. A white, since they were having fish. Probably.

For a moment after she hung up, she sat pondering what she had just done. Her phone rang, she saw a number she didn't recognize, and she picked it up. It was Kent. "I forgot to ask," he said, sounding sheepish. "Is anybody else coming?"

"I don't think so," Meg said. "Why, do you want somebody?"

"No, no," he said. "I just want to make sure I bring enough wine."

"It's just you and me," she said. "If that's okay."

"It's very okay."

Almost immediately she had regrets. She wasn't even sure she liked Kent. She couldn't recall anything in his favor from the hours they had spent on the day they went hiking. Not really. He was nice-looking, she thought. In a sandy-haired way, pleasant to look at. He was in shape, as she had learned on the hike. She herself struggled to keep her weight down, and she thought it was very important to go to the gym.

She had serious reservations about his involvement at the mission. Not that she held anything against its work. In fact, she had contributed once or twice—usually fifty dollars, which was her personal minimum for charities. But working for the mission meant living off charitable gifts. Meg didn't want to think about the homeless. She didn't want to hear about them either, and if you don't want to hear about a man's work, what does that say?

Well, she had gone with her impulse, and now she supposed she could not get out of it. She ought to feel distressed, but actually she felt vaguely jubilant.

* * *

Friday evening, right at 6:00, the doorbell chimed and Meg, still in her apron, welcomed Kent. He held a bottle of chilled wine, a white burgundy, and he pecked at her cheek. The dogs rushed him. He did not seem bothered, even when they jumped up on him. He said he liked dogs. Meg had not quite expected him to arrive exactly on time, and she wondered whether he was the type to park around the corner waiting for the exact moment.

Very rarely these days did she cook, and certainly she never cooked using a recipe. This afternoon she had enjoyed playing homemaker, preparing a special meal. She had found a recipe for Cambodian fish fillets, which she had just put in the oven. She had made fiddly hors d'oeuvres from figs and goat cheese and honey. She had a green salad and a loaf of bread, and she had chilled a bottle of wine just in case Kent forgot. The evening was warm so she had set a table on her deck, with candles ready to light when it got dark.

"You have a beautiful house," Kent said, probably just out of politeness, but she thanked him and offered him a tour. He seemed interested but said very little as she led him around, other than to murmur, "Beautiful," or "Very nice." She wondered what he really thought. Meg had grown up in a traditional home with carpets and curtains and dark furniture, and part of her regarded that as the true elegance. However, she felt much more at ease in the beach-hotel ambiance she had adopted, and she had no intention of changing it.

Kent seemed most attracted to her back yard, where they settled in green padded patio chairs around a small round table where she deposited the hors d'oeuvres and brought two wine glasses and a corkscrew. She generally bought screw-top bottles because she found corkscrews difficult, but Kent's bottle was traditional, so she wanted him to open it. She noted that he struggled with the cork before popping it out. She asked him to pour and he did; they both sat back.

"I was really surprised you called," Kent said. "After our hike I thought I probably wouldn't see you again."

"I knew you would think that. I wasn't very nice that day, and I wanted to make it up to you." Meg had thought carefully about these lines; she had even said them out loud, practicing how they would sound.

He looked down at his lap. "Well, that's very nice," he said, then looked up at her and smiled. "The day was kind of a disaster, wasn't it? I'm not very good at this sort of thing."

Meg wasn't sure that she had ever seen his smile, but it was a dazzler. When he smiled at her, all the weight of his worries dissolved and he had the look of a four-year-old at play.

"You should smile more," she said. "It suits you better than that worried expression you wear most of the time."

He looked at his lap again, then turned a more pained smile on her. "I should," he said. "You're right."

She heard the buzzer and went to take the fish out of the oven. She was working on the salad when he poked his head in the kitchen and asked if he could help. She told him no, she couldn't talk and cook at the same time, and she'd rather that he just waited on the deck. "Eat some more of those figs, if you like them. I'll be done in no time."

She was pleased that he had offered. Greg's only contribution in the kitchen had been to pour his own Cheerios into the bowl she set out for him. When he tried to barbecue, he got so angry at the meat she had to take that job away from him.

While Meg did final preparations, Kent sat on the deck enveloped in gloom. Her apology—or semi-apology, she had not really said she was sorry, had she?—made him feel worse. He was stuck between the powerful feelings of being near an attractive woman, who had invited him into her beautiful home to feed him and talk to him, and his dread that it could lead to nothing. When Meg had opened the door, he had been taken aback by her physicality. She was a presence, he thought, a bomb, so vital and dimensional. She was a living force. She was a woman. When he leaned toward her to kiss the air by her cheek, he caught her scent and had to restrain himself from reaching out to clutch her.

He leaned back in his chair and looked into the translucent sky, streaked with the faintest of clouds. He might explode from the opposing forces within him. It was physical, of course, but it went deeper than that. He wanted to talk to her. He wanted to blurt out his guts. No chance he could do that.

He was beyond playing his cards right. He just wanted to survive this.

Meg appeared with two plates in her hand, trailed closely by both dogs. She had shed her apron and Kent couldn't help noticing her shapeliness. She had dressed in slacks and a loose top that made her look young, younger than she was. "I hope you do like fish," she said. "This recipe is an experiment."

They began the meal in silence, interrupted only by Kent's appreciative noises. He could not remember the last time he sat for a meal with a woman. It was a wonderful, vulnerable feeling. He determined to enjoy it while it lasted. He did not see how it could.

The easiest thing was to talk about their kids. Meg remembered Andy and Suzanne from grade school days. She even told a story about Suzanne at a Vacation Bible School, when she had begun by painting her face and then went on to begin painting her whole body.

Kent enjoyed listening. Meg's children obviously were extraordinarily important to her. He wanted—this realization streaked through him like electricity—to be part of that, to know her kids when they came for dinner, to have his own kids join them too. One happy family.

He told himself to stop fantasizing. It didn't help.

Meg talked very freely. She had raised her kids without any interference from Greg, and she felt closer to them than to practically anyone. It didn't mean a lack of conflict. Meg disliked Eve's partner Brenda, who was a high-drama individual. Meg couldn't understand why Eve put up with her. Meg told Kent about this conflict, once again closely observing his reaction. Any repulsion of her daughter because of her sexual identity—or for any other reason, really—would be the end of him.

He listened; he didn't gush or overcompensate. He seemed very calm and measured.

She asked him what he was passionate about. The implication seemed to be: if not your children, what?

By this time they had finished their meals. Meg had not moved; the dirty plates still sat on the table in front of them. The dogs had settled at their feet, under the table. The sun was gone, and the light was dying. Meg lit the candles. A light and chilly breeze had kicked up, and it wouldn't be long before they needed to move indoors.

Kent was uncomfortable with the question. It felt like something from a job interview. He wanted to tell her that he was passionate about his kids just as much as she was; he would do anything to regain them. But he wasn't ready to go into that again. He realized, anyway, that he could answer in another way.

"To be perfectly truthful, my passion is to see people change. That's why I love my work. Sometimes I almost regret it, because it's brought me a lot of trouble. I think my marriage failed largely because Alice didn't like the ministry and didn't want to be part of it, and I couldn't leave it. I couldn't take a regular nine-to-five job, no matter how much she wanted me to. And I think later on it kept me from being close to my kids, too. I was distracted from paying them the attention that they needed. Especially after they became teenagers and it wasn't as simple as taking them to Chuck E. Cheese."

Kent raised his eyes to look directly at Meg. His face was full of woe. "Meg, I can't help it. Ever since I was a little kid I've wanted to be a minister. I should say, hoped to be a minister. I never claimed that I deserved it. I just longed for it. I longed to help people at the deepest level of their souls. When I lost my church, it felt like I had been cruci-fied. I don't know if I can lose that again."

Meg was taken aback by this confession, and she lifted her eyebrows and expanded her eyes. "Why would you ever lose it again?"

Dusk had fallen far enough to obscure his eyes, but his gestures were broad and visible even in the gloom. "You know about this woman who is suing the mission? Have we talked about this?"

"You told me a little. You seemed very worried, but I didn't get that you could lose your job."

He told her about his woes with the board, the meeting with David Stearns, the problems with funding. He tried to rein in his feelings and tell it factually—it seemed unseemly to spill it all in front of her—but there was a nerve-wracked quality to his telling. Meg was the sort of woman who listened actively and was full of advice, but this once she had nothing to say. She had started the whole thing by asking what he was passionate about, but she was not quite prepared for the result.

But did she hate it? She felt queasy about the mission. She felt sorry for the homeless, but she didn't want to get closer to them. Seeing somebody begging perturbed her; she wanted to get away from it.

She found herself moved by Kent's emotions, however, which were visible even in the twilight, and audible despite his attempts to speak casually. She had been married to a man who had only one emotion: anger.

He is a good man, she thought, and though virtue had never been something she looked for in a man, she found it appealing in him.

"Why don't we go inside," she said. "It's getting cold."

Kent helped gather the dishes and carry them into the kitchen. On their way in the French doors, they got tangled together for an instant as Meg tried to let Kent go first and he stopped and started and stopped again. She put out a hand and it found—by an accident—his chest. Spontaneously she let it rest there for an instant.

It took two trips to get all the dishes inside. They did not touch again, but Meg thought she felt electricity when they passed each other. She wondered what she was doing.

Meg had bought sorbet and some lace cookies from Trader Joe's. As she spooned out the sorbet into dishes, Kent leaned against the stove and continued talking. It felt like a complete release. He was speaking openly, spilling his thoughts, his anxieties, his woes, and he felt tenderness in the room. He didn't know Meg very well, but she was warm.

She handed him his bowl but lingered by him. She put a finger up to touch his cheek. "I'm sorry it's such a hard time," she said. Then, unexpectedly, she pushed up against him and kissed him. Involuntarily, Kent put a hand on her, as though to steady her or to fend her off. But this quickly became a grip holding her to him, and his lips moved to hers.

The dogs joined in, pushing up against them both. Rach, the Russian wolfhound, stood on his hind legs and licked at Meg's face. She pushed him off.

"Wait," Meg said, and separated herself. She took Kent's dish and set it on a small lamp table. Then she returned to his side and insinuated herself against him.

"Meg," Kent said. "Should we?"

She ignored him and cradled his head in her hands.

In short order they were on the sofa, hot against each other. Kent had his hands on every part of Meg, and she him. Excited by the physicality, both dogs leaned in, putting their heads and then their front paws on them. "Get off!" Meg shouted and pushed them both away.

She smiled at Kent. "Not you."

They were not novices; they remembered how to do this. Kent had begun to unbutton, his fingers fumbling on large, tight buttons. The dogs were back, plunging in on top of them. Kent was oblivious to their presence—everything was composed of bodies pushing against each other—until he realized that Cheerio was humping his leg. He stopped himself, flung Cheerio away, and stood up. He was breathing hard. He shook his head.

* * *

After he went to the bathroom, washed his face, and stared into the mirror, after he cooled down, they sat across from each other and talked about it. They had both come into adulthood believing that sex should wait for marriage. That was the policy impressed on them in the conservative churches they grew up in. Neither one had precisely managed to live up to the ideal before their marriages, but they had stayed close enough to it to feel justified in passing on the same wisdom to their children. Not that the children had followed it. Times had changed.

Meg had switched to her business-only persona. She was angry enough at being thwarted, but she squelched that, or rather, expressed it through a stubborn assertion that there was nothing wrong. "We are both grownups," she told Kent. "I don't think anybody follows those rules we grew up with. Of course, if you don't want to get involved, you can just say so. I'm too old to be playing games."

Kent felt so utterly miserable he could barely speak. He too had been thwarted, which left him agitated and unhappy. More deeply, he feared that any chance at happiness was flying away. For just a moment he had glimpsed—or so he thought—a new life.

"Meg," he managed to say, "I do want to be involved with you. I just think we are getting way ahead of ourselves. We hardly know each other, and I'm probably too attracted for my own good. I don't want to rush into something we will regret."

Meg was leaning forward with her elbows on her knees. She looked ferociously intent, but in reality she just wanted to end the conversation. She found the whole business humiliating.

"What I regret is that we are having this conversation."

Kent could easily have given up at that point, apologizing and going off to lick his wounds. That, however, was not his nature. He was a plodder, a very tenacious plodder.

"Don't you believe that people should wait?" he asked. "I don't want to hold back any more than you do, but don't you think it's best? For the relationship? I'm afraid of spoiling everything."

He struck a vulnerable point: she didn't really know what she thought. The shift in the culture had eroded her certainty, but it hadn't quite reversed it.

"I'm too old to worry about that," she huffed. "You want to know what I think? I think it's just sex and we are adults and we aren't going to spoil anything. But I don't know. I just know I hate this conversation and I want to end it."

He felt the chill. "You want me to leave?"

"Well, what else is there?"

He stared at his feet. He was seated in an uncomfortable basket-shaped chair that wanted to thrust him backward with his nose in the sky; to compensate, he was sitting on the very edge. "Meg, I just want you to know that I'm very attracted to you. I'd like to see you again."

"I don't know about that," Meg said.

"Then think about it," he said, standing up.

14   LIFE SKILLS

Jake called from the downtown mission on Wednesday morning, asking Kent if he could substitute in the Life Skills class. The regular instructor, a retired middle school science teacher, had called in sick.

"Sure," Kent said. "What's the subject?"

"They're on sexuality," Jake said. "That's one reason I thought of you. It's hard to get somebody who can teach on that."

The call came at ten in the morning, so Kent had several hours to be distracted by it. The topic put him immediately in mind of his Friday night with Meg.

He had taught the subject many times, when he was the mission program director. There was always a colossal mismatch between the biblical recommendation of a chaste, sober life and the untamed experiences of the men in the program. A classroom at the mission offered very little possibility of philosophy, or even sociology: it came down to personal testimony. The men would go there immediately, incredulously asking: can anybody really live like that? Kent did not want to be a hypocrite.

He nurtured this worry while doing paperwork, gradually coming to realize that hypocrisy was not his deepest concern. The itching question was whether he still believed the old story. He had been disturbed to learn that Meg did not. It was one thing to know that everything was different now, to read in the newspaper about surveys of young people, even of young evangelicals who had sex and lived together without thinking of marriage. It was another to find the same philosophy in a woman of your age and life experience, an attractive flesh-and-blood woman bearing down on you like a 16-wheeler.

That was a funny comparison to make of Meg, he realized. Maybe he was afraid of her. No, not her, but the life that she appeared to offer if he climbed out of his rut. He did not know where he might end up. Things happened when you opened up, and not only good things.

When you get to a certain age you think you have everything settled. It wasn't necessarily so.

But no, he thought, Jesus is my life. That was settled. Saying it to himself might be a bit of magic. But it had carried him through bad times before.

* * *

When he got to the Sixth Street mission, Kent parked across the street and felt himself relaxing almost immediately. He nodded at a half dozen men loitering on the sidewalk, trying as he always did to be a gentle presence. Entering the narrow front door, he introduced himself to the man behind the glass and said he would go up and say hi to Jake.

He had mentored Jake ever since he came to the mission, but they always kept a certain formality between them. Jake still seemed morose, but Kent didn't feel he could ask personal questions directly. He asked a more general question: how were men at the mission getting along? Jake's response surprised him: his face fell even deeper into a slump, and his skin turned strangely darker. He shook his head and could not immediately speak.

"I haven't told you," Jake said in a subdued voice. "Sam? Did you meet Sam?"

Kent tried to remember, and then did. "The little guy? The kid?"

Jake nodded. "He died. He OD'd. We heard on Monday."

"Where?" Sam was one of four men who had left the program planning to make a fortune working on the oil wells in North Dakota. Kent hadn't heard anything more about him since the plan blew up. He knew that some of the men came dragging back to Santa Rosa with their tails between their legs.

"In Modesto," Jake said. "That's where his family lives. He went home after the fracking thing fell through."

"How did you hear?"

"His dad called. He left a message at the desk. He said he drowned."

* * *

Kent's class, the third of the afternoon, was required for all first-phasers. They slumped into the bare classroom, filling the back seats first, as though to keep as distant as possible from whatever medicine the teacher might prescribe. After a prayer, Kent asked them gently whether they had talked about Sam. For a few minutes it seemed as though he had waved a wand over them, turning them to stone.

"Anybody?" Kent asked.

Elvis, who had taken a front-row seat wearing a pearl-buttoned western shirt and a leather vest, spoke up. "We talked about him in chapel."

"You all remember him?"

"No," Elvis said, "these guys are first-phasers. He left before they arrived. It's guys like me, who have been around this place a very long time"—he smirked as though he had made a joke—"who really knew Sam."

"For those of you who didn't know him," Kent said, "he was dealing with some very serious problems but he left early, thinking that life would be better outside."

"With me," Elvis interrupted. "He left with me. We thought we could get to North Dakota and make a ton of money working up there, because of this frack thing. We never even made it out of San Francisco."

Kent nodded. "I'm not trying to put any blame on Sam or anybody else, but to point out that he thought he was ready to be out on his own. This program lasts for ten months or more. For most of you that is a very long time. Believe me, I've watched a lot of men go through it. You can get really sick of it. My point is that the program is ten months long because it takes at least that long to learn what needs learning. You'll be sick of this place and you'll think you won't ever relapse. That's when you need to trust that other people know what is best for you. Stick with the program, and you will reap the rewards.

"Now if I could make a very smooth transition, I think that's also true of what we are talking about today, sexuality. When you are with a woman who attracts you—and let's be honest, sometimes every woman does—your instincts are to get as close as you can to her. You're just drawn, like you have a gigantic rubber band pulling you to her, and especially to her body. But the word of God says no, that's not how you do it.

The word of God says to treat the women like sisters, to honor them, to protect them, never to take advantage of them. That's a hard lesson for a lot of us, and it goes against our instincts. That's why we don't allow any fraternizing while you are here. Guys sometimes ask me, 'What do you have against women?' They think we are acting like women are poison. Women aren't poison, but bad relationships are poison."

Somewhere in the back of the room someone made a comment, too low and too quick for Kent to catch it, and it was followed by general laughter.

"What was that?" Kent asked, but nobody would say.

"Women are not poison," he went on, and once again there was low laughter. He had to wait a beat to go on. "God gives women to us men as our helpers and our soul mates. But you have to get things in the correct order. Number one comes knowing them as sisters. Number two is discerning the special one God may have for you. That discernment takes prayer and godly counsel. Number three is courtship, and it comes only after you have made a godly discernment. In courtship, you get to know each other better with the agenda of learning whether you can become life partners. Number four is engagement, when you have committed to each other and you are making proper plans for marriage. That might mean reserving a church and planning a celebration. That might mean getting your debts and your legal issues under control so you don't bring any of that into your marriage. That might mean getting some premarital counseling about finances or family life. Only after all that comes number five, you get married, and then you begin to enjoy life together physically. It's a long process, men. It might be six months, it might be ten months, it might be two years. Yet it's so very much worth it because it builds a solid and wonderful life together."

By this time hands had gone up around the room. Kent dreaded the questions. How come his marriage hadn't been a solid and wonderful life together? Then there was his dinner with Meg. The men in New Life didn't know about that, but he couldn't get it out of his mind. It was true that he had pulled back before he got in too deep. But he wasn't following the steps he had just given out, and he wasn't sure he could honestly say he wanted to.

He picked one of the hands because it belonged to Charles, a lanky, good-hearted, simple-minded man with a handlebar mustache. Charles had a face unbroken by lines of worry or stress; he possessed a lovely smile that seemed to rise up out of the depths of his soul. He was now in his third time through the program.

"Say now, Kent, can I ask you a very personal question?"

"Of course." Kent wished he could say no.

"Well, you said you don't take advantage of the woman. But suppose you are with a girl and you are really attracted and it looks like she wants to, you know, do it with you. I mean, she is showing all the signs. Sometimes they say no when they mean yes, but you know what she is thinking. You know what I mean? Now how can you say to her, 'We are on step one. I can't even touch you. You're just supposed to be my sister.' I mean, isn't that being mean to her? I don't know if she will be happy with that."

Kent was relieved that it was a question in the abstract. "Charles, you know, you are right; it's possible you are going to hurt her feelings. But sometimes you can't make everybody happy. The thing to ask is, are you doing the right thing? That's what a man has to do. Because if you do, in the long run it is going to turn out all right."

Charles had his hand up again, and Kent acknowledged him.

"I don't see how it can turn out right in the end if she gets her feelings hurt and she just goes away with some other guy who is willing to go ahead when you aren't. I mean, women do that. I mean, they have feelings just like we do. I mean, they like to do it too. You know?"

When Charles had referred to women having feelings, some chortles exploded. The class was all attention.

"Charles, that's a great question. I think this turns into a question of your faith. You're right—there's no guarantee that a woman will be happy if you follow the Christian path. They not only have feelings, they have lust!" At that word, a burst of hilarity detonated. It spread and died and then rebounded again. Kent hadn't meant to ignite that kind of reaction. He was caught off guard. Some of the men couldn't stop laughing, even when they tried to stifle it.

Kent waited, smiled, waited more. "Well, it's true," he insisted, which led to another outbreak of mirth. "Charles, it comes down to, do you trust God? If you do, you'll obey him and I believe you will reap great rewards."

The room was buzzing. From the back, somebody parroted, "GRRREAT rewards." The men loved it. They were laughing with excitement.

Chet, who sat in the front row, was a stutterer. "That g-g-gal will give you g-g-g-great rewards!" He threw his head back, delighted with his joke, and the men applauded him, brimming with smiles.

"You think it's funny," Kent said, "and I guess it is. But I'm serious."

"G-g-g-g-reat rewards!" It was a voice from the back, he didn't see who.

Kent held up his hands and the talk diminished, though it did not end. He noticed a slender young man had his hand up. His cheeks were indented and covered with a rough scrag of black beard.

"Yeah, what's your name?" Kent asked.

He looked at Kent with hostility. "What does that matter?"

"I guess it doesn't matter. I just like to know the names of people I'm talking to."

Looking more carefully, Kent realized that the man was practically emaciated. He continued to stare at Kent until he shrugged and said, "I'm Tim. You said we should listen to the word of God. What word of God were you referring to?"

"I was referring to the Bible. This is a Bible-based program."

"You said the word of God says not to take advantage of a woman, to honor her, not to get sexually involved until you are married. Where does the Bible say that?"

"Okay, good question, Tim. Let's start by looking at First Corinthians six, verse..." Kent opened his well-worn, soft-covered leather Bible and found the passage. "Verse thirteen, in the middle. It says, 'The body is not meant for sexual immorality, but for the Lord.' And in verse fifteen it clarifies, 'Do you not know that your bodies are members of Christ himself? Shall I then take the members of Christ and unite them with a prostitute? Never!' Basically it says, you can give yourself to the Lord, or you can give yourself to sex. Choose one."

Tim didn't bother to raise his hand, he just blurted out, "That's talking about prostitution. Where does it say that you don't have sex with your girlfriend?"

Everybody was talking, as though they couldn't help themselves. The noise in the classroom was becoming an uproar. Kent struggled to make himself heard. "I think that verse applies, Tim. It's saying that your bodies belong to the Lord. Whether it's a prostitute or your girlfriend, sex is the same."

"It's all lust!" a deep male voice shouted out, and everybody laughed. The uproar continued.

Tim was shaking his head.

"Okay, Tim, let's hear from you. You don't agree. Do you agree with Hebrews when it says, 'Marriage should be honored by all, and the marriage bed kept pure?'"

"We're not talking about marriage," Tim insisted. The noise abated slightly because the men waited to hear from him. "We're talking about sex with your girlfriend. Marriage is different. So is prostitution. You're mixing up different things."

"I don't think so," Kent said, raising his voice as loud as he could without shouting. The noise was overwhelming and he couldn't make it go down, even when he stopped and held his hand up. He was losing the class, he realized. Maybe he had already lost them.

For a few moments Kent stood with his hand up, his eyes scanning the room, looking for possible allies. He caught Elvis, with a big grin on his face, laughing with another man and high-fiving him. "Elvis," Kent called. Elvis turned toward him. "Shhh!" Kent said, putting a finger to his lips. He smiled encouragingly and Elvis smiled back, then stood and began waving his hands.

"All right, you guys, listen up! Kent is our teacher and we need to listen." He managed gradually to bring the room back under control.

With all eyes on him, Kent had to think what he would say.

"Look," he said. "Tim has a decent point. People in the Bible didn't have the same exact issues that we do. They didn't go on dates. Girls didn't date; their fathers probably kept them locked up.

"But Tim," Kent said, addressing the scruffy, scowling young man, "or anybody, find me one time when the Bible says it's okay to have sex without being married. It doesn't talk about the exact situation Charles is describing, but if you've read the Bible much at all I think you know what it would say.

"I have to admit, I haven't lived a perfect life. I'm divorced. I've never talked about this before, not to anybody. My marriage didn't work out, and I am not proud of that fact. But here's the thing. The fact that I missed makes me all the more determined to hit the target. Because can you imagine it? Really, try to think about it; you are married to a woman who loves you and is faithful to you because you love her and you are faithful to her. Don't tell me that isn't a beautiful thing. Don't tell me that in your heart of hearts you don't want that. I think what the Bible is trying to say to us is, don't settle for less. Don't compromise. Stick to the program, just like you're sticking to the New Life program. Charles, don't settle for a one-night stand, or even a one-month fling. Go for the prize. It's so valuable. It's worth a lot."

For a long moment the room was quiet, and then Elvis said, "Charles, man, it's not really suffering to keep your pants zipped." He meant to get a laugh but only got chuckles.

Charles had a look on his face like he had swallowed a pint of sawdust and was trying to cough it up. He was sincerely confused.

"Yeah, okay, Kent, of course like any man I would like to get married, but you know, I don't really understand what's the harm in it. I mean, if you get to know a girl, and you make her happy, does that disqualify you? I mean, what's the harm in it? I don't get that."

Kent sighed deeply and said he appreciated the question. "But Charles, I'm going to disagree with you, because I see a lot of harm. People who play around before they are married are going to play around after they are married. You know what that leads to. Marriages break up. Kids grow up without their fathers. How many of you men grew up with that? That doesn't even touch on STDs and diseases of that nature, which wouldn't even exist if people only had sex when they were married.

"But sure," Kent said, "you see people who fool around, and they sometimes seem to have pretty good marriages. I can't deny that it's possible. I don't believe it's the best way, though. I don't think it's nearly as successful as what the Bible is recommending.

"Look, Charles, Tim, all you men, you have to decide for yourself if you want to follow this way that the Bible gives. I believe it's for our good, but nobody can force it on you. This is a Bible-based program and we are committed to making sure that every person who goes through the program understands what the Bible recommends for their life. God knows our makeup and he loves us and wants what's best for us."

A young man in the back of the classroom raised his hand. He wanted to know why Kent thought his marriage had failed. It was the question that Kent had dreaded.

"That's getting a little personal," Kent said, a sad smile frozen on his face. "It takes two people to make a marriage, which is why step two says you should pray and seek counsel about the right one. I tried to do that, but things happened between us that I don't want to go into. They were harmful, and we couldn't get past them. It was the worst thing that's ever happened to me, and that's one reason I'm talking to you about this subject. I don't want you to go through anything similar."

* * *

As Elvis slowly worked his way out of the classroom, he jogged his head back and forth as though "Yes" and "No" were rolling around inside like silver balls. He couldn't imagine how Kent's plan would work in real life.

Would he and Angel ever get together again? He had been calling her most nights on the house phone, but she usually didn't pick up and he didn't like to leave a message.

The trouble with Angel was, there was so much water already under the bridge. He would never get to take Step 1 with her. Or any of the steps. They had already stepped all over everything. He wanted to be with her, but it had begun to dawn on him that it might not work out.

Elvis went upstairs to shed the vest he had put on in the morning chill. He had been placed back in the 12-man room after his collision with Manolo and Richard. As he opened the door, he was surprised to see Peter Anderson lying on his bunk. In the course of putting his vest into his cubby, he realized that Peter had not been in class.

"You sick?" he asked.

Peter did not answer, so he repeated his question.

"No."

"Then what are you doing up here? You're supposed to be in class."

Peter sat up in bed and stretched. "Nobody elected you Pope."

"I'm not trying to be the Pope. I'm just telling you what the rules are. Which we all agreed to."

"So not everybody buys into that."

"Buys into what? You signed an agreement, didn't you?"

"But people have their own interpretation of that."

"Like who?"

"Like people who are on Leadership."

Elvis stopped what he was doing and turned to stare at Peter. "Manolo."

Peter shrugged.

"You've been talking to Manolo?"

Peter shrugged again.

15 MEG'S HUMILIATION

On Friday, Meg Fletcher received a very short note from Kent Spires. It was handwritten on a simple folded ivory card, and it read, "I am sorry for the misunderstanding. It must have been awful for you. It was for me. I have a lot to catch up on in this changing world. I hope I can see you again." He had signed it, "Sincerely."

It had been a week since the dreadful dinner date. It occurred to Meg to wonder why, if he was so sorry, it had taken him so long to say so. Nonetheless, she was touched by the gesture. She had very little exposure to men who apologized, let alone men who wrote handwritten notes on ivory cards.

She got the note as she was running by her house to change for yoga. Twice a week she went to Operatic Yoga, a class she had found on the internet. Meg had grown up in a military home, her dad a Marine-turned-cop. She first heard opera as an adult at a women's retreat, bunking with a roommate who adored it and knew everything about it. Meg rolled her eyes when her roommate played it in the bathroom. But subtly, over the weekend, it got under her skin. When she got home she bought a "best of" CD and listened to it in her car, when no one was around.

She made no claim to be an aficionada. She had only attended an opera performance once, and she recognized only the most famous arias. She listened when she needed a jolt of pure, unrestrained musical emotion.

Operatic yoga was an anonymous social experience where they did their poses to ear- and emotion-shattering sound. There was something perfect about it: over-the-top passion entering through Meg's ears and exiting through physical rigor.

Meg had been an athlete in high school, playing softball on a traveling team (she was a pitcher). She disliked exercise but nevertheless went to the gym religiously, staying trim. She would never be described as skinny, but she was in excellent shape and enjoyed the challenges of yoga. When the silvery voices soared and glistened through the sound system, with everyone in the room intent on their own performance, Meg felt as happy as she ever did. She liked that nobody talked. She liked pushing her body to see what she could do. She adored the extravagant music.

She still felt humiliated by Friday night. She had made herself vulnerable, against her own good judgment, and had been rejected. It felt worse than that: she had been jerked short as if on a leash. And then all but told that she was immoral. At the thought of it she grew angry again.

What softened her was not just the note of apology, but the recognition that Kent had acted according to the way they had been raised. From that perspective, she knew, Kent had done what was right, for her benefit as well as his. Part of her felt that those restrictions had long since lost validity, but if she got off her high horse she could see that there was more than one way to look at it. A man who censured her would be deeply offensive, but a man who had simply not changed with the times could be sweet. The note, Meg thought, swung the argument in favor of sweetness.

Should she reply? That went against her instinct. Humiliation could not be brushed aside. She felt a rush of resentment as she remembered again what he had put her through.

She was in a very strenuous pose, needing to concentrate. Her muscles began to tremble with the exertion, while on the stereo a tenor voice soared to astonishing, muscular heights. Meg had no idea what the words meant, but she knew they had to do with love, and with suffering. It was the most glorious sound.

16 RAVENOUS BEASTS

On the same day that Meg listened to rapturous songs of extravagant love, Kent was gathering papers to go into another emergency board meeting. His secretary Marci was acting arch, pursing her lips and making comments as though to herself about how the Sonoma Mission in all the years had never had money problems like these, and she had to wonder whether God's favor had been taken away. Kent knew that he needed to sit down and give her his undivided attention, but he felt like the proverbial one-armed man nailing shingles on a chicken coop in a hurricane. He kept putting papers down on the table by the copy machine and then getting confused so he could not put his hand on the one he needed. This while he tried to throw in the occasional word to placate Marci—and while he reached out to shake hands with unsmiling board members as they trickled in.

Kent was able to regain focus once he reached the boardroom. Michael Tilden, the chair, cut an austere and impressive figure in the black suit he always wore. He opened in prayer and then explained to the gathered members—all 15 had arrived—that they had just over a week left in the month of July and as of today they could not meet payroll. He turned the meeting over to Kent for a more detailed explanation.

Kent had further troubles handing out the financial reports. In collating them, he had somehow gotten mixed up, and now he had to sort them again while everyone watched. Two of the men sitting on his side of the huge oak table offered to help and tried to, but he was sure they would just confuse him more. He fended them off.

Finally he was able to pass around the documents. When Kent looked at financial statements, he always felt as though he were deciphering hieroglyphics. In this case, however, anybody could read the evidence. They had almost no money in the bank and income was extremely low. Their only assets were the buildings.

A feeling of hopelessness came over Kent. These men, whom he had hand-picked for the board, too obviously had given very little sustained thought to the mission. Listening to them hypothesize about his fundraising efforts, he was reminded of a row of parrots in a pet store, squawking and talking. The sick secret was that they weren't providing any sizeable gifts either. They didn't know that of each other, since giving was confidential, but Kent knew it.

"I have been involved with this ministry for twenty-five years, if I count right," said Charley Imwalle, a short, gentle soul who had the sweet appearance of a Hollywood gremlin. "And gentlemen, I don't hear anything about prayer. I am just asking myself, what's wrong here?"

He went on in that vein, remembering fondly the challenges of 2008, when the economy crashed and people couldn't give like they had. He led them all the way back to 2001 when the towers fell and donors were scared and hanging on to their money. Kent thought Charley was positively enjoying the memories.

"We got through those times," Charley said, and his demeanor became stern. "But this is different! Something is different here, and we need to understand what that is."

Kent's weariness had grown profound, so much that he felt he could barely lift his chin to talk. "Charley, I think what's different is that we've been sued. You can't keep people from suing you if they are determined to do it. You're helpless."

David Stearns butted in immediately. "You could suspend the man who's behind the complaint."

"Yes, you could do that," Kent said, his inertia almost overpowering. "But I'm not prepared to sacrifice a man's life for something he didn't do."

They had been over this ground before. David acknowledged as much with a glowering expression.

Joe Marconi jumped in and offered a truly unexpected idea. "I tell you what," he said. "This may seem crazy, but I think we should close the mission down."

After a stunned silence, David asked, "What? Why?"

Kent was staggered. Joe was someone he would think of as a friend. Joe had a kind heart. He would occasionally drop a note with some encouraging words.

"We'll find out!" Joe said. "We'll totally find out." He stopped as though he had explained himself.

"Find out what?" Kent asked, mystified.

"Find out whether anybody wants the mission." A slight stutter took over when Joe got excited, as he was now. "Heck, find out whether God wants it. If we don't have any money, we have to close it, right? Well, why should we wait?"

To Kent's amazement, some of the board seemed to consider this seriously. They asked solemn questions about where the men would go after they closed, and whether the board would offer severance pay to the staff. But Joe's proposal also lifted others out of their lethargy. Serge Williams, who owned a downtown jewelry store, declared stoutly that he wasn't going to be the one who closed down a place of God; two other men asked plaintively how they could give up without a fight. Kent kept a neutral expression on his face. He wondered who they thought would be doing the fighting.

David argued that something needed to be done, therefore not enough was being done, therefore laziness or incompetence must be involved, or both. The board veered back into familiar territory, evaluating Kent's job—as though they directed the mission by critiquing his performance.

Michael, the chair, invariably spoke in a formal way that would seem more suited to New England than to northern California. He said he would suggest that it might be valuable for Kent to step out for a moment. He turned toward Kent. "I think, Kent, that we need to have a very candid discussion about the approach you've taken. I want everyone to speak freely, and that's hard to do when you are present. Would you mind, Kent?"

Kent went to sit in his office, nodding to Marci as he passed her desk. He felt sure the board wasn't going to fire him, because then they would have to take responsibility themselves. Still, the very idea amazed him, that they would consider removing him after his years of serving and renovating the organization when they just showed up at meetings and talked. That they would even discuss such a thing.

At the moment he hoped they would let him go. Then he could leave this mess behind.

Or maybe he wasn't the subject at all. Maybe they thought it would be easier to discuss Joe's proposal to close the mission without him there. Kent was still amazed that Joe had suggested such a thing. As though you could just close up, and maybe later open again, like a garage door. It seemed so unlike Joe.

They took a long time, which didn't help alleviate Kent's anxiety. Finally Joe came to get him, wearing a confusingly goofy smile.

"I think it worked," Joe said in a whisper, after carefully closing Kent's door behind him.

"What worked?" Kent asked.

"My proposal to close. I was hoping that would give them a jolt. I think it did."

Kent stared. "You weren't really wanting to do it."

"Nah. Nobody wants to close the mission. But they didn't know that until I goosed them." He grinned broadly now. "I got them stirred up."

"You sure did," Kent said, feeling a glimmer of hope. "You got me stirred up. I didn't know what you were trying to do. But what about me?" he asked. "Do I still have a job?"

Joe was a high school teacher, and now he looked like a teasing high school boy, full of pleasure in hiding information from people who want to know. "I'm not telling you that. These are confidential deliberations."

When he reentered the boardroom, Kent knew right away. If they were going to fire him, they would not be able to look at him, and there would be an ungodly ugliness in the room. Instead, nothing had changed: the same dullness and depression continued.

Michael summarized. "Kent, we made an important decision, and of course we want you to fully implement it. We want to issue a bold call to all our Christian community to pray for our financial situation. We intend to reach out beyond those who already support our work, and put the situation in front of the entire family of God. We're going to ask some of the pastors to organize special times of prayer. We feel that there must be spiritual forces involved and we need to fight the battle on spiritual terms."

Kent breathed a deep, cleansing breath. "Who is going to organize it?" he asked. "I might be able to help him."

"We'll talk about that," Michael said. "You and I can discuss how to move ahead."

Kent nodded. He knew what that meant: they expected him to do it. He wasn't entirely unhappy with that. If he organized it, he could do it in a way he could live with. It wasn't a bad idea to ask people to pray.

After a closing prayer, there were handshakes and cheerful farewells all around. *The truth is,* Kent thought, *if the mission goes down, none of them will lose any sleep. They'll be sorry for about five minutes.*

David Stearns didn't get out of his seat as the others exited. When he and Kent were alone, he spoke. "We had a vote of confidence," he said. "You won by a single vote. There were four abstentions. Six to five." He stared into Kent's face with fierce, bristling attention.

"I assumed you were doing that," Kent said. "Thanks for letting me know. Was there one particular issue?"

David scowled. "Jake, of course. You've made that the issue."

"I think you have," Kent said.

"Well maybe I have," David said. "Our troubles would disappear if you would deal with him."

Kent saw no reason to respond to this. He stared silently at David.

"You survived this round, Kent," David said while looking toward the door. "I wouldn't count on surviving the next one."

"I suppose not."

Kent parted from David without another word. He felt guilty for that. He hated that any animosity would linger between them. But he couldn't think of a thing to say, so he left it alone.

Marci handed him a note. It had a telephone number, with "Meg" written under it in Marci's slanted, spidery script.

"What's this about?" he asked.

"She called. She said there was nothing urgent."

Kent stared at the note as though it would reveal more information if closely examined, then realized that Marci was watching him. He hoped he wasn't flushed. "Meg's an old friend," he said. "A Facebook friend. We used to go to the same church, years ago."

He knew that wouldn't placate Marci. When she got on to some idea, she stuck to it.

"I'm taking the rest of the day off," he told her. "You can go if you want."

"Oh, no," she said, her lips pursed in disapproval. "I have a lot of work to catch up on. What do I say if someone calls?"

"Just take their name and number. I'll call later."

17 THE FIGHT

From the first, Peter was puzzled by the change he experienced on the day of his breakthrough. Some sun had shone in his eyes, he had crumpled to the sidewalk, and afterward, for no reason, he found himself interested in other people. He had no idea why.

He was surprised to discover the other men in the program treating him as a friend. Elvis, particularly, talked to him every day. A cloud of positivity traveled with Elvis, so that Peter was exposed to an environment he hardly recognized.

Peter felt the change dissipating as time went on, however, as though he had a pinhole leak. What had really happened to him? He toyed with the possibility that the sun in his eyes had triggered something like a stroke. Perhaps that was what religion did. He did not know. He was not a dogmatic thinker. All he knew for sure was that something in him was drifting back toward how he had been.

Elvis must have seen it too, because he began to tag along after Peter and bird-dog him with questions. It irritated Peter, and he told Elvis to get lost.

"Okay, I will," Elvis said, "but only after you tell me what's going on."

"There's nothing going on. What could possibly be going on in this place?" As he said it, Peter felt his growing repugnance toward the mission, which showed the wear and tear of thousands of homeless men. It lacked a single note of elegance. It smelled of cleaning fluid and floor wax and rot.

"Hey, man, I don't mean this place; I mean what's going on in you."

Peter scowled and shook his head. He didn't want to discuss that. He didn't know how to discuss it.

The fight at the softball game caught Peter by surprise. It was true that Casper's plans for the team annoyed him. Casper was the team captain, a tall, bony electrician. He played a decent first base, looking as awkward as a crane but making the plays. This was his first year in charge of the team, and he was trying to change their cutoff assignments. Instead of having the third and first basemen cut throws to the plate, he wanted the second baseman and shortstop to retreat to do it from their positions, while the third baseman and first baseman backed up the bases. He had copied diagrams of the proper positions for all cuts, which he distributed to the team at the Saturday practice.

Peter had never taken kindly to coaching, and Casper was clearly an idiot. However, Peter saw no reason to react. Let other people bark and protest.

That would be Elvis. Before the Tuesday game, Elvis told Casper nobody had ever cut the ball that way. This didn't make any difference to Casper. He kept saying, "A softball team isn't a democracy, Elvis."

Other players told all parties to cool it. They did, but in the third inning it resurfaced. Their opponent, North Assembly, loaded the bases with two out, and the next batter whacked the ball into the outfield. It went to their left fielder on one bounce, and he fired quickly to the plate. The catcher was yelling cut but there was no one there to do it. Instead the ball hit a divot ten feet in front of home plate, took a crazy hop, and went to the backstop. By the time the catcher retrieved it, three runs had scored and the batter was on third base.

Casper rushed across the infield, shouting at Peter, who was short-stop and should have made the cut. Without contemplation Peter clocked him. It felt good to do so—so good that he smashed him again. That was all, two good pokes, like the swat you might give a dog if it jumped up and stole food.

As far as Peter was concerned, it was practically nothing. He couldn't even call it a fight. It was just a whack at a guy who deserved it.

* * *

Jake called Peter to his office the next morning. He confirmed to Peter that the rules were the rules: violence always meant that you choose to leave. He got Peter's phone from storage and dangled its plastic bag toward him. "If you want to charge it up, you can," Jake said. It was an iPhone, the latest version. He couldn't remember seeing such an expensive phone at the mission.

Peter shook his head. "I just want to get away from this place," he said.

"Okay. I'm sorry it didn't work out. We'll have to report this to your probation officer, so you had better get in touch with him yourself."

"Sure," Peter said.

"I think you still have some time to serve."

"Just a week or so," Peter said.

"If you don't mind my asking, what are you going to do?"

He shrugged. "Don't know."

18   BIG HURT

Kent's phone rang—not his desk phone, but his cell, which he had to fish out of his pocket. He saw that it was his daughter. He heard a sound more like a winter storm than a human voice: Suzanne wailing and choking.

"Dad!" she sobbed. "She's not moving! I can't tell if she's even breathing!"

"Who?" he asked. "Who are we talking about?"

"I tried to wake her up but she won't move. I think she's dead!" Suzanne sounded like she was gargling salt water while crying.

"Suzanne! Listen to me! Where are you?"

"In the studio!"

"What studio?" Then a glimmer of light struck him. "Is it your mom?"

"Yes! I kept calling her and she didn't answer, and so I came by, and I found her. I think she's dead. God, I can't stand it!"

"Suzanne," he said. "Listen to me. Call 911. Can you do that? Hang up on me and call 911. Tell them to send an ambulance, and then do whatever they tell you to do. That's the best thing right now. Call 911. Do you understand? I'm going to hang up so you can call. Suzanne, tell me if you understand and can do that."

She made some sound, which might have been an affirmative, but he wasn't sure so he repeated himself. "Suzanne, if you understand and can call 911, say yes, so I can hear you, and then I'll hang up."

She said yes. He hung up.

He knew only approximately where Alice lived now, somewhere miles across town. He picked up his phone and dialed Meg's number, hoping, urging that she pick up. Meg lived on that side of town and he thought he remembered that she knew where Alice lived. If Meg didn't answer, he would call again, twice, three times, as many times as it took to get her.

But she did pick up. He cut past any small talk and told her about Suzanne's call. "Could you go over there right now?" he asked. "I don't know what is happening but Suzanne didn't sound like she was capable of handling it. I told her to call 911 and I hope she did. I'll get there as soon as I can but I would feel a lot better if I knew you were going."

"Okay," she said. Meg was all business.

"You know where it is."

"Yes," she said. Before he got out another word she said, "I'm on my way," and hung up.

* * *

As Meg turned on to Bardot Road, she heard the wail of the siren behind her. The ambulance and its flashing lights made a scary amount of noise for quiet suburbia, pulling up fast past her and then into the drive. Meg parked alongside. A man in a blue uniform with gold piping and a large, square plastic name tag was already trotting toward the front door.

"I think she's around back," Meg yelled toward him while running for the wooden gate on the side of the house.

Meg bolted up three steps to the studio door and jerked it open. A young woman gaped at her with a face blotched red. For a moment Meg thought that she was the injured one.

The first responder was already silently sliding past Meg and onto the floor beside the body, which Meg only now saw. Unlike on TV, there were no blaring alarms, no shouting. The med tech said nothing but placed one hand on the throat and left it poised there for a moment, his whole body a still life. Then he grasped the body firmly and turned it faceup. It did not look like Alice. The left part of her face over her eyebrow had caved in like a spoiled grapefruit, and her nose was a flat, bloody shape like a yard mushroom that has begun to disintegrate in the weather. Worst, one eye was open but there was no life in the eye.

A second man in the response team had made his way in the door, carrying a heavy pack. The responder who knelt by Alice said, without looking up, "We're going to need the stretcher. And the police." The second man dropped his pack and went back out the door.

"Can I help?" Meg asked. "I know CPR."

"When?" he said. She saw that he had brown, wavy hair, long enough to hit his collar. He looked like he was in high school. "When did you take it?"

She had to think. "Ten years? Twelve years?"

He said, "I'll handle it," without looking at her. Then he seemed to have a second thought and said, "It's hard if you haven't done it for a while."

Meg noticed a dark, glistening substance underneath Alice—blood, thick, almost black, and glinting in spots as though covered by a plastic film.

Meg became aware of Suzanne beside her. Pulling her eyes away from Alice, Meg looked at the horrified face. She turned Suzanne's head away from her mother and wrapped arms around her. "Let's move away," she said. "Let's let this man do his job."

* * *

By the time Kent arrived, the police had blocked off the street. He parked down the block and walked toward the house, stopping before being told to do so by the sturdy policeman who was eyeing him.

"It's my daughter in there," he said.

"She was the one who was hurt?" the officer asked, as though only casually interested.

"No, the one who phoned it in. My girlfriend is there too. I can see their cars from here." He could, in fact, make out Meg's car in the driveway. Meg wasn't going anywhere, since the police had parked behind her.

The cop gave his head a slight shake. "I was told not to let anybody in there. It's a crime scene now."

"Crime" had not figured into Kent's thoughts. "What kind of crime?" he asked.

With another miniscule shake of his head, the officer declined to give out any more information.

The street was a dead end off a county road. The houses were ordinary ranch-style homes, without much hint of personality. And yet, the police officer said "crime."

He could call Meg. She might pick up and tell him what was going on. Maybe she could even arrange to get him past the cordon.

"Hi," she said. "Where are you?"

"I'm standing outside. The police won't let me go past. Where are you?"

"I'm in the studio. They want to ask some questions."

"How is Alice? And Suzanne?"

"They're gone. They took Alice to the hospital, and Suzanne went with her. I think she calmed down, but who knows. You should go over there. I'd go, but she doesn't know me."

"What about Alice?" he asked.

Meg hesitated for just a beat. "I don't know. She had a pulse, according to the first responder. A med tech, I think. I can't tell one uniform from another. She had been beaten up, she had lost quite a bit of blood, and she was completely out of it the whole time I saw her. I don't know," she repeated.

Then, "Did you call your son?"

"Not yet," Kent said. "I wish I knew more. What do you think happened?"

"Somebody beat her up," Meg said. "Maybe it was a robbery. Though this is a funny place for a robbery. In her studio, no less."

Kent let out a deep sigh. "Okay," he said. "I'm going to the hospital. Can you come with me?"

Meg hesitated again. "Sure," she said. "If they will let me leave."

He overheard some words. It went on for a minute or more and he was just about to try to get Meg's attention and tell her never mind, she could join him later, when her voice came back on. "Okay," she said. "I'm on my way."

"We'll have to take my car," he said. "At least I think so. You're blocked in by police."

* * *

During the journey, they hardly spoke. Kent tried to ask Meg for more information, but she cut him off. "I've told you everything I know." She seemed to be concentrating hard on something else.

Everything he thought to say was a blind alley, a stupid cliché or an annoyingly false hope. He ought to be thinking of Alice or Suzanne—praying for them. Perhaps that was what Meg was doing. The truth was that he could only think about Meg and what to say to her. Even though she wasn't talking to him. He knew this was wrong, but he couldn't help himself. Meg dominated his thoughts.

He knew he couldn't go into the hospital, which would seem strange to Meg. She couldn't possibly understand all that had gone on, and continued to go on, in his tormented relationships. He couldn't face his daughter today, not with her mother on the brink of death. Suzanne might well be hostile, and even if not, seeing her and seeing her mother would be overwhelming for him. He didn't want to draw attention to himself with an emotional reaction. Something so much more significant should be on all of their minds.

When they reached the hospital, Kent pulled up to the entrance to let her out. "Aren't you coming in?" she asked.

"I don't think so."

"Why not? You should see Suzanne, at least."

He shook his head. "I'll let you go ahead. I don't want to be in the way."

"You aren't going to be in the way. She's your daughter."

"You go in and if you think she wants me, tell her I'll gladly come. But I think she'll want to be with her mother." He looked pleadingly at Meg. "I don't want to be in the way."

"What does that mean?" Meg asked, but she wasn't sure that Kent heard her. He had already turned his attention back to the road.

As soon as he pulled away, she recognized that there was no point in going in the main entrance. She would find Alice in the ER, if they let her go beyond the waiting room. Meg didn't care if they did. The idea of staring at Alice's battered body made her queasy. But she thought she should see Suzanne.

Kent's behavior mystified her. What kind of father took off like that? He ought to be here.

She walked around the hospital perimeter to the ER. It seemed like miles of parking lot, designed with no thought of anybody making this journey on foot. Once inside the sliding doors, she glanced around the mostly empty waiting room and found, in a far corner, a station with blue-clad personnel behind glass. She got one of them to look at her. "My friend Alice Santorini was brought in half an hour ago," she said. "Could you tell me where she is? Or her daughter?"

The woman to whom she addressed these questions had brown hair pulled back sharply into a ponytail. Her skin had been worn down by sun until her neck was a ring of furrows. She did not even look up at Meg but scanned her computer screen as though she were searching for answers. Eventually Meg realized that a reply was not forthcoming. She asked again.

"She's here," the woman said testily.

"Where can I see her?" Meg asked. "And her daughter."

She felt a hand on her arm and turned to see that it was Suzanne. She must have been in the waiting room all along; Meg had missed seeing her in her quick scan.

Suzanne did not smile or say a word but led Meg away from the window and out of the room into a wide hallway. Rooms flanking the corridor were dimly lit. Through glass doors Meg could see shadowy figures and pulsing lights in red, green, and white.

Suzanne kept going until turning into a windowless room that remained brightly lit. Meg's eyes came to a single bed. Alice seemed to have shrunk to the size of a child. Her head was neatly bandaged and the blood was gone, but her skin was gray. She did not look like she was sleeping; she looked like she was dead. Meg could not detect the slightest movement, though the machine by her side showed a silent progression of mountains moving across its screen.

"They're stabilizing her," Suzanne said. "I don't know your name."

"I'm Meg. I'm a friend of your parents', from years back. Your dad called me. He was across town, and I live nearby, so he thought I could get there sooner than he could. Of course, I wasn't needed, thank God. You had already done everything."

Suzanne was staring at her mother and she looked as though she might fall down. Meg put out a hand and felt Suzanne's wrist trembling.

"Your dad asked me to tell you he would come if you wanted him. He didn't want to be in the way."

Suzanne did not answer. Her eyes were on the machine throwing mountains across its screen.

"Your dad will have to come back to get me," Meg said. "I left my car at your mom's."

"Oh, I'll take you," Suzanne volunteered, and then said, "Wait. I don't have a car either." She giggled, the first sign that she was not catatonic. When she smiled, Meg realized that she was a beauty.

"Maybe your dad will give us both a ride. I think both of our cars are at your mom's."

"My brother could come."

"That's one of the things I wanted to ask you about. Have you called your brother?"

"Not yet."

"Your dad said he didn't want to get in the way, but he'll come if you need him. He told me to tell you that."

Suzanne looked as though a wave went through her. She seemed as fragile as a burden of leaves floating on the water. "Maybe it's better if he doesn't come."

19 SITTING WITH A GHOST

The situation seemed so emotionally jagged that Meg stayed on. She could feel Suzanne's unease. Meg watched her surreptitiously, trying to make sense of her and her family.

Here was a daughter who stayed with her mother in her hospital room, but sat on the far side of the room. Here was a daughter who didn't want to see her own father. Where was her brother? What kept him?

Alice's face was a clay color with an underlayer of green. When Meg took one of Alice's tiny, cold hands, she got no detectible response. Alice's hand felt as limp as a squid. Meg perceived a very faint motion in her nostrils as Alice drew breath.

"Can you come talk to her?" Meg said to Suzanne. "They say people can hear."

Prompted, Suzanne slowly approached.

"It might be good for her to hear your voice. A familiar voice. I doubt she knows mine."

"What do I say?"

"It doesn't matter. Just tell her you love her, tell her how you found her, tell her what you have been doing. She's your mother; I'm sure she wants to hear anything you tell her."

Meg withdrew to give Suzanne space, and she tried not to listen too obviously. Suzanne ran out of words in a few minutes and stood staring at her mother's face, then abruptly returned to her chair.

"It's hard, I know," Meg said. She was tempted to place a hand on Suzanne's shoulder. "Hard to see your mother like that."

Suzanne lifted her head, wearing a sulky expression. "I feel stupid, talking to nothing."

Meg nodded. "Are you close to your mom?" she asked.

Suzanne's eyes were wary. She didn't answer.

"I'm not trying to pry. I'm sure you care about her or you wouldn't be here. You wouldn't have gone to her house to check on her." Meg did her best to say this in a motherly, accepting way.

"We don't always get along."

"You could probably say that about every mother and daughter under the sun. The important thing is that you're here."

"My mom raised me. My dad was...nowhere."

Meg raised her eyebrows. "That's why you don't want him to come?"

"Something like that."

"It's not because of something he did to hurt you."

"Of course it is. He left our family."

* * *

Andy came in, quietly hugging Suzanne and going immediately to their mother's side. He was tall, like his sister, and more sandy-haired than blond. He stared at his mother without expression for several moments, then cupped a hand on the side of her face. When he came back to Suzanne, he glanced inquisitively at Meg.

Suzanne introduced him, and he asked Meg how she knew his mom. "We went to Sonoma Grace together," Meg said. "When you were just little. I knew both your parents."

"Yeah, I've heard my dad refer to you."

"Oh, how nice," Meg said.

"Dad called her when I called him about Mom," Suzanne said. "She lives near Mom and she came right over. She was there before the ambulance."

"Thank you," Andy said, looking Meg in the eye. "So you've stayed in touch with my parents all these years?"

"Your mom more than your dad. But recently, your dad found me on Facebook and we reconnected."

"Well, we appreciate it," Andy said. He seemed considerably older than Suzanne. Was he thirty? He seemed more settled and secure. "Thanks for being here," he said. "Don't feel like you need to stay any longer. I'll be with Suzanne."

Meg hesitated. "Your dad said he would come if you wanted him. I have to call him for a ride home; do you want me to ask him to come in?"

Andy glanced at his sister, who gave her head a slight shake. "No, I think we're fine. Tell him hello for me."

"Do you know anything about her?" Andy asked Suzanne once Meg had gone. "I've never heard Mom mention her."

"No, nothing. But you said that Dad told you about her?"

"Yeah, he came by a couple of weeks ago and mentioned that they have been going out."

Suzanne scowled and made a chuffing sound.

"Why, what's wrong with that?"

"I don't know. I just don't like it. Dad's not in high school."

Andy shrugged. "He's still alive."

"I don't want him acting like Mom."

"Anyway, he told me that Meg wasn't interested and they wouldn't be going out any more."

"Then what are they doing right now?"

"Suzanne, for heaven's sake. If he brought her, he needs to give her a ride back to her car."

Suzanne continued scowling. She was quite lovely, even when she frowned. As Andy knew, she could become furious in an instant. Just as quickly, she forgot what she was angry about, or at least denied it.

After the divorce, Andy had abstracted himself from the drama, plunging into school activities; Suzanne became a handful of hot energy, enraged at whatever crossed her. Her mother understood; she partly approved.

"Do you know what happened?" Andy asked. "With Mom?"

"I have no idea," Suzanne answered, and told him about her repeated calls. "Somebody attacked her, I guess."

"A thief?"

"What would he steal?"

"He might think that Mom had money. She always acted rich."

"You're talking about her in the past tense," Suzanne complained. She glanced toward her mother, but quickly looked away.

"Sorry. Have you talked to the doctors?"

Suzanne's face crumpled, but she shook her head. "Nobody wants to say anything."

"They have to say something," Andy said.

"One doctor—I don't know her name—said that Mom had a severe brain trauma, and that the first 24 hours were crucial. She said they would know more tomorrow, depending on how she responds."

They were silent for a few moments, looking down at the floor. When their parents divorced, they had been just 7 and 11 years old. It felt to Andy as though they were alone again, orphans.

"Why didn't you want to see Dad?" Andy asked.

"I don't know. He can't do anything to help, can he? I know Mom doesn't want him around."

20   ALL KINDS OF REVELATIONS

Marci brought in the sorted mail, and the first folder Kent opened had four checks in it: one for $50, two for $35, and one for $125,000. He stared at it, looked away, and then looked again. He thought he had misread the zeroes. Picking up the check as though it were a living creature, Kent marveled. This was the last thing he had looked for. Good God, he had no faith. He had lost faith in what God could do.

He felt an impulse to kneel at his desk, but he restrained himself. What if Marci came in?

Ordinarily she stapled checks to the notes that came with them, but this time there was nothing. He almost called her to bring him the envelope, but first he looked more carefully at the check. It was business-size, with a printed address from Wine Country Products, on 7th Street in Santa Rosa. Kent couldn't place it. It wasn't on their list of donors, he was sure. He looked at the signature, an illegible scrawl.

The check had a phone number, so he picked up his telephone and punched it with some trepidation. He only wished to say thank you, but he was nevertheless calling into the unknown. He heard the phone ring and then change gears, starting a different ringtone. Most likely he was being forwarded to an anonymous voicemail. Should he leave a message? He didn't want to give out information about the gift; you never knew who might be listening. The phone rang five, six times, while he pondered what to do. He decided he would say something about having questions regarding an item he had received in the mail from Wine Country Products. He would give his first name and the phone number, without mentioning Sonoma Gospel Mission.

Instead of a recording, he got a voice—a low woman's voice, speaking sotto voce. "Hello?" she said.

He asked if he had reached Wine Country Products. The voice said yes.

He identified himself as Kent Spires, saying that he worked for a social service agency, and he'd like to speak to someone who might know about a gift they had received in the mail today.

"Kent," the voice said. "It's me." She spoke in an ordinary voice now.

"Meg?" He suddenly remembered the name Wine Country Products, and the location in the Brickyard. "Meg? Are you the one who wrote this stupendous check?"

"Who else did you think it could be?"

Embarrassed, he said he hadn't put it together. "I forgot the company name. Meg, what a gift. Are you sure you can afford it?"

"It's fine," she said. "I'm glad to do it. Listen, this isn't a good time to talk; I'm in the hospital."

For a second time his mind flipped over: he had temporarily forgotten about Alice. It took him a moment to gather himself. "Thank you for going there," he said contritely. "How is she?"

"The same," Meg said. "Nothing has changed, at least not that I can see. Your kids are here. They're talking to her, holding her hand. They haven't seen any response."

"What does the doctor say?"

"Your kids say she won't make any prediction. Alice's brain doesn't seem to have any bleeds or strokes. The doctor told your kids that there's a good chance she'll come out of it, but it's very difficult to predict. She said to keep talking to her and touching her."

Kent felt boggled with the shame of forgetting. Alice wasn't his wife anymore, but she was the mother of his children, who were evidently sitting by her side day and night. He was squirming with excitement over the check, but he had to pull back and join Meg's somber mood.

"Did you tell Suzanne I would come anytime she wanted?"

"Yeah. I told you, remember? She didn't seem to want that. You probably should call her."

Kent thought he heard an implied rebuke.

"I did," he said. "I'll call again. I was just thinking I need to do that. Thank you for being there. And thanks for this stupendous check. We'll be able to get through the crisis thanks to you. I can't believe you are doing this."

It was just beginning to sink in—not just that they had the money to go on, but that Meg of all people had given so extravagantly. Why had she done it? He couldn't recall that she had ever given a substantial gift, if she had given at all.

"I have to go," Meg said. "Don't worry about the check; I'm glad to be able to help."

"Okay," Kent said. "You're now our biggest donor."

"Right," Meg said. "Maybe you'll come and see me."

After they hung up, Kent stared at the check and thought seriously that he ought to tear it up. Meg hadn't given it to help the mission; she had given it out of pity for him. She probably felt guilty because she didn't want to see him anymore. The check was a way to buy him off.

He almost did tear the check in two, but then he remembered her last words about coming to see her. It was a strange thing to say. Did she mean it? If he tore up the check, it would be an insult.

Like it or not, he had to take the money. Meg had given it to the mission. He should leave his pride out of it.

21   AMBUSH

For the first time in memory, Kent looked forward to Friday's board meeting. He had not told any board members about the remarkable gift, thinking he would wait while Meg's check cleared. Two days later something even better happened: the developer came to his office and admitted that the lawsuit had been contrived to get them to sell the building. Kasha's suit would be dropped, he said. He even apologized.

It was such good news. Kent wanted to celebrate but he had nobody to celebrate with. Further, he was naturally cautious. When news seemed too good to be true, it might in fact be too good to be true.

Several board members phoned in with excuses. Kent was gracious, as always. What choice did he have? He couldn't make them come. A children's Sunday school song kept circulating in his mind: "I cannot come to the banquet, don't trouble me now; I have married a wife, I have bought me a cow."

The majority did show up, however, looking as though they were at-tending a funeral. Michael Tilden, the chair, had the suave, sad manners of a mortuary director. He called them to order and asked one of the younger members to open their time in prayer. Kent prepared himself to be called on for his regular report.

Instead, to his surprise, Michael said that some important questions had arisen. He turned to David Stearns, who glared back at him, looking harsh and uncomfortable, and said that Don Markens would introduce the subject.

Don seemed surprised at that, but he nodded and then sat for a moment pursing his lips, apparently thinking about what he would say. "I think we should start by establishing the facts," he said, and turned toward Kent. "Kent, you came here about twelve years ago, after your divorce. Is that right?"

Kent nodded slowly, unsure where this was heading. "Fourteen years, actually."

"You were a pastor at Sonoma Grace, but they felt you had to leave because of that divorce?"

Kent nodded again.

"Kent, we understand that you are dating a woman some of us know, Meg Fletcher. She's also divorced. Is that information accurate?"

By this time Kent knew that his happy bubble was being popped, though he could not see what was coming. "I've been out with Meg a few times. Yes."

Don turned back to Michael and suggested that they ask Kent to leave while they discussed his situation.

"What situation?" Kent interjected. "I can't see that Meg Fletcher has anything to do with this board."

Michael and Don looked at each other, both hoping the other would speak. David Stearns spoke up instead; he couldn't help himself. "Meg Fletcher doesn't have anything to do with us, Kent, but you do. We need to discuss how your reputation affects our work."

He was flabbergasted. "My reputation? What are you talking about? Speak plainly."

David leaned back in his chair and squinched his eyes closed, then opened them. He learned toward Kent with a searching look. "At your age, if you are dating someone, you're thinking about marrying her. You can't deny that. Divorce has serious consequences for many of our supporters, and divorce and remarriage have even more. It's our responsibility as a board to consider the reputation of our leaders before it becomes an issue, not after the fact."

Kent looked around the room, trying to understand what was happening. Was this a setup that the whole board was in on? Nobody wanted to meet his eye.

"If you're going to be discussing my reputation," he said, "I want to be in the room to hear it. I think I have a good reputation, and I have a right to hear any allegations made against me. You can't discuss my reputation without giving me a chance to defend myself."

It occurred to him that he could end the discussion by saying that he was no longer dating Meg. But the whole subject offended him. He was prepared to defend the principle of remarriage, if it came to that, and he was reasonably sure that hardly any churches in Sonoma County would struggle against it. Was David suggesting that he couldn't even date? That going out for coffee with Meg besmirched him and the mission with him? Why hadn't they come to him to talk it over? The whole thing was wrong. He felt outraged and abused, and he was in too delicate a state to put up with it.

Michael looked at David inquiringly, and David shrugged. "Very well," Michael said, "we'll have a discussion with Kent present. It might feel awkward to speak frankly with Kent hearing, but I have to remind you that we have a duty as board members to support and protect the Sonoma Gospel Mission."

David jumped in. "I want to say that this doesn't have anything to do with Kent's personal reputation. It's a question of how our supporters view his divorce and remarriage. I can't see why he needs to be here to be part of that discussion. We're not really talking about him."

Nobody said anything to that. The room seemed to hold its breath. Finally Michael looked at Kent and said, "Kent? How do you feel about that?"

"It feels pretty personal to me," Kent said. "I'd like to stay."

"All right," Michael said. "I'm going to suggest we have an open-ended discussion. Anybody can speak or ask questions. David, do you want to get us started?"

"Yes," he said. His face had turned into a mask of determination. "I'd like to make a motion. I move that we ask Kent Spires to submit his resignation, with immediate effect."

Obviously startled, Michael asked if there was a second. After a pause, Don said, "Second."

"Good," Michael said. "David, I think you should begin the discussion by explaining why you want Kent to resign."

"Sure," David said. "It's really very simple. It's our job to protect and advance the Sonoma Gospel Mission, and I'm convinced that Kent has become an obstacle to that. Understand..." He swiveled toward Kent. "I have nothing against Kent. I think highly of him as a human being. But we are in a crisis, and he has been an obstacle to resolving that crisis through his unwillingness to remove Jake from his position. In addition, I've learned that when we had an excellent opportunity to sell the property for twice what it is worth and build a new facility with money left over, he didn't even consult with the board. I just learned about that, almost by accident. Now, this. If we were to become known for serial divorce and remarriage, I feel sure that we would lose credibility. Maybe not with everyone. But certainly with some. With the financial challenges we already face, I think that would almost certainly prove fatal. We are on the brink of disaster. We need to act now, not after it's already a fait accompli. I personally don't think we have any business telling Kent how to conduct his marital affairs. I wouldn't dream of treading on such personal ground. I merely assert that the time has come to realize that we have a problem and to act decisively on it. I believe we need new leadership."

Kent, who had been internally strong to this point, crumbled inside. He knew David had a point. He had become an obstacle. He was adrift, and he very nearly held up his hand to voluntarily say so. Everything seemed suddenly dark; he had lost his bearings, and he ought to quit now. Before he did, he remembered: the problem was gone. The lawsuit had disappeared. Meg had given them money.

For that matter, he was not going to marry Meg.

He said nothing. Some deeply stubborn reserve made him hold his tongue. This board could ask him to resign and then discover for themselves that they had done it unnecessarily. Let them.

Discussion followed, mostly about why David thought that it would be so bad if Kent remarried. "Geez, it's been fourteen years, didn't you say? That's a long time to wait. Nobody is going to blame him." That was John Brown, a compact, nut-brown man in his eighties. But Serge Williams, who owned a jewelry store out in Rincon Valley, said that some of the really conservative churches could be sticklers about divorce. To which Charley Imwalle said, "I don't think those churches do anything for us anyway, do they?" Nobody knew how to answer that. Kent could have told them that Charley was right, but since nobody asked him, he held his tongue.

Robert Green, a school vice principal, wanted to know who would run the mission if Kent left. Don spoke up for the first time since seconding the motion. "Well, at David's suggestion I talked to one of the pastors in town. I won't mention his name, but I think you'd all be pleased. He seemed very interested."

"Wait," Serge said. "You offered him the job? How could you do that?"

"No, no, I just wanted to see whether he was open. No, I didn't offer him any job."

Kent ran a roster of pastors through his mind. If their churches were going well, they wouldn't want to leave for the mission. If their churches were in trouble, they might want to move, but would that be the kind of person that David and Don had in mind?

Finally somebody called the question. Michael took a voice vote, which was divided. Michael could not tell who was in the majority, so he asked to see a show of hands. It actually wasn't as close as Kent had expected. Last time he had (so he had been told) won by a single vote; this time it was by two. After Michael counted the votes and announced the result, a period of silence followed.

Finally Michael stirred himself. "I suppose we should carry on with our regular business. Kent, can you give us your report?"

As he stood to speak, Kent realized that he was trembling. He thought that he had remained calm through the discussion, his expression neutral, his eyes tracking from one speaker to the next. His hands gave away the truth. For an instant he wondered whether he could carry on in this job for another day. But then he gathered himself and remembered what he had to say.

"I'll be brief," he said to the board. "I bring good news on two fronts. First, as a result of conversations with Buddy Grace, the developer, the suit against the mission is not going forward. Apparently Buddy and his lawyer Adam McLeod had persuaded Kasha to file the suit as a way of pressuring us to sell them the Sixth Street property. The lawsuit never had any basis in fact, as Buddy admitted. He apologized for the trouble he had brought us, and particularly that he had inflicted on Jake, who was the person falsely accused in the suit. Buddy apologized to Jake and has indicated that they won't pursue the lawsuit. He's willing to make a public apology.

"The other piece of news is that a donor has given us a gift of $125,000, with no strings attached. That should let us get through this financial crisis. I'm hoping that our donors will soon forget about these phony charges against the mission and that we'll regain their trust. I feel confident that the Christian people of Sonoma County believe in what we are doing."

He took questions, and there were a lot of them. Most he couldn't answer yet, such as what kind of publicity would let people know that the lawsuit had been dropped. He said he would be happy for suggestions. (Kent had a good idea that the best thing would be more phone calls—hundreds of them.)

David Stearns raised his hand and asked who the big donor was.

"It's an anonymous donor," Kent said.

"I think this board can keep the information private," David said. "I'd like to know so that I can thank him."

"I'm afraid I can't give out that information," Kent said. "Anonymous means anonymous."

"I'm not asking you to publish it," David insisted. "If you know who gave the money, why shouldn't the board?"

Kent managed a smile, one he hoped looked genuinely gracious and not smug. "I think you know the answer to that, David."

22 NO SURPRISES

Meg visited Alice in the hospital every day. Walking down the corridor in her squeaking rubber soles, she felt like an interloper. She had never been close to Alice, and she was not a relative.

She went every day just to see that Alice was alive. Also, she went hoping to see Alice's children. (They were Kent's children too, but better to think of them purely as Alice's, who had done most of their raising.) Whenever they appeared, Meg tried to back away and leave them with their mother, but Andy invariably urged her to stay. She thought she understood why. It was wearing to occupy a room with the unmoving body and beeping machinery of someone you love. Having another person in the room made it easier to endure.

Andy was tall and skinny, with a goofy way and a winning smile. She felt guilty for liking him more than she did her own son. This boy she could dance with. It was bliss to simply *like* young people.

The two of them, Suzanne and Andy, seemed very alone perched on the edge of Alice's bed, holding her hand; or sending each other out for a Coke or a sandwich. Kent should be here, she thought. On Saturday, their third day in the hospital, she brought it up again with Suzanne. Would she like her dad to come by? Suzanne's dark eyes looked down and away, and then she said no. Meg would have liked to ask her why.

Meg couldn't help imagining her own kids in a comparable situation. They were more gregarious, uproarious and disruptive. They would not fade into the background. Their friends would show up. The hospital staff would love them or hate them.

Still, she liked these two. On the fourth day, she ran into Suzanne again and didn't have anything to say to her. Alice was unchanged, so still and so ghostly that Meg could barely imagine her coming back to life. As Meg prepared to leave the room—she never stayed long—Suzanne stopped her.

"I wanted to explain about my dad," Suzanne said. "I'm not mad at him, you know. But he and my mom are like oil and water, and I hate it when I have to see them together. My mom wouldn't want him here."

"I wasn't thinking that he would come for your mom," Meg said. "I was thinking he would come for you and Andy."

"We're doing fine," Suzanne said.

Meg made herself study Alice's small form. It was a way of acknowledging that she still lived, that her body mattered as the seat of life, even though it was easier to pay attention to the machines.

The flesh had turned green and yellow down Alice's nose and around her eyes. Her head was still bandaged, so Meg could not see the area where the skull had been crushed. Her limbs remained splayed as the last nurse had left them. She didn't squirm. She lay absolutely still. Even her breathing was silent and invisible. Meg put a hand on Alice's arm or her back, she spoke to her, she prayed out loud. They said it was good to bring something familiar, something that the sleeping brain might recognize. The Lord's Prayer was the best thing she could come up with. Alice remained as still as a wax candle. She didn't mumble or flicker her eyelashes. She barely breathed.

On Monday, the police interviewed Meg. They came to her store unannounced and asked a bunch of questions about Alice. Brian was there; he kept leaning in to listen. The lead questioner was a young woman of Asian descent, pretty in a tight, athletic way. She cut her hair too short, in Meg's opinion. Accompanying her was an officer in his late middle age, who said very little. Meg got the idea he was the more experienced policeman, perhaps overseeing the young woman's training.

There wasn't a lot to tell them. Meg rarely saw Alice, and they weren't really close. Alice's ex had called Meg after his daughter found Alice unconscious; he had asked Meg to go over because she lived nearby and knew where the house was. It took the police some time to understand the sequence and the relationships. They wanted to know how they could contact Kent, and she told them about his role at Sonoma Gospel Mission.

Was Alice seeing someone? Not that Meg was aware, but then, she probably wouldn't know. Meg mentioned the gallery where Alice sold her paintings and sculptures in Healdsburg; she said the owner might have some contacts for her. Otherwise, she was not able to offer much.

On Friday Alice's door was open, and as Meg entered, she saw that Suzanne stood in the middle of the room looking down at the floor. Her hair was a golden taffy color. Suzanne quickly raised her head and snapped back to life, but to Meg's eye she looked wan and harried.

"You all right?" Meg asked after they had touched in a polite hug.

Suzanne wagged her head. "All right. This is hard, you know? I don't want to lose heart but I wish that there was some sign."

Meg nodded and put a hand on her upper arm. "Wish I could help," she said.

"No, you're great. I appreciate your coming."

"Is there anything I can do?"

Meg didn't expect an answer to that, but after a pause Suzanne raised her eyebrows and said that this was probably stupid, but could she go and check Mom's studio to make sure everything was all right? She and Andy planned to go by the house over the weekend, just to water the plants and collect the mail and make sure everything was okay, but she wondered whether there might be anything left in the studio that would be upsetting. She was sure she would be fine, she said, but would Meg mind going by to see?

Some blood? Meg thought. Or maybe stuff left in disarray, a reminder of the violence? Meg had no idea how the police would leave things.

"You haven't been there since you brought your mom to the hospital?"

"No. Andy went to lock up, but he didn't go inside."

Meg walked from her house first thing on Saturday morning, taking both of the dogs because she thought it might be eerie to enter the empty studio. It was a 15-minute stroll down the hill from her front door, the last stretch on a narrow tree-shaded road that had no shoulder or sidewalk. She had to keep a close eye for cars, and when she heard one coming, she had to drag the dogs off the road and yell at them to sit. She had meant the dogs to be a calming influence, but in these circumstances they actually made her jittery.

Still, she was glad she had them when she walked around the house, letting herself in the gate, and proceeded through the garden to the studio. She tied the dogs up outside. In just these few days, the grass had grown shaggy and the place had a deserted aspect. She couldn't stop herself from thinking that whoever had hurt Alice was still on the loose. He might be here as well as anywhere. That was all nonsense, but still, when she pulled out the key Suzanne had given her, unlocking the door while the dogs pulled and whined, she felt unnerved.

Fog had come over the hill during the night, and so despite the studio's large skylight and plentiful windows, the room was dim. She found its smell strange and unpleasant, a sour chemical odor with bite. It might have been paint, or glaze, or whatever artistic substances Alice used, but she didn't remember smelling it before, and she didn't like it. She wondered if it was the smell of blood. Meg found the light switch and felt better when she could see clearly.

There was nothing. She could see no sign that anything untoward had happened here. It did not even have the tidied look; it seemed as though perhaps Alice had walked out just moments before, leaving some signs of her work in progress: a painting on an easel, some unfinished clay figures on her workbench. Where Suzanne had held her mother, where the blood had pooled, there were no remnants of violence. Perhaps she could see some slight staining on the tight oak flooring, but that might be her imagination, too.

She walked around the room, flipping through a stack of canvases, examining the workbench more closely. It all seemed perfectly innocent. Surely the police had been over all this carefully.

Well, she could let Suzanne know that she had been here, and there was nothing to fear. Meg was glad that she could do something for Suzanne. It really was nothing. Whatever had happened was most thoroughly over.

Meg was just ready to lock up and leave when she noticed the kiln. It was a curious mechanical thing, something between a stove and a safe. She had never really seen a kiln to look at. She went over and fiddled with the door. How hot had Alice said these things got? Was it 4,000 degrees? You wouldn't want it open when it reached that temperature.

It had a double latch, which she undid. She swung open the small, heavy door. There was something inside, a sculpture, one of Alice's small heads. Meg took it out—it sat snugly in her hand—and saw that it captured a man, strikingly sharp-featured. Green glaze had been dumped over it, and orange on top of that; a knife-shaped notch had come out of the right cheekbone. Strange and alienating stuff that Alice had been working on. Why was this one left behind? There were no others in the studio. She assumed they were all on sale in Healdsburg.

She placed the head carefully back in the kiln and closed the door. She would have to tell Suzanne that it was there.

23 SHE CALLED

After 14 years, Kent had grown accustomed to feelings of loneliness, as well as to the accompanying phantoms of relief: ideas of family togetherness or a new career or—in this case—love. He thought often of lonely Jack Lewis and his concept of Joy, that Elysian delight that could only be experienced when you were not chasing it. (*Surprised by Joy* was a book he read again and again, trying to find a portal into Lewis's life.) Kent hoped that by averting his gaze from Meg, he would stumble into Joy.

He hoped for Joy, but in his heart of hearts he knew it would never happen. All optimism had been scrubbed out of him by the Brillo pad of experience.

Kent was determined to stay clear of Meg. He considered himself a gentleman, and she had told him to give her space. She had also become the mission's biggest donor. Though he couldn't exactly put his finger on what would be wrong with romancing a contributor, he knew it felt wrong. Furthermore, some members of his board believed that a divorced man had no business going out with anybody. Kent didn't agree, but he wasn't anxious to court opposition. He had decided to stop seeing her, insofar as it depended on him.

It was Saturday night, and he was watching a public television special on the national parks when the phone rang. He stared at the caller ID, not recognizing the number, and waited four rings before deciding to answer. He didn't recognize the voice at first, either. It was Meg. He had to ask her to wait while he turned down the TV.

"Are you all right?" she said.

"Yes, yes."

"Have you been running?"

"No! I'm sitting here watching TV."

"You sound like you are out of breath!"

"Oh," he said, "it must be allergies. I'm fine. How are you, Meg?"

He had not talked to her since receiving the contribution. He had, naturally, written her a warm thank-you, but there was no reason for her to acknowledge it. Talking to her now raised all kinds of mixed feelings. It was easier for him when they had no contact.

She told him she had been to Alice's studio. "Your daughter asked me to go and make sure everything was okay. I think she worried that there might still be some signs of the attack. So I went by this morning. Everything was fine, but in the kiln I found one of Alice's sculptures. I've been thinking about it and I'd like you to see it."

After hanging up, Kent stared at the muted television for a long time. Portraits of nature glided over the screen: snow on fir trees, and a little bird with a bright eye, and wind whirling snowflakes through a canyon with wedding-cake walls. Was Meg signaling that she would like to have a relationship after all? It seemed like a flimsy excuse for her to call.

On Sunday morning, Kent found himself parked on the curb in front of Sonoma Grace waiting for her to appear, as they had arranged. Sonoma Avenue was quiet, except for the dull pounding of the church band inside the walls. Kent had already attended his own Lutheran service.

The sleek sign for The Barn was new to him. He looked at it with a neutrality that surprised him. Apparently Ross had given Sonoma Grace a new name. Kent wasn't repelled by it, nor was he impressed by the brushed chromium and swooshing logo. He didn't really care one way or another. In a funny way, that was a relief. It was also sad, the fading and tattering of the fabric of his former life. At one time this place had been his heart.

Meg appeared at his passenger door, stooping to look in, smiling. Kent resolutely kept his eyes on her face. "I came out while they were still singing the last song," she said. "Did I startle you?"

He didn't know how to answer. Did he look startled? What expression was he wearing?

Kent had thought of one thing he wanted to say, and he went there immediately. "I wanted to thank you for your kindness to my children. Andy told me you are visiting Alice, and I think it means a lot to them."

She waved a hand. "You know, it's funny, I started going to see her because I was the first one to get to her house, other than Suzanne. I've never been that close to Alice. Then I noticed that she doesn't get very many visitors, so I thought I should keep it up. It's not a big deal. The hospital is near my showroom, and I don't stay long. You have nice kids. I like them."

"They must like you, too," Kent said. "Obviously, if Suzanne asked you to go to her mom's studio for her. Thank you. I can't really claim much credit for them, but they are nice people."

* * *

Kent had never seen Alice's studio, but when he entered it behind Meg, he felt a strangely familiar resonance. It must be that he felt Alice. They had been married for ten years, after all.

"What's wrong?" Meg asked him. "Are you all right?"

He nodded. She was staring at him as though he had giant spiders on his head, but he didn't mind. He liked to look at her.

"I'm not sure I can explain," he said, "but there's something of Alice in this room. I have a lot of sick memories associated with that."

"Did you fight here?" Meg was still staring at him. Her eyes were lively and dark, her body limber and fluid. Not beautiful, but beautifully alive, as he remembered thinking before.

Kent shook his head. "No, I've never been at this house. She moved here after we split. But something in the room is just her. I'm not wanting to be negative about her, you know, and I realize you are her friend, but there's a lot I'm still getting over."

"Okay," Meg said, looking at him with an expression he couldn't easily categorize.

"Come over here," she said. At first he thought with alarm that she was making an overture, but almost immediately he recognized that she was only inviting him to approach a big metal box. He had not noticed it when he came in, and he did not know what it was until Meg told him. She opened the door with a complicated latch and pulled out a sculpture, about ten inches tall.

Kent knew from somewhere that Alice was doing sculpture. He didn't like her paintings, and he found as he appraised the sculpture that he didn't like this any better. A cold violence came through it. That had to be something of an artistic achievement. Wasn't that the point of modern art, to draw a response?

"Do you like that?" he said to Meg.

"It's interesting," she said. "I don't think I want it in my living room."

"Somebody must," he said. "I think she's done well with it."

Then, "Why did you want me to see it?"

She screwed her mouth, as he had noticed she did when she had something significant to say. "I had a thought I wanted to try out on you. It was in her kiln, and I wonder whether that means it was the last one she did. The most recent, I mean. And then I thought that maybe this head is modeled on the man who attacked her."

"Let me see," he said, and stepped close to Meg, taking the head from her hand. Yes, it was very realistic. It might be modeled on a real person.

"Why don't you talk to the police about it?"

"I did. I called them on Saturday, after I found it. They didn't seem interested."

"And what am I supposed to do?" He suddenly felt a little hostile.

She shook her head. "I don't know. I guess I was hoping you might recognize who it is. You know a lot of people."

He looked at the head again, and something in it did strike a spark of familiarity.

"You mean I know a lot of homeless people."

She said nothing.

"And do you think Alice was in the habit of mixing with homeless men? I don't think so."

"Maybe not," Meg said. "I guess it's a stretch."

It was almost as though the sculpture was speaking to him, pleading for recognition. He began to suspect that eventually a name would come to him.

He took a picture of the head and promised Meg that he would show it to a few people at the mission. "It does look familiar to me," he said, "but I don't know from where. I've met a lot of men over the years."

He drove her back to the church, where she said a pleasant but ordinary good-bye before getting out and walking away. No looking back. No suggestion that they see each other again.

At the light on Farmers Lane, he looked at the photo on his phone. For some reason, it looked more three-dimensional on his small screen than it had in the studio.

He suddenly made the connection. No doubt 15 years had changed appearances, but Kent felt a sureness of recognition, the un-erasable memory of a face. It was the boy whom he had caught with Alice. The boy he had rescued and sheltered, who had rewarded him with the most flagrant betrayal possible. It made him cold to think of it. This boy had come back to Alice, and this time he had tried to kill her.

24 RAW ANGER

Kent looked at the photo time and again. Sometimes he was sure, sometimes he thought he was imagining things. It was a sculpture, after all, not a passport picture. Could somebody else from that time confirm the boy's face? He tried to think, but the only person was Alice.

Everything important to him—his children, their mother, his years of suffering—seemed connected to that photo. Monday morning he went to the downtown mission. Meg had suggested the sculpture might be of a homeless man, and though Kent was operating on a very different assumption, he took it up with Jake just in case. At one glance Jake identified Peter Anderson, who had been in the New Life program for a short time and then left after starting a fight.

"You're sure?" Kent asked, stunned at the confirmation.

"I'm sure," Jake said. "That's him. You can ask any of the men."

In the afternoon, Kent showed up unannounced at Meg's showroom. Meg regarded his outfit—a tie under a blue V-neck cable-knit sweater, in a shade that did nothing for him—with a dollop of pity, as a woman will regarding men who have no idea how to dress. She was also annoyed by his general clumsiness. He could have called to say that he was coming.

Such annoyances were quickly put aside when Kent told her that Jake had recognized the face. He didn't go on to explain that Peter Anderson was the boy who had caused his marriage's failure. She didn't need to know any of that. He was almost sure she had never met Peter, and she probably didn't know his name.

"When did he leave the mission?" Meg wanted to know.

Kent wagged his head from side to side, as though he were coating the inside with a plastic seal. "That's what gets interesting. He left a day before Alice got attacked. And nobody has seen him since."

"And there's no doubt?" Meg asked. "I mean, there's no doubt it was the same man that Alice sculpted?" Meg flopped down on one of the leather sofas.

"I asked around," Kent told Meg. "I asked quite a few of the guys in the mission. When I showed them the picture of the sculpture, they said it was him. Immediately. Without hesitation. I even walked the streets around the mission and asked a few people. Some of them could recall his face but he's disappeared. He told Jake when he left that he was all but done with his probation, but when Jake called the probation officer he found out he has months still to serve. He's required to report, but he hasn't. He's just gone."

"How would Alice even know somebody from the mission?"

"They all said Peter seemed really different," Kent said. "Like he was a spoiled rich kid. Very entitled and out of place in the mission."

"So you're saying he might have some overlap with Alice's social circle."

Kent shrugged. "I'm not saying anything."

Meg found a deep pool of impatience toward Kent. Why did he have to use that "I have no idea" routine? Did he really think she would believe he had no idea?

Kent was pretending to study her displays. She was tempted to ask him his favorite use of lavender. That would not really be funny. He was saying something and she had not listened. "What?" Meg said.

"I was asking if you know anything about Alice's social circle. People who might know of the contact she had with him."

"You want to follow them up?" Meg knew as she said it that it was an unpleasantly aggressive thing to say; it probably seemed to mock him.

"Well, no," he said. "Maybe the police would be interested."

"The police aren't interested in much. When I told them about the sculpture, I'm not even sure they wrote it down. And look what we've found now."

"I don't know if we've found anything, Meg. Could be a coincidence."

Why did he act this way?

"We found that a man who might have been the last person she saw disappeared about the same time as she was assaulted. And that he was someone with a criminal record. I'd call that something."

Meg had seen Alice covered with rust-colored blood, she had sat by her bedside to watch her breathe. Alice might die yet. How terrible for some stranger to come into her home and beat her. How could she defend herself? Alice was tiny.

"Are you crying?" Kent asked, with a voice full of concern.

"No!" She wiped her forearm across her face. "No. I'm just thinking of what Alice went through."

He said nothing. He had his hands clasped behind his back, not knowing what to do with himself.

"Come sit down," she said. As soon as he moved, she felt an urge come over her: she wanted him nearer, she wanted to reach out a hand to him. But she didn't.

He came over, hesitantly, lifted his pant legs at his knees like an old man, and sat down.

"Why don't you take that tie off?"

"Why?" he asked. "Does it bother you?"

"You're not at work. You don't need a tie."

He took it off, rolled it, and stuck it in his pocket. It was a cheap tie. If it had been silk, she would have made him take it out again; it would get spoiled jammed into a pocket.

"I want to tell you something," she said. "I'm sure you don't know. I don't even know why I want to tell you, but I think I should come clean with you. You okay with that?"

"I don't have any idea what you're going to say."

He was a kind man, she knew, but at the moment he seemed like a generic man, an exasperating man. Alice must have rebelled against that pious, above-it-all attitude. Meg remembered how it felt to be stuck in a marriage where your life meant nothing. With Greg it had been literal: he thought women were objects to move or manipulate. It might have been worse for Alice, married to a man of principle. She must have wanted to scream. There was no discussion with principles. There was no living with principles.

"Right. True. Well, when you and Alice were starting to come apart, Greg and I were too. Alice and I talked about it. We shared. I told you that I'm not really close to her, but for that little time I was, because we shared a secret. Who else could we talk to about our marriages? Not anybody in our Bible study. Not anybody in the church. Not our parents. We talked to each other, because we both realized where we were heading."

"You talked about this *when?*" He sounded cold, and scared.

"Oh, I don't know. All along. As soon as we realized we were going in the same direction. We would say little things even when you were around, and lift our eyebrows, and stuff like that. You were just too busy with important things. You never guessed."

He didn't say anything. Meg found it hard to believe that he could look at her with that level gaze, like he was listening to a lecture.

"What I need to tell you is that I egged Alice on. I encouraged her."

"Encouraged her to what?"

"To be independent, first. To open her eyes. To see her options. We talked about all that, and she was encouraging me, too.

"But what I'm not so proud of. She told me she had the hots for that boy who was staying with you, and I encouraged that, too. I didn't see any harm in it. I was angry at Greg, and angry at men because of Greg. I thought all men were like him. What happened might have happened anyway, but I was wrong. I thought, *We won't hurt anybody because we are grown-up women.*"

Meg was astonished when Kent, peaceable Kent, got to his feet, swept out his arm, and knocked over one of her displays. Bottles of olive oil shattered in a fabulous crash. The spicy, herbaceous smell filled the air. Kent had tried to catch the display as it tumbled, and now he was holding his hand, as though he had injured it.

"How could you do that?" he asked. "Tell me how?"

"Don't shout at me," she said.

He throttled it down. It was almost worse, the way it hummed in his throat, like something caught there and choking him. "Why did you tell me now? It brings back such awful memories."

She was not frightened. Frightened was what she felt with Greg when he got out his guns.

"No, don't cry," she said. "I can't stand that."

"You have strange standards," he said.

She shook her head. "I thought I needed to come clean if we were going to be friends."

He had gotten control of himself, barely. He stood in a pose like Frankenstein's monster, his back curled, his head lowered.

"Well, it's just sick. You don't know how sick. And I don't want to tell you. Whether we are friends or not. There are such awful memories."

She got to her feet and put out a hand to touch. "Who knows?" she asked.

"Nobody knows," he said. "Nobody needs to know. It's nobody's business." He looked at her with venom in his eyes. "Nobody's business now, and it was nobody's business then. You really screwed up."

25 REMEMBERING

On Saturday, Kent was up early. He was no good at sleeping in, and his favorite time of the day was the dawn hour he spent with his cup of coffee. Lately—for the last five years at least—he had abandoned reading the newspaper (sports section first) for time to sit on his front porch and watch early light on the massive slopes of Mt. St. Helena. Some days the mountain looked very far off, but today it seemed to be just across the apple orchard.

His week had been long and wretched. After he stormed out of Meg's showroom, he drove out to Spring Lake and followed trails far up into the hills, farther than he had ever gone, until he was disoriented and foot-weary. Hunger pangs finally drove him down the hill to his car, and then to In-N-Out, the burger place. He relieved his hunger but not his mind.

He kept on furiously replaying his conversation with Meg, rehearsing what he should have said to her: crushing comments loaded with bitterness. He was still doing it now, five days later.

This was nonsense. He knew he could not say anything like that.

What kept reentering his mind was a memory that he had tried to cordon off. This was the true cause of his fury. He had never told it to anyone, and he never would.

He had come home from work earlier than usual, had found the house deserted even though Alice's car was in the driveway. He remembered so clearly the eerie, museum-like quiet as he walked through the kitchen, into the living room, down the hallway. He thought that Alice was in the bathroom, but that door was open. Then he saw a light under the door of their guest bedroom, where Peter was staying until he could make peace with his parents. Kent knocked and when he got no answer, he opened the door.

There was Peter, the boy with the luxuriant, long hair, sitting on the edge of the bed. Peter's face was contorted with pain or fear, and he was breathing heavily. He looked like he was having a heart attack. Alice was on her knees in front of him. Kent's immediate, unfiltered thought was that Alice was giving first aid. Then he saw that Peter's pants were unzipped and pulled open, exposing him. Even then it took one, two, three moments before Kent understood what he saw. He said, "Excuse me," turned on his heel, and left. He went through the kitchen, out the door, got into his car and drove away. Even while doing it, he felt like it was fake, a scene from a movie. He did not come back home until late that night, and when he did, Alice was gone and the children were gone and so, of course, was Peter.

The next day Alice came back, sauntering in unannounced. He knew she had taken the children to school but he did not know where she was staying. She made no apologies and offered no explanations. She told him that he should find a place to go. They were standing in the kitchen, him leaning on the counter as though he needed it to keep his feet under him. In the only act of protest he made during the entire proceedings, Kent asked her why he should leave. Why didn't she find a place to go? She looked at him with the expression that a tax attorney might use with a client who suggested that he didn't want to file. "You can't take care of kids," she said. "You have too many important things to do."

It had taken him months, even years, to investigate all the forms of insult implied in that single comment. At the time he simply took it as true. It never occurred to him that in a matter of weeks he would have no pastoral responsibilities.

He lost everything, including his own sense of innocence. He gradually came to know that he was at fault for inviting Peter to live with them.

He could claim to have been naive. When the church's youth director asked if Peter could sleep in the youth room for a few nights because his parents had thrown him out of the house, Kent automatically invited him home. Had he even consulted with Alice? He doubted it. In those days he thought he had an absolute obligation to offer his help to those in need. He thought that faith meant throwing caution to the winds. It took him years at the mission to learn that it wasn't always good for people to get what they asked for.

He brought Peter into his home, trusting that all would be well with his wife and his two young children. When he thought of this now, he felt ashamed. He had been so cocksure he knew what he was doing.

Later, resentment grew. His wife committed adultery, and he lost his kids, his home, and his calling. *Explain the justice of that to me.* He never said this to anybody. He didn't complain. He carried fifty pounds of sand with him wherever he went. He missed his children terribly, but when he saw them he could hardly bear to look at them, he felt so full of shame and sorrow. He was so tired at night that he fell asleep still dressed, sleeping fully clothed through the night. He found it difficult to move his tongue and jaw to talk.

That was his condition when he took the job at the mission. It would be weeks before he discovered that he had fallen into the one place where he could be mended. He was with men who had lost more than a wife and family and job; they had lost their way. Kent had the privilege of holding them as they put down their feet to find something solid to stand on. That something was Christ, but Christ as his regular church-goers had never known. As *he* had never known.

It was not the 12-step program, or the rules and organization of the program—those were tools. It wasn't even the men: they came and went. Not too many of them were able to put together sober lives for long. Jake was a rarity. What made the mission for Kent was the actual place: dingy, leaky, too cold or too hot, full of frustrations and longings and the smells of men who had slept in the rain. This place was a sanctuary where he, desperate, found Christ. It was a holy place. He was not going to sell it and move to a new, clean spot on Sebastopol Road, not unless he got instructions from God.

But Meg. God, how he wanted her. In ways and for reasons that he could not fathom, except the obvious fact that he was tired of being alone.

She had egged Alice on to infidelity with the very same boy who had tried to kill her. Every time he thought of it, he reverted to anxiety and fury. He realized, at the same time, that Alice would have left him anyway, sooner or later. In the ignorance of his youth he had mistaken her completely. She was not sweet and never had been, though everybody called her that. She had a will that would run down whoever stood in her road.

Which explained, perhaps, why she had invited Peter Anderson home, again. She thought she was invincible.

In that sense, the adultery was incidental. Peter had been merely an accomplice to Alice's leap toward freedom. He had merely sped them down the inevitable path.

That didn't mean, however, that Kent felt no pain. He wished Meg had just kept her memories to herself. They didn't need to bare their souls. Leave it alone. Nothing good was going to come of their relationship, anyway. Surely by now she could see that.

26   AT THE HOSPITAL

Meg entered Alice's hospital room quietly and slowly, as she did every morning. From the doorway where Meg paused, Alice looked like an oversized doll. Her bed and her monitoring equipment dwarfed her, taking up most of the space. Advancing to Alice's bedside, Meg saw the oxygen tube coiled under her nose and the IV taped to her wrist. Everything was silent, except for the regular hissing of the air mattress, inflating and deflating to prevent bedsores.

It had become Meg's usual routine to visit Alice in the early morning, when she rarely saw anyone else. She passed by Starbucks for coffee, then made a quick stop at the hospital. Parking was easier at that hour, and she found Alice's room a refuge from the usual hospital bustle. Meg would grasp Alice's hand and say hello, pronounce her name, sit with Alice for five minutes, drink her coffee, say the Lord's Prayer out loud, think about her day, and be gone.

By now she was not really sure why she went. She felt some low-lying compulsion, probably related to the fears of a single woman that nobody would visit her if she were in similar straits.

More than two weeks had passed since the assault, and Alice showed no signs of recovery. Presumably the hospital staff shifted Alice's position regularly, but every time Meg visited, she had her face pressed into the mattress, so that the back of her head and her mussed hair were the only visible part of her head. Meg tried her best to address Alice personally with her few words, but the idea that Alice was a being who could comprehend became harder and harder to sustain.

Nevertheless she visited. Generally, the visit didn't much affect Meg's emotions, but for some reason it had crashed down on her yesterday morning. Alice's stasis finally penetrated. Only dead things don't change.

She had wept, with no one there to see her. Perhaps those feelings had been a factor in asking Kent to meet her here this morning.

He had appeared at her business, the first time she had seen him since the horrible encounter. He stared glumly at her, hanging back and holding out an envelope. She made him stay while she opened the thick, white paper. It was a card with a silly picture on it, an old black-and-white photo of two fussily dressed ladies riding a tandem bicycle. Inside it read, "It's hard work to pedal together. Sorry."

He had written by hand, "I hope we can forgive each other and be friends."

She held the card with both hands and looked at him. Neither one of them could force a smile. "Thank you," she said. "I hope so too."

Then, for a minute or more, no one spoke. She didn't want to bring up the horrible day again.

* * *

It was not like Kent to shout at someone, and especially a woman. His row with Meg shook him, not only for what it was but for what it meant about his personal state. Fourteen years after the fact, he had still not achieved serenity—far from it. He managed to fill his life with many things. But when the memories awoke, as they had with Meg's confession, he experienced the pain as fresh as yesterday.

He told his Saturday morning Bible group about a "little altercation" with Meg. He gave them no details, only that she had said something that made him angry, and now he regretted his reaction. It was hard for him to say even that much, but his confession seemed to come as a relief to the other men. They had talked over so many heavy things that morning, including a cancer diagnosis and a prostate operation that had all but castrated one of the men. Kent's troubles seemed lighter and more familiar. They all knew what it was like to make up to a woman after a quarrel. Someone suggested flowers. Rich suggested he write a note. "Get a funny card," he said. "Add a serious handwritten message."

Kent found himself in the nearest CVS, looking through the long aisle of cards for something that could speak to Meg. It had to be funny but not boorish, and it should communicate fondness or appreciation without being romantic. These qualifications turned out to be extremely difficult to fulfill. He went through almost every card in the store, finally choosing the old black-and-white photo. He took it to Meg's place of business.

He didn't expect to find her there on a Saturday. He had intended to leave the card and go, but after an awkward silence, Meg asked him if he would go see Alice with her tomorrow morning.

He didn't know what to say. "I don't see the point of that," he said. "And anyway, I don't think Suzanne wants me there."

"You won't see Suzanne," Meg said. "I go in the mornings to avoid people, and I've never seen her then. I don't see anybody."

"But what would be the point?" he asked. Did she think she somehow could resolve his long-ago disaster with Alice?

"Do it for me," she said.

Now, on his way to the hospital, he wondered what she wanted. Was it something to do with her guilty conscience? Was she trying to make up for the part she had played in breaking them apart years ago?

What it meant, all together, was that she was not done with him. This realization came to him like a moon rising on a dark night.

* * *

The hospital building was new, an aggregation of glass rectangles. Kent marched right past the reception desk, past the uniformed girl who tried to give him a name tag, past the signs indicating room numbers and departments. The corridor was paved with wide, dark planks of hardwood. Recessed lighting ran the length of both walls, softly illumining the air. Kent plunged past a nursing station, looking straight ahead. Halfway down another corridor, he encountered his children, coming out of their mother's room. It was the last thing he had expected, and he almost stopped short. It dismayed him. His first thought was that he had been tricked.

"You're here!" Suzanne said, and ran up to hug her father long and ardently. She looked radiant. Her blond hair was piled on top of her head in two wide swirls, and the eyes she trained on Kent were luminous. This was the girl who had said to keep away?

Meg came out of the room now, having heard the commotion.

Andy hung back, tall and gangly, a little smile budding on his mouth. When Suzanne let go, he moved forward to shake Kent's hand. "Did you come to see Mom?" he asked.

"If that's all right," Kent said, looking at them both.

"Of course it's all right!" Andy said. "Why wouldn't it be?"

Kent looked abashed. "I understood that you thought I should stay away."

"Oh, Dad," Suzanne said, as though the idea was such nonsense.

Suzanne had attached herself to her father's arm like a sprig of mistletoe. Meg wondered if she had completely misread the situation. They could not be happier together.

"So how is your mom doing?" Kent asked.

"I don't know," Suzanne said. "The doctors don't seem to know anything."

"They tell us to talk to her," Andy said. "We don't know what she hears."

Meg saw Kent's troubled face as he glanced to his right at his son.

"I'm so glad to see you here," Suzanne said. "What made you come?"

"Meg asked me," he said simply.

Meg regretted that attention had turned her way. "I just asked him to come along for me. I didn't think we'd see you."

Suzanne had already wrinkled her forehead. "For you?"

"I come to see your mother every day, you know. Yesterday it got to me. I was feeling so sad, and then your dad happened to come by my business, and I..." She stopped there because she still did not know how to explain her motives.

"Are you two a number?" Suzanne asked.

Meg forced a little smile. "I wouldn't say that."

"Meg and I are friends," Kent said. "We've known each other a long time."

"And you just drop by her business?" Suzanne asked in that same tone.

Meg could see confusion on Kent's face. "I did yesterday," he said. "I don't know if I've ever done that before. I was dropping off a card."

"Is there something wrong with our being friends?" Meg asked.

Andy stepped forward, as though to protect his sister. She was not to be protected. Her face contorting, she said to Meg, "My parents' lives are not your business. You don't need to visit my mom. You don't need to be asking my dad to come with you. This is our family, and you're not a part of it."

In the moment it never occurred to Meg to back away. "Good grief, Suzanne, what are you talking about? Nobody is trying to join your family."

"Then why are you visiting my mom every day? You don't even know her! You told me that yourself."

"Suzanne!" Kent said. "Meg has known your mom for 20 years. I think it's very kind of her."

"And to ask you along to comfort her." Suzanne shook her head in disgust. "You may not see what's going on, but I do."

"What do you see, Suzanne?" Meg asked. "For heaven's sake, what do you see?"

"I see that you're trying to come between my parents."

Meg made a face. "Good grief, they are divorced."

"And so are you. So stay away."

"This is stupid," Meg muttered. She turned to Kent. "Kent, I'm sorry I pulled you into this. I'm going now. You can sort out this nonsense without me." She turned and walked toward the entrance to the hospital.

After a moment of hesitation, Kent said to Suzanne, "That was ridiculous." Then he followed Meg.

He caught up with her as she went out the doors. Meg was walking briskly and she resolutely didn't look at him. She went right past her car and plowed through one of the medians, planted with pink petunias. After another section of parking, she reached a walkway. She didn't know where this led but soon found that it meandered past large sculptures made from boulders strapped together with rusted iron bands. It was a new space, sprinkled with saplings that had been staked out.

Kent kept pace beside Meg but said nothing, and she did not have anything to say to him. She walked the length of the sculpture garden, until the path bent back toward where she had come. She saw that the situation was becoming preposterous and stopped. "All right," she said to Kent. "Why are you following me?"

"I want to apologize for my daughter," he said. "That was completely uncalled for."

Meg shook her head impatiently. "I can handle your daughter."

"Okay," he said. His eyes were searching her face. He had only once seen her angry before, and that was when he was too furious to observe. Her flushed face alarmed him, but he couldn't help noticing its warmth.

Meg cast her eyes into the sky, speaking as though to the clouds. "Your daughter is very protective of you and her mother. I'm sorry I walked you into that."

"I can handle my daughter," he said, and smiled at her. Meg could see that he was trying to draw a smile in return, but she wasn't going to give it.

This, she thought, *is what comes when you get involved with a man*. In a moment of weakness she had asked him to come. It resulted in insults and anger. She was split off from Alice's children, made into an alien. She would never be able to visit Alice again.

"I'm very glad that you asked me," Kent continued. "It's the first time I've felt like I can do something for you. Or be something for you. And whatever Suzanne says, I appreciate that you've been visiting Alice."

She recognized that it was quite a speech for him, normally a man of fewer words, and not prone to making himself vulnerable.

"That's great," she said. "But the bottom line is that I have no business here and I have no business with you here. Let's chalk it up to experience."

He didn't respond, whether to agree or disagree, so she started for her car. He walked beside her, periodically glancing her way. Meg found herself growing irritated by his bird-dogging. She wanted to put this scene out of its misery. She was tempted to say something cold but restrained herself. He hadn't asked for this. She had asked him to come, she remembered. Nevertheless she was extremely ready to be done.

At her car she turned to face him. "Let's just forget this. It was a bad idea, and I'm sorry for it."

His light halo of frizzy hair seemed to glow around his head. She almost laughed, he was so serious. He looked like he might cry.

"Don't be sorry," Kent said. He dropped his eyes as though embarrassed. "I don't know what I'm doing, but I want to be near you all the time."

Meg stood up a little straighter. "I don't see that happening," she said. "Every time we are together it ends badly. I think we better learn our lesson."

She opened her car door and paused, leaning on it, before she got in. "I know I asked you today," she said. "I'm sorry for that. Sorry for your trouble. Now go in there and make it up with your children. They are glad you came."

27 HIDING PLACES

Elvis was assigned to guest services, which meant he had constant contact with the homeless men who came on a daily basis for a meal and a bed. He checked their stuff into storage when they arrived for breakfast; he checked them in again in the evening if they came for a meal and a bed. He would regularly get called to the front desk to see if the mission could supply an extra sleeping bag, or a pair of boots, or to ask if he could get somebody a sandwich because they had missed breakfast.

Of course, some took advantage of the generosity. Some were belligerent, acting like customers who had paid for services and wanted things done to their satisfaction. Some couldn't think straight: they talked in cloudy shapes. You always had a few who would scald you with their insults or take a poke at somebody who looked at them wrong. You had to deal with all that.

Overall, though, guest services brought a lot of satisfaction. Elvis particularly liked it because he was such a friendly guy. He would talk to anybody. Also, he needed the stimulation of being on the jump. Elvis got in trouble when he was bored, but he was never bored by guest services. The regulars learned to like him. That kept him even more active, because when they liked somebody, they asked him for stuff. Elvis bent the rules to help them out. What might be a no from somebody else was more often a yes with Elvis.

Glenn was a regular guest, and Elvis often helped him lock his bicycle in the yard and put his bags of recyclable cans and other stuff in a safe place. Glenn looked like a hermit, with his leathered face and wild hair and beard. He was always explaining some way that the world had failed him. Nonetheless, Elvis had taken a shine to him, and Glenn reciprocated by heading straight for Elvis when he wheeled his overloaded bicycle through the gates.

"Got some dope for you," Glenn said on Monday. He was early for the breakfast hour, being fussy about how his stuff was stored, and wanting plenty of time.

Elvis didn't understand his use of the word "dope." He told Glenn he couldn't bring that stuff into the mission.

Glenn looked at him. "When were you born?"

"March 11, 1985," Elvis said. "Why? You planning to buy me a gift?"

"That explains why you don't know the meaning of 'dope,'" Glenn said. "You're just a baby. You're not necessarily an idiot after all."

"Well thank you," Elvis said. "What is the meaning of 'dope'?"

"It's something I know and you don't."

"Exactly. That's why I'm asking you what it means."

Glenn cleared his throat. He could not see his way through this verbal confusion, and he was not anxious to spill his inside knowledge, since he believed holding it gave him a clear advantage, something he rarely had.

"That guy who got kicked out?"

"Which one?"

"The one who got kicked out for fighting."

"What about him?" Elvis didn't know who Glenn could be talking about. More than a few men got in fights and were asked to leave.

"You know. The slick one. The one you were looking for."

Elvis clicked. "Peter?" he asked.

"I don't know his goddam name," Glenn spat out.

"Watch your language. You mean the one who was always dressed up," Elvis continued.

"Yeah."

"What about him?"

"I saw him."

Now Elvis was showing some attention. "Where? When?"

"Last night. He was over by Teevax."

"What was he doing?"

"He was just walking down the street, minding his business."

"How did he look?"

Glenn paused before answering. "A little messed over."

"You mean like he was sleeping rough," Elvis said. "Like he needed a place to wash."

"Maybe." Glenn wagged his head back and forth. "You still looking for him?"

"I don't know. I think so. If you see him again, let me know, will you?"

When he had a minute after breakfast, Elvis went upstairs to tell Jake. Jake called over to Berger Street to inform Kent.

"What do I do if he comes to the mission?" Jake wanted to know.

Kent puffed up his cheeks and blew out the air. "Well, talk to him. Make him welcome. The police don't know about this, do they?"

"No. I thought about calling them, but they really haven't shown any interest."

"You can't really blame them, can you? It's a stretch."

Jake said he thought they should at least interview him. "He must have been one of the last people to see her."

"Yeah, that's what we think, but I guess the police aren't impressed. I mean, somebody found a weird sculpture that seems to resemble him. That might not be that convincing."

"I think it is," Jake said. "I mean, it looks exactly like him."

"To your eyes," Kent said.

"To my eyes."

Since Sunday, Kent had been reliving his ongoing debacle with Meg. He was angry at Meg for dragging him there, and livid with his daughter for her treatment of Meg, and all at the same time his mind was surrounded by the hopeless feeling that he was no good at anything. Plus, he suffered with lovesickness, a malady without a cure.

After Meg drove away, he had not gone back into the hospital. He was too furious, and he wanted to avoid any interaction that might go wrong. But of course, the delay only made it more difficult to initiate contact now.

He had been toying with calling his daughter at her office. Should he start with an apology? It would have to be a non-apology apology, such as, "I'm sorry that you were so upset," or "I didn't mean to make everything harder for you and your brother." He thought Suzanne owed Meg an apology, but he wasn't in a position to start there.

It occurred to Kent that the news about Peter gave him another point of entry. Kent looked up Suzanne's work number.

"Hi, Dad." Her voice was grim, and she didn't ask him how he was.

He told her about the news on Peter, and when she didn't respond, he went on. "It's not much to go on, but as far as I know it's all that we have."

Her curiosity got the better of her. "What do the police say?"

"I don't think they're interested in Peter. At least, they don't act like they are."

"So what's the point? If they aren't interested?"

"I don't know," Kent said.

"Seems to me that if this Peter were walking down Fourth Street in his pajamas it wouldn't do us any good, if the police don't care. I'm sure they would have found him if they really wanted to."

"I don't know about that," Kent said.

"So Dad, what are you doing? Why are you even telling me this?"

"I thought you would like to know." Kent almost went on to say that if she didn't want to know, he wouldn't call her, but he managed to stifle that. "It's not much to go on, but it's something."

"And what are you going to do with it?"

He had never experienced this toughness, verging on meanness, in his daughter. Not that they had spent so much time together in recent years.

"I think I'm going to look for him," Kent said.

"Where?"

"I guess I'll start out in the places where homeless men sleep. I know those places pretty well, you know."

* * *

Kent remembered Glenn from years ago; Glenn had been a constant fixture when Kent ran the program. When he went to the mission, he couldn't find Glenn, however. The men in the New Life program didn't remember seeing him leave after breakfast, and nobody Kent talked to on the street recalled encountering him. That was one of the mysteries of the homeless, how they appeared and disappeared. You might think somebody was as rooted as a tree on a certain corner, but when you went to look for them they were gone like the morning.

"You want help looking for the dude?" Elvis asked helpfully. "We could check under the bridges, and places like that."

Kent first thought to accept, but he pulled back when he considered what he might be stirring up. He didn't want the whole men's program wandering around Santa Rosa telling stories to whomever they met.

The day was going to be brilliant. Shops were starting to open, lights were coming on inside the plate-glass windows, but there wasn't much of anybody on the streets. Customers from the Flying Goat spilled out to the sidewalk tables but they were quiet, absorbed in their phones as they sipped at their paper cups.

It had been years since Kent patrolled the encampments. When he first joined the mission, he had some of the men take him around. He made a point to introduce himself to anybody they found, telling them (if they were inclined to hear) about the services the mission offered. Sometimes he got an earful about crappy treatment, and there were some who wanted nothing to do with religion in any form, but most people were appreciative.

Toward the south of town were multiple places to shelter: culverts, freeway overpasses, small brushy enclaves caught in no-man's land between a parking lot and the railroad right-of-way. In the early days, he would go looking for men who walked out on the program, to try to talk them into returning. He learned the location of every hiding hole, and he took pride in finding the men, talking some of them into coming back into the program. Eventually, though, he realized that if you talked them into it, they weren't likely to last. They had to want to be in the program, to want it definitely and perhaps desperately. Bring half-convinced men back in and they could pull others down with them.

No doubt God pursued addicts, but Kent wasn't God and he had come to their present policy by hard experience. You left of your own free will, and you could stay away of your own free will. Guys just disappeared without notice, and you had no idea where they had gone. They were welcome back to the mission after 72 hours, but nobody was going to go out looking for them.

Kent started his search in the knot of freeway ramps where Highway 12 met 101. He remembered that there was a hidden niche invisible from the street. You went up an embankment and squeezed through a concrete opening that was barely wide enough for one person. This opened into a dim space rimmed with ivy and roofed by an onramp. There was room, he remembered, for a dozen people there.

He couldn't find the right embankment. There had been a dirt pathway through the ivy and the oleanders, but it seemed to be gone. Kent was certain that such a perfect, hidden spot must still be in use, but he circled the streets looking for access without success. He even scrambled up a dirt embankment, searching. Finally, he gave up, and decided to walk the railroad tracks.

Along the railway, Kent found his way through short overgrown pathways, going slowly and with lots of whistling and humming so as not to surprise anyone. Most of these spots were just big enough for a handful of people. Some of them appeared to have been lost and forgotten: where he was sure there had once been an encampment, he found high weeds, or bushes that had completely filled up a space.

You had to look carefully, though. Sometimes he found an entrance that looked too small for anything larger than a cat, but when he called out, somebody called back. He didn't go in if he wasn't invited, but he did say he was looking for Peter Anderson and described him. At best he got vague replies that sounded more like wishful thinking than real information. Most people claimed to know nothing. They didn't sound like they wanted to help.

It made him temporarily happy, to be wandering through this urban wilderness. He knew how to be polite, to respect people's privacy, to treat them with the same respect he would show anybody in suburbia. Some of the people he met wanted to talk. But none of them shed any light on Peter Anderson.

He traipsed over a large area, bushwhacking his way into obscure corners of brush and low-hanging trees. While some camps had disappeared, others had grown up to the size of Robin Hood's village. The setting could be almost park-like, with tall trees overhead and clear ground around dome tents. He found some very friendly people in those environments. They knew all about the mission; most of them had at least eaten meals there.

More usual were the messes, however: camps strewn with garbage, with multiple fire pits and frayed plastic ropes strung from trees. In one of these Kent encountered Gil Nichols. He didn't recognize him at first, but Gil knew Kent immediately and started talking as though picking up a conversation from ten minutes ago. Gil was short and weathered, with a long skinny neck and a snub nose. He wore layers of clothes even though the sun was getting warm.

"Dammit, do you remember Ronnie?" Gil asked. "He still owes me money. You seen him? I guess not; he took off, didn't he? Well, it's been too long. How are you? How is the missus? The girl I was with, you probably remember her, she's not around anymore. She went back to Chico. Good riddance—she never cooked. I'd rather have a dog. I haven't got a dog, though. Can't keep 'em; they run off. You got to feed a dog." Gil stopped in mid-flow, as though he had suddenly realized that the tap was on. He scrutinized Kent. "You remember me?"

It was an occupational hazard. Kent had seen thousands of people come and go from the mission, and they all thought he should remember them. "Help me out," he said. "I'm forgetting your name."

"C'mon, you know, don't you? You're just figging me."

"I know, but I can't quite get it," he said. "Help me out. My memory is no good."

"Well, it's Gil. Gil Nichols. You saved my life."

Actually, when it came down to it, Kent did remember him. Looking at him carefully, he could see the face of the young man who had come in completely wasted with heroin, who had detoxed in his room and screamed for two days about worms. That must've been ten years ago.

"So how are you doing, Gil? How are you staying alive?"

"Well, I'm clean, most of the time. I'm not saying I'm perfect. I haven't got it all together yet. Sometimes I stray. Everybody does, right?"

"Can I sit down?" Kent asked, and when Gil nodded, he took a seat on the ground. "So, it looks like you're getting by, but just barely."

"That's about right. I've had jobs, and I was able to clean up. I lived in a motel once for weeks at a time, when I had a job at a salvage company. But I can't seem to stay with anybody. They don't tolerate the tricks I play."

"What kind of tricks, Gil?"

"Well..." Gil laughed to himself. "I don't always get there on time. Sometimes I don't feel good and I just sleep it off. And when I go in to work, they just tell me to come back at the end of the week to pick up my check. That's happened a few times lately."

"You ever think about coming back to New Life? I think there's more to learn."

Gil shook his head. "I'm not going back to that place."

"Why not?"

"I just don't like it." The friendly self had vanished. He was scowling. "Too damn much religion. I hate that music. I can't breathe down there."

* * *

Kent came out of the tracks by the foot crossing at Jenkins Avenue, finding his way through the neighborhoods to the creekside trail. There was a new paved path there. Almost immediately he located an encampment on a bank overgrown with live oak and alder. It was out of sight above the trail, disguised by shrubby oaks and hemmed in by a broken-down redwood fence that looked ready to collapse. Kent spotted a pathway winding through the trees. To follow, he had to bend down under limbs and at one point go on hands and knees. He found a light blue dome tent with a royal blue tarp stretched over it. Two ancient and worn leather chairs were set by a blackened fire ring. Plastic garbage was strewn about. Kent called out a hello as soon as he saw the camp. No one answered. Several times he called out as he circled the camp, but he could feel as well as hear that it was empty. He extended his palm over the fire pit but found no warmth. He decided against looking into the tent. That could be construed as trespassing.

Farther down the trail, he entered areas he was sure had once housed people, finding no trace of habitation. Brush and poison oak could grow in a hurry, and it had been many years since he last explored this environment. In some spots, blackberries had built an impenetrable wall. In other places, you could not worm your way through the poison oak. At first Kent wished he had gloves, but then he realized that no one would regularly pass through a thicket that required them.

He found a large encampment in a spot where two streams came together and the trail wandered away from the water. The camp probably was underwater in the winter rains, but now people had spread out through the woods. Kent counted half a dozen different shelters, and judging by spots rubbed bare by human passage, people threw down blankets or sleeping bags in other spots.

One family—a man and woman and three small children—were scattered around a rectangular structure made with blue tarps and plywood. The woman looked to be knitting. Kent waved to her and she waved back.

From the edge of a steep drop-off to the stream, Kent could see a man with his feet in the water, leaning against a tree. When Kent waved to him, he gestured for Kent to come down to the waterside.

"I know you," he said to Kent. "Where do I know you from?"

"I don't know. My name is Kent Spires. How are you doing?"

"I know you from the gospel mission! Don't I?"

"That's probably it. I ran the program there for years. Were you a guest?"

"I was in the New Life program in 2005. I graduated. Don't you remember me?

"You must look different. What's your name?"

"Al Ziegler. Yeah, I graduated in 2005, in November. I didn't have long hair then."

When Kent looked closely at his face, he thought he remembered. The name seemed familiar.

"You living out here?" Kent asked.

Al pursed his lips and screwed up his face as though to offer a facial shrug. "Yeah, when I graduated I had a job in an auto body shop. Down on Berger, near the thrift store. I was there for seven years. But that ended a couple of years ago and I can't afford any place. I'm sleeping in that orange pup tent." He gestured vaguely up the hill.

"You can't get on at another auto body place?"

Another facial shrug. "You've got to have references. I know my stuff; I even have my own tools. If you need your car fixed, I can do it. But they all want references."

"So I take it you didn't end on good terms at the place on Berger?"

"No. They loved me. I was like their number-one worker. Don, the guy who runs it, he told me so. I was clean all that time. Then my mother died, and I was pretty bent out of shape by that, and after the funeral one of my cousins offered me some meth to smoke. You know how that goes."

"I do," Kent said. "I'm afraid I do."

"It's crap," Al said. He seemed to want to say more, but he stopped.

"You ever think about coming back?" Kent asked.

Al just looked at him.

"Lots of guys come back," Kent said. "You could start over."

Al dropped his eyes and stayed silent, as though he were studying the turbid flow of the creek. Eventually Al said, "I think it would just end up the same way."

"I'm sorry about your mother; that's a hard blow for anybody," Kent said. "But wouldn't she want you to bounce back?"

Al still didn't look at him. "There would always be something, wouldn't there?"

Kent waited. When he saw that no more would be said, he nodded. "There would always be something. You're right. Things get thrown at you. It's too much for anybody, but nothing is impossible with God. If you came back, that's what we would focus on, I think: how to get better in tune with God."

The comment made Al look up. "You know, I had that. When I left the mission I definitely had that."

"God hasn't moved."

"Maybe not, but I don't hear him anymore. I've tried." Al bent his arm at a sharp angle and scratched his back. His face seemed to relax. "That year I was at the mission was the best thing that ever happened to me. I'm grateful, man; don't think I'm not. I'm very grateful. I wish the whole world was like the mission."

"It's still there. You could come back any time."

"Well, I might. I just might."

Kent said he was looking for someone. He picked his way down to the creek bed and showed Al the picture of the sculpture. "Sorry that this is all I have, but it's actually a pretty good likeness. His name is Peter. He's young and he tends to dress in nice clothes, dressy clothes."

Al studied the picture. "Yeah, I've seen him. I can't tell you where, but I know that face. He's around. He's definitely around. What do you need him for? He steal something from the mission?"

"No, nothing like that. There's just some questions we want to ask him about a woman who was hurt."

"Okay, I'll watch out for him." As Kent made his way cautiously up the bank, Al said, "I mean it about the mission. I appreciate it."

"Thanks. Give it some thought. You are always welcome."

* * *

As the day wore on, Kent's hopefulness dropped. His chances of finding Peter were small to begin with, and the farther he went, the smaller they became.

The camps looked the same as they always had. Everywhere was an accumulation of trash that was precious to somebody. He found only a few people occupying the sites. They left during the day, taking with them anything they didn't want stolen. If you really needed to find someone, you should come near dusk.

Underneath the visible city was a suburb of people who had exhausted everybody—relatives, friends, agencies—who would help them. They hung on to a shopping cart or a plastic tarp as though it were treasure. Kent's encounter with Al reminded him that his work sometimes made a difference. These were the people God had sent him to, and God had sent them to him. They kept him sane. They kept his feet on the ground.

Kent followed the creek path all the way to Fulton Avenue. He could go further, of course. He could go all the way to Sebastopol, if he wanted, but he knew that nearly all homeless encampments were closer to the center of Santa Rosa, near the library and soup kitchens and places to panhandle. He turned back. He was foot-heavy by the time he reached City Hall, near where he had begun, but he carried on east. The creek branched, and as it grew smaller, it disappeared into culverts and reappeared.

He could not look everywhere. Santa Rosa was surrounded by hills, with an almost infinite number of possible hiding places. Annadel State Park was on the edge of town, with ample space in its oak forest for thousands of campers. The thing was, the homeless liked convenience as much as anybody—or even more, since they usually were on foot.

He didn't know about Peter, of course. Peter was a mystery.

The day had been swallowed up, a breeze had begun to come off the ocean, and he had eaten nothing all day. The time had come to wrap up his search, and he had no regrets in doing so, since by now he knew his chances of finding Peter were minuscule. He had one more place to look: the woods below Community Hospital. The hospital had been closed for several years, moving to a new location on the outskirts of town, but its public lands included a surprisingly large wooded area with a small stream and a pond, sequestered in a dip that you couldn't see from any road.

By the time he reached the deserted hospital, he was genuinely tired. He had been on his feet all day. Kent crossed the road and began making his way through the storage buildings and clinics that ringed the main wards. Somewhere back here was a mental wing, he remembered; he had visited it once after one of the men broke down and started beating his forehead against the dishwasher.

Kent found a pathway around what appeared to be a repair yard, strewn with broken-down equipment. Behind was a field: grasses sloping down to brambles of blackberries, with head-high willows behind. In the low evening light it looked golden and wild. The pathway disappeared and then picked up again. It led by a small, murky pond. Kent remembered this. He scanned around the pond for the tall trees. They were up a hill.

As he climbed, the path grew clearer and firmer, then branched. He chose to go right. He was now cut off from signs of any buildings, any roads. The light underneath the trees was dim, almost dark. But the path underfoot had been packed hard, and there were ruts from bicycle tires. He thought he was near something.

The path split again. He chose right, and in thirty yards he came upon a camp. It was a small clearing in the woods, a level spot just big enough for a green square-sided tent. Someone was there: he could hear the hiss of a gas camp stove.

"Hello?" he called, feeling slightly spooked by the dark woods. "Hello?"

Nobody answered, so he moved ahead. When he was ten feet from the tent, he said hello again, and this time he got an answer. "Hey."

"Can I come in?" he said. "I don't want to bother anybody."

"Come on in," the voice said.

A man with blond hair was bending over a pot, stirring something. An open bottle of wine sat on the ground beside him. "What do you want?" he asked, turning his head.

It was Peter. Kent could not be mistaken. He was, of course, no longer a teenage kid. Peter was dressed, incongruously, in tight red jeans and a navy-blue shirt that looked as though it was made of silk. He had on loafers. He was dressed for a wine-tasting tour.

Kent had braced himself for this encounter. He had worried that he would be overcome by emotions. In the event he was calm, almost clinical.

Peter held his eyes with the slightly hostile gaze of someone facing an unwelcome intruder, but with no hint of recognition. That surprised Kent: Peter loomed so large in his memory, but he perhaps did not feature in Peter's mind at all. Kent's breathing came fast, and he was rigid with excitement, but he forced those symptoms down. If Peter did not recognize him, that was to the good.

"Sorry to bother you; I'm just exploring," Kent said. "You're staying here?"

Peter just stared at him, as though to ask, "What do you think?"

"I've only been up here once before," Kent said. "Fifteen years ago, probably. I didn't mean to bother you."

"Okay," Peter said. He didn't look hostile or particularly suspicious. He gave the sense that you were on the level of the stuff he was cooking.

"Do you know the best way to get out of here?" Kent asked.

Peter unbent slightly. "Which way did you come?"

"From the hospital."

"You really are lost," Peter said. "If you go down the hill, you'll come to the road."

28 AWAKENING

That same late Monday afternoon, Suzanne Spires sat in the clammy pleather bedside chair, watching her mother's monitor. Suzanne held a paperback novel that she had read to her mother for about half an hour, until she tired of it. Suzanne did not really believe that Alice heard anything, but she was following the doctors' encouragement to keep providing stimulation.

Alice had never encouraged emotional closeness; she was not a huggable mother. Nevertheless, Suzanne and her brother Andy practiced a fierce loyalty to her. After the divorce, all three of them had worked to present themselves as easy and careless, living in a nice house, dressing well, going on real vacations, and doing it so gracefully that no one would guess the cost. They never discussed what they were doing, or why.

Alice wasn't much for communicating. Suzanne, for instance, never understood why her parents divorced. She never knew why her mother kept them at such a distance from her father, why his presence was so carefully calibrated and monitored. He must have done something awful, Suzanne assumed, but she did not ask. If she edged up to the subject with her mother, Alice shut down the discussion immediately, as though it was distasteful.

That family silence bore down on her now. Suzanne felt the terrible burden of feeling alone in a hospital. She rarely saw the doctors caring for her mother, she did not know their names, and it seemed as though she and Andy encountered a different set every time they met. Her mother's treatment plan was extremely hazy to Suzanne. It seemed to amount to "wait and see," although the doctors never said that. Medications and test results were their language. Suzanne never got the opportunity to ask the most basic questions, such as, *What are we looking for? What is going on?* Before she could get her wits about her, the doctors were gone.

"Do you want to hear some music, Mom?" Suzanne asked. At the suggestion of one of the nurses, she had gone out to buy a portable CD player, to provide musical stimulation. She had been stumped as to what CDs to play. Suzanne couldn't remember her mother ever putting on music or commenting on something she enjoyed. Or didn't enjoy, for that matter. Suzanne had settled on the Beatles' #1 album and a selection of Christopher Parkening. She was already tired of them. Besides, who knew if her mother heard anything at all?

She put on the Beatles. "Love, Love Me Do" began, with its reedy harmonica riff. How remarkable that the song had first been performed before her mother was born. Suzanne turned up the volume.

The movement she caught out of the corner of her eye was so slight that she did not know what she had seen. She scanned the room, and her eye came to rest on her mother, who was as still as a wax statue. Something seemed different, however. Suzanne looked more closely. She got up from her chair. Her mother's eyelid fluttered.

"Mom?" she said, going close and hovering just over Alice's face. "Mom, it's Suzanne. Can you hear me?"

Alice opened her eyes. She did not look at Suzanne; her vision seemed to float upward, like a woman gazing at clouds. The Beatles were singing "She Loves You."

"Mom? Are you awake?"

Alice's mouth curled into a smile. She focused her eyes on Suzanne. "Where am I?" she asked in a voice smudged by lack of practice but perfectly intelligible.

"You're in the hospital, Mom. You've been unconscious for two weeks. Oh, we have been so worried about you."

A look of perplexity spread over Alice's face. "What happened?" Again, that smudged articulation. She moved her eyes over the rest of the room. She started on another word and stopped. It was too hard to complete. She closed her eyes.

Suzanne leaned forward and grabbed her wrist. "Don't go!" she said. "Talk to me."

Alice opened her eyes again. "I want to sleep," she whispered.

Her first day awake was a jumble. She wanted to rest, she craved darkness, but they would not let her go. So many watched her, touched her, talked to her. She would sleep and they would wake her up for nothing. Someone did bring food. She could only eat a little, but the taste and the sensation of swallowing reawakened her more than any of the touching and prodding did. This was an act of resurrection. The second time they brought a milkshake. She had never tasted anything so wonderful. She wanted more. She wanted solid food. She asked for a pulled pork sandwich. That seemed to confound them, but she insisted on it: that was what she wanted. When it came, she could only eat two bites. But what bites.

Suzanne always came when she called for her. She told Alice that she had been assaulted. By who, she wanted to know? They couldn't tell.

Someone had tried to kill her. They said she had been unconscious for weeks. Where? In this hospital room, they said.

"Alone?" she asked. "Was I alone?" She asked because she had a powerful wish not to be alone. She did not want Suzanne to leave her even for an instant. Whenever she felt her absence, she grew anxious. She asked for her and was not easy until she came.

"No, never alone. I was here. And Andy came."

"That's all?"

"Your friend Meg came almost every day."

"Meg?"

"Meg Fletcher. Dad's friend."

"Where was I before then?" Alice asked.

Suzanne said she had found her in her studio. "I called Dad. I didn't know what else to do. It was terrible, Mom. You can't even imagine. I thought you were dead. Dad called Meg, and she came to help. And then the ambulance came and brought you here."

"What did your dad do?" she asked.

"Nothing," Suzanne said. "He just called Meg."

"And she has been here every day?"

"Almost." Suzanne paused to calculate whether she should explain. "I ran her off yesterday when she came with Dad. I think they have something going on, and I didn't want to deal with it."

The idea of Kent and Meg was complicated. "Meg, with your dad? I can't see it."

Suzanne just shrugged, which was useless because Alice was on her back with her face pointed at the ceiling. She was thinking of that shadow, the person who had tried to kill her. She wondered whether she could ever be alone again. Could she ever again feel safe?

But she had not been alone here. Her children had stayed near, and Meg. Why had Meg come? She could remember the sound of Meg's voice, like a lullaby lilting over her sleeping head. She could almost hear it now, Meg's soft tones, a woman's voice. And prayer, Meg saying the Lord's Prayer.

They allowed her to sleep, but first she got Suzanne to promise she would stay. "I want you here when I wake up," she said, and managed to squeeze Suzanne's hand.

But Suzanne was not near when she awakened. The lights were low. It was night, she thought, though the hours were hard to keep straight. She called out and it was Andy who answered.

"Where's Suzanne?"

"She went to get some food," he said. "She'll be back."

"Aren't you working?" she asked, and stroked his hand.

"Trying," he said. "I told Suzanne I could spell her. She doesn't want to leave you."

"I'm fine," she said, and let go of him. Staring up into the dark ceiling, she tried to force her mind to reconvene. She had been assaulted, and though nobody had asked her, they were sure to want to know who had done it. They had found her in her studio. Who had been there?

She rarely had guests at the studio. Maybe somebody had just happened on her, had stumbled on her alone. Why would he do that? She knew it was a man. How she knew, she could not say.

Then, quite suddenly, a door opened in her memory. She could see the face before she remembered who it was. He was very good-looking, very striking. A small man, lithe, quick and smooth in his movements. He had a name. Peter.

He had come to the studio so she could sculpt him. Ordinarily she worked from photos, but he wanted to model. Why? She never considered that. She had trusted him because she had known him before.

She had known him when he was just a boy.

Her whole history with Peter came to her then.

They had met again after so many years at an art show at the Sebastopol Center for the Arts. That jumped out at her with sudden clarity. He had been pouring wine, a job usually performed by kids. Peter was no longer a kid. She had recognized him before he remembered her. She knew him by his face, by his head. She could see him sculpted, his eyes blind, his countenance frozen. She asked him whether he ever modeled. He didn't know what she was talking about. She explained. She gave him her phone number, and said to call. He never called.

Of course, she remembered that he had been the one who knocked over her marriage to Kent like a house of cards. That didn't matter. He was only a head. Long before she began to paint, she was drawn to such. Faces could inhabit her mind, even if the person remained a white cloud behind the mask. So it was with Peter: she hardly knew him. As far as her marriage was concerned, he was incidental. He had lit the fuse that blew up her little prison.

In the darkness, with far-off sounds of medical carts moving, of footsteps in the corridor, of a just-audible beeping in some other room, she tried to think. He never called. How long had it been? Weeks? Maybe months. She had given him her phone number. She felt that he was attracted to her. She wanted him to model. She was not closed off to other possibilities; they would have to see. She thought he would surely call, because he was attracted. She had felt it.

The rest was a blank. He must have called. She was sure that she had sculpted him there. When? She did not know. These events floated away.

Alice felt lonely, and she called out. "I'm here, Mom," Andy answered. "What do you need?"

"Nothing," she said, settling down. "Where's your sister?"

"She's not back yet. She went out for food."

"Yeah, you said that."

Perhaps Suzanne could help her put the pieces together. But Suzanne did not like it when her mother invited men home. She did not approve of her lifestyle. Suzanne was conservative, like her father. Not a church person like him, but strict in so many ways. She could not tell Suzanne about Peter. Her attitude would be exhausting.

29 LETTING DEFENSES DOWN

Tuesday morning Meg woke early, which gave her time to luxuriate in her 600-thread-count sheets and under her puffy down comforter. She was not given to sleeping in, but there were days when she liked to lounge. One of the dogs was snoring loudly. Meg stretched out very quietly. As soon as the dogs realized she was awake, they would be all over her.

Today, she thought, she would talk to Brian about internet sales. Thinking of him warmed her, made her fond. They needed to sit down for a conversation, rather than pecking at each other. He had such beautiful eyes. They would take as much time as they needed. Her Bible study met tonight. That was her only commitment.

Meg did a half-hour workout in front of the TV screen before showering and doing her makeup and hair. Even with that she drove down the hill ten minutes earlier than usual. She got her coffee at Starbucks and decided to go by Alice's hospital room. Suzanne never came in the morning, so why, Meg thought, should she give up her visits? She resented being sent away from the hospital. She had been grinding on it ever since.

She had read enough articles in women's magazines to know that children often harbor hopes that their divorced parents will reunite. Fourteen years was a long time to sustain such an impossible dream, but what else could explain Suzanne's outburst? It had been bizarre how eager she had been to bring in her father to see Alice, especially after keeping him at arm's length for weeks. And bizarre how she turned on Meg when she got the idea that Kent was going out with her. It made Meg wonder whether her own children longed to see her and Greg back together. She did not think so, but surely the human mind was a locked box teeming with oddities. Nobody who knew Kent and Alice could imagine them married in the first place, let alone remarried. Except, perhaps, their daughter.

Meg walked into the hospital with her paper coffee cup, expecting five minutes of peace while she sat by Alice's bed. She swung open Alice's door with her free hand and was startled to find Alice sitting up in bed and looking at her. It was a sight so unexpected that Meg could not speak. Tears began gushing from her eyes and she scuttled across the floor to grab Alice, who winced.

Horrified at the pain she must have inflicted, Meg stepped back. "God, I'm sorry," she said. "I just can't believe it. You woke up! When did you wake up?" She put out a hand to caress Alice's arm.

Alice had closed her eyes and now lay back against a propped-up pillow. Meg silently stroked her arm, with tears continuing to streak her cheek.

A short, wide nurse came in with a clipboard. "How are you this morning?" she asked. Then she looked. "You're up!" she said. "Nobody told me! That's great!" She stopped six feet from the bed and asked again, "How are you feeling this morning?"

"Not that well," Alice said in a low voice. Her eyes were still closed.

"Well, honey, you took quite a knock. You've been sleeping for three weeks. Did anybody tell you that?"

Alice nodded.

The nurse addressed Meg. "Are you family?"

"Just a friend."

"Well, probably a good idea to keep visits short." She turned toward Alice and stood looking at her monitor. "It's looking good," she said. "We'll have you up and out in no time." The nurse wrote something on her clipboard. "Have you had anything to eat?"

Alice nodded again. "Oh, I see," the nurse said, looking at the whiteboard over Alice's bed. "You ate all that, huh? Did it stay down?"

Alice nodded yes, still with her eyes closed. Meg thought she looked like a ghost. She had no color or flesh on her.

"That's just the thing, sweetie," the nurse said. "You need the calories. I wish I could give you some of mine." She moved toward the door. "Well, I'll be off. I'll check in later, but call if you need something. Better keep the visit short," she warned again, looking at Meg.

When she was gone, Meg advanced to the bedside again and took

Alice's hand. It was an action she would never have taken with Alice under other circumstances, but it seemed natural now, and Alice did not pull back. Her hand seemed flimsy and fragile, like a balsa-wood model you could crush with your fingers. "Has anybody told you what happened to you?" Meg asked. "Do you remember?"

"Suzanne told me," Alice said. "She said you were there."

"Not to do anything. The paramedics arrived at the same moment I did, and they had it under control."

"And Kent called you," Alice said, with her mouth turning very faintly toward a smile.

"He knew I lived near you. He was way across town when Suzanne called him."

Alice stayed quiet momentarily, her eyes still closed. "I heard you," she said softly. "When you visited. I heard you. Thank you for visiting."

* * *

As she walked to her car, Meg felt a powerful urge to draw Kent into what she had just experienced. For one thing, she doubted anyone had told him the good news; and for another, she felt jealous for him to know that she had not stayed away after Suzanne banished her from the hospital. She wanted to tell him—or somebody—that she rightfully belonged there. It did occur to Meg to wonder how she had come to prize her power to visit Alice, who would hardly have counted as a close friend. But she swiped this thought to the side.

Kent's reaction surprised her: his voice stuck so he was unable to speak. Meg thought that perhaps after all his daughter was not entirely wrong; perhaps he did still hold a flame for Alice.

Kent could have told her different. What he felt was more akin to the rush one gets from witnessing a near miss on the freeway. It was the jet-engine roar of death passing by.

When he recovered his composure, he asked for information. No, Meg had not seen Suzanne or anyone else. She had been making her regular morning visit to Alice and found her awake. Alice could not have been awake for long. Even the nurse had been caught unawares.

Kent felt as though some soft dark wing had been lifted from him. Dimly in one corner of the horizon, he could see a light.

Yesterday he had seen the man who might have killed Alice. While still a boy, he had stolen Kent's life.

"I have news for you," he said to Meg. "I found the man she sculpted."

"Where?" Meg asked.

"In a homeless camp up near the old hospital."

"So what did he say?"

"Oh, nothing. He doesn't know who I am. I just asked him for directions, and he gave them."

Describing it brought Kent back to that moment: in the falling dusk, in the forest, far from the nearest street or house. A man who was capable of murder. A man who had seduced his wife. Or been seduced. He would never know. He didn't want to know.

"Did you tell the police?"

He paused, thinking how he could explain. He planned to call them, but had not done so yet. "They haven't shown any interest in him."

"But now that Alice has woken up, it might be different."

That made him stop. "I hadn't thought of that. You think she remembers him?"

"Maybe," Meg said.

"Did you talk to her about it?"

"No, I wasn't there long. She could barely talk."

* * *

That night at her Bible study, Meg broke into tears while describing Alice's situation. The emotion took her by surprise. True, she had wept when she first encountered Alice awake, but hours had passed since that shock.

It was not the damage done to Alice that got her. It was the realization of her own vulnerability. She was a strong woman, but nearly any man was physically stronger. That made her weep—weep for sorrow and for anger. Violence came so close.

She hated being so weak as to cry, and in front of everybody. But just as she began to shake her head and reprove herself, she realized that her friends were weeping too. First it was Patricia—who knew that Patricia could cry?—and then gentle Suzette and Evelyn. It spread until the whole group was dabbing their eyes, wiping their noses. The paroxysm passed through them, went away, came back.

"Why are we all crying?" Patricia wanted to know. She began laughing, so it was hard to distinguish between tears and glee.

After they got control, they went on with their regular time together. They didn't talk about Alice anymore and they certainly didn't talk about the blubbering.

Nevertheless, when she arrived home and her dogs romped over her, Meg did ponder it. Why had they all wept like hysterical women?

30   STAKEOUT

Very much to Kent's surprise, the police officer who took his call was quite interested in information about Peter's whereabouts. He carefully noted Kent's name and number and thanked him. Less than an hour later, a detective called to ask if Kent would show him the spot where he had seen Peter.

It caused a mild commotion when two police cars appeared at the Berger Avenue thrift store. They would hardly have been noticed at the downtown mission; but the police never visited Berger Avenue.

Kent got in the back seat of one car—two uncommunicative police officers rode in front—and directed them across town to a service road entrance off Chanate Avenue. Chanate was narrow, with houses on the left and woods on the right. The police stopped with their flashers on, half their bumpers spilling out into traffic. Four officers got out, bulked up with equipment. Kent wasn't sure what to do with himself while they huddled and talked together. He stood on the curb ten feet off, waiting nervously.

One of the officers, who had introduced himself as Jeff, told Kent they were ready. Kent led them through a heavy metal gate and up the service road. It ran through trees tall enough to block the sun, ascending farther than Kent had remembered, following a stream until it ended in a turnaround. From there they took a narrow footpath, climbing steeply.

When Kent thought they were near the camp, he stopped and informed Jeff. All four officers gathered close around Kent. One of them held out a hand flat, signaling that they should be quiet. Then he lifted his chin forward along the path. Kent could feel the hair prickling on the back of his neck.

The camp was, in fact, a little farther along the trail than he remembered. Kent had begun to worry that he had taken the wrong turn when he came around a bend and saw it. One green square-sided tent almost filled the small site. A little litter lay scattered about, including one empty wine bottle. Kent felt almost embarrassed as he led the officers into the clearing.

"Anybody here?" one of the officers called. Nobody answered.

Jeff, the detective, went to the tent and whacked the flat of his hand on the front. "Anybody in there?" he asked.

He knelt and opened the flap, which was not zipped. "Nobody," he said.

"Is his stuff there?"

"Yeah. He'll be back."

The four officers stood around staring for a while. To Kent they seemed to move too slowly—in fact, hardly at all. He didn't know what they were waiting for. One of them, a thick man with a beefy red face, circled the outskirts of the camp, kicking at debris. They might be looking for something but not very actively.

"What are you going to do next?" Kent finally asked Jeff.

Jeff looked at his watch. It was late afternoon. "I guess we'll leave a couple of us here. He'll be back."

"So you're going to stake it out."

Jeff shrugged. "I guess. We'll just wait for him."

* * *

That night Kent tried to get back into the book he had been reading on the Inklings, C.S. Lewis' friends, who typically met in an Oxford pub. Their drinking had kept Kent off them for a long time. He had been raised a teetotaler, and fourteen years of working with addicts and alcoholics had done nothing to loosen those convictions. Only gradually had Kent become inured to the alcohol in Lewis's life. Kent had grown fascinated by the Inklings, who met together week by week to talk about books and read from whatever they were writing. Kent would have given almost anything to sit in one of those evenings.

Still excited by the search for Peter, he had a hard time concentrating on the book. He put it aside and called Andy. "Did you hear the news about your mother?" he asked when Andy answered.

"That she's awake? Yeah, I heard. Suzanne let me know yesterday."

"Oh, good. I just heard this morning, and I had a thought that maybe nobody told you. Have you seen her?"

"Yeah, I went by last night. And today at lunch, too."

It gave Kent intense pleasure to hear his son's voice. "How did she seem to you? Is she going to be okay?"

"She seemed okay, but I think it's too soon to know for sure. I mean, she's not saying much. She has her eyes closed a lot of the time."

"Does she remember what happened? Or who did it to her?"

"I can't say. She hasn't told me."

It was stilted. Kent asked all the questions and Andy answered very briefly. After hanging up, Kent wondered whether Andy had acted distant because the subject was his mother. Kent would like to ask Meg about that, if he ever had the chance to be with her and Andy in the same conversation. Which seemed extremely unlikely. Andy had not told off Meg the way his sister had. But then, he had always been a less extreme character. It didn't mean he didn't share her opinions.

Kent had mentioned the search for Peter, thinking Andy would be interested, but it had been almost like the CD skipped a track. Andy gave no reaction. Surely he cared about the man who had assaulted his mother and nearly killed her. The non-reaction depressed Kent; it occurred to him that Andy would care more if the information wasn't coming from his father.

There is nobody so alone, Kent thought, as a divorced man.

He knew this state of mind was not good for him. He got depressed if he sat alone wondering about his children.

Kent thought of turning on the TV, to see if anything was on. He finally took his Bible off the table. Opening to the psalms, he began to read them aloud, cries of woe and betrayal, hymns of exultant victory. It steadied him; it gave him a horizon to gaze on. He was quite aware that he would prefer hope that arose from his everyday life instead of from long-dead poets.

At any rate, he had accomplished something. He had found Peter. Nobody else, he thought, would have found him. There was some justice, surely, in his being the one to locate him and turn him over to the police. Kent thought again of his brief interaction at Peter's camp. How could it be that Peter had not recognized him? But he had aged since then. And he had a beard now. That was probably it.

It was funny to think that nobody else would know the deeper story. The police might ask Alice how she had come to know Peter. They might learn that she had been acquainted with him when he was just out of high school, but they needn't know the details, unless Alice chose to tell them. And why would she? After keeping the secret for so long, why would she tell it now?

31   ALL THE MEMORIES COME BACK

In the morning, Kent sat on his front porch and watched the light slowly stain the mountain and the orchard. He had woken up unusually early, in time to see the last pale stars dissolve as he sat with his coffee. Then the silhouette of Mt. Saint Helena took on depth, the trunks of apple trees emerged out of gray shadows, and lastly, green came back to the earth. For Kent, the slowness and the beauty were reassuring, like a tonic chord bringing a song to its end.

He had slept deeply, waking to turn over and remember the psalms he had read before bed. The words did not stick to his mind. What stuck were the juxtapositions of strife and security, incredulous howls and brassy confidence: God will surely this, God will surely that. He thought of it as he sipped his coffee and watched the world reappear. The earth offered this good news, daily.

After 45 minutes he realized he was cold. He got up to get a jacket, and as he put it on the idea occurred to him: he should go and see Alice. He could tell her about finding Peter. This early he would see no one else. He could be in and out without any friction.

The instant this idea came, he shied away from it. Was he operating on an outdated reflex, the desire to please her?

He *did* want to please Alice. She had hurt him and crushed him, and yet, there was a part of his soul that leaned her way. He did not know whether he would ever get over her. After fourteen years, you would have to doubt it.

Then he thought: *it doesn't matter. Don't scrutinize your motives; follow your instincts. When has caution ever rewarded you?* He decided to go.

On his way to the hospital, he nearly turned back. How many years since he last saw Alice? Why should he see her now? The questions made him miserable. He was not at a good place in the road for a U-turn, however, and so he kept going. His momentum carried him forward, into the hospital parking lot, and then he went inside.

She was lying on her side and did not look up. She must have thought he was a medical person. Her little body seemed tiny and vulnerable, tucked in that bed. He felt nothing. No anger, no regret, no longing.

"Hello, Alice," he said.

She turned with no sign of surprise. "It's you. What are you doing here?"

"I heard from Meg that you woke up. I was really glad to hear it."

She said nothing in reply; she just looked at him. Her face was not hostile; it was simply expressionless. That was Alice, as he had experienced her over the years since their divorce. She was business-only. He held nothing against her for that. It saved him a lot of wasted emotion. But it was not easy to talk into such indifference.

"I came to tell you that I located the man who might have assaulted you. I was able to lead the police to his camp. Did Meg tell you about him?"

"Meg Fletcher? I've barely seen her."

Alice's face did not show it, but she grew immediately alert. She had kept her memory of Peter to herself.

"I understand you don't remember what happened," Kent said.

She shook her head. "What makes you think you know who did it?"

"Is it all right if I tell you, then? It won't upset you?"

She shook her head again. "Of course not."

"Meg found a sculpture in your kiln. I think Suzanne asked her to go and check your studio before she went there. Meg thought maybe the sculpture was modeled on the last person to see you. She showed the sculpture to me, and I knew the face, right away. Peter Anderson. I suppose you remember that name."

She would not give him the benefit of surprise. She just looked calmly at him, through him.

All of a sudden Kent was furious with her, all over again.

"Have you been in touch all this time?" he asked. He didn't want it to be true, but he had to ask.

She shook her head, no.

"How did he find you?" he asked.

"That's not important," she said. "It was just a chance encounter. How did you know where to look for him?"

"I didn't. I was lucky. I had a picture of the sculpture and I showed it around the mission, in case somebody had seen him. It turns out he was staying there, and he left the day before you were attacked. I thought that was a pretty strong coincidence, although the police haven't been very interested. I figured that if he was at the mission, he might not have a place to go. Monday I went looking for him, and I found him at a homeless camp up by the old County Hospital. This time the police seemed interested. They staked out his camp."

"But they haven't caught him." Alice felt a cold streak through her heart, a vein of hatred.

"I don't know. I haven't heard."

"Do you have the sculpture?" she asked.

"No, Meg gave it to Suzanne, I think. But I have the picture I took. You want to see it?"

He had put it into his shirt pocket. When he offered it to Alice, he recognized her agitation for the first time. "Alice," he said.

Alice's mind was still stunned from her injury, and thoughts had a sinuous, shadowy quality to her. The photograph of the sculpture, though, had the effect of grabbing her with pincers. Peter Anderson. She had no memory of making the sculpture, but she remembered him. Yes, she had brought him home to sculpt his head. She remembered.

"Alice," Kent was saying. "Alice, what's happening?" He had come close, watching her.

She handed the photograph back, as though she couldn't wait to get her hands clean from it. "I remember. I remember now what he did."

"Oh," Kent said.

"Would you call the police? I'd like to know whether they have him under arrest."

"Yes, I will," he said. "Can I leave you for a minute? Are you all right?"

She nodded, and he walked out into the hallway. He had an aversion to talking on the phone in front of others, and he wasn't sure what it would be like for Alice to hear him talking to the police.

It took some time, but after being put on hold several times, he was connected to Jeff, the officer he had taken to the camp. Just as Jeff came on, Suzanne and Andy appeared. He waved to them and signaled that he was on the phone. They nodded and went into the room.

"Do you want to come down and identify this guy?" Jeff asked.

"You got him?"

"Yeah, he came in last night. He didn't put up any resistance."

"What did he say?"

"He didn't say anything. He denied knowing anything. If you want to come down and identify him, you'll need to get here soon. We can't hold him without more evidence."

"You mean you're going to let him go."

"We don't have any choice. We've got nothing solid."

"Jeff. Don't let him go. The woman he assaulted woke up."

"I know she did. We interviewed her yesterday."

"I didn't know that. You didn't show her the sculpture, did you?"

"Why do you ask?"

"Because I showed her the picture of it this morning, and all her memories came back. It's Peter who assaulted her. She remembers now."

"You're sure?"

"Very sure. Do not let him go."

* * *

In her hospital bed, Alice thought of Peter and that night. She had been in her studio, sculpting, when he called. She didn't recognize the number, but she answered the phone anyway. His voice was lovely. Peter reminded her that he had seen her at the art show. "Do you still want me to model?"

The face was the thing. She wanted to sculpt it.

"Sure," she said, "If we can arrange it. When did you have in mind?"

"What about right now?" he said. "I'm free. But you'd have to come and get me. My car's in the shop."

That gave her pause. She didn't often bring men home. She was always careful.

"Why are you calling me now?" she asked. "It's been weeks."

"I lost your card. I stuck it in my wallet, and it must have fallen out. I just today found it underneath my desk."

"Oh," Alice said. "Where's your office?"

"My desk at home," he said. "I work down in Los Altos, but most of the time I telecommute."

They made arrangements for her to pick him up at Courthouse Square, on the Fourth Street side. In the car she watched him with an artist's eye, assessing how the lines of his face would translate into clay. She appreciated the quick, foxlike way he moved. He might have been a dancer.

"Do you live alone now?" he asked.

She told him she did, but the question raised her guard.

Alice wasn't a worrier. She had never been robbed or threatened, and she believed herself to be worldly wise. What Peter asked could be construed as merely innocent curiosity. She felt no such curiosity about him. He had been just a passing moment, long ago. Perhaps curiosity was to be expected from him, though, since he had been so young. She might loom larger in his life than he did in hers. She put her concerns aside. She didn't worry.

Alice had taken him around the side of the house, straight to the studio. He didn't need to see inside. He looked around the studio as though he was thinking of buying it. She wondered if he was himself an artist. She didn't ask; that wasn't her style. But she watched him.

She soon saw that he knew nothing about modeling. She was brusque with him in telling him how to pose, in scolding him when he moved.

"I can see why you'd rather have a photo," he said.

"Why?" she said.

"Photos do what you tell them. They don't move."

"You think I'm bossy?"

He didn't even smile.

Something he said, or perhaps just something in the way he posed, put her off. His face made a wonderful subject—it reminded her of a figure on a Grecian urn—but when she was done, she found she had no interest in him. He watched while she glazed the head and put it in the kiln. He was curious why she maimed it, and she felt no interest in explaining it to him. She probably was curt.

It must have been obvious that she wasn't going to ask him to stay. Nevertheless, he tried. "Can I cook you dinner?" he asked.

"Did you bring some groceries?"

"No, but I'm a good cook. I'll bet I can make something great from what you have in the house."

She turned down the corners of her mouth and shook her head.

"You don't like me, do you?" he asked.

"Did I say that?"

"No, but you're not very friendly."

"You're not my friend. You're a model."

He shifted the ground and asked for payment. That turned her to ice. She had no use for beggars. "You called me," she said. "I didn't call you."

"You're going to sell that thing," he said. "It's my face. You can't use my face without paying for it."

"You offered it."

"Well, I'm taking it back," he said. "Let me see that thing."

"Don't you touch that kiln," Alice said. "It's too hot to open."

He hit her so quickly, so improbably, that she never got a hand up. It was a blow to the side of the head. She remembered the surprise of it, the sense of impossibility.

That was all she remembered.

Now, in her hospital room, alone while Kent called the police, the experience built in her like a wall of water, like a wave about to break. She had no memory of the violence, other than that initial strike, but the impossible outrage of it, the rage of it, washed through her. She felt fury over helplessness, over the privilege of male aggression that put her in the hospital for weeks and walked away. She had no words for it, only a swirling, hot darkness behind her eyes.

Then her children walked in together. They looked at her strangely. She must show her agitation, which she never revealed. They showed their alarm by going to her, one on each side of the bed, Suzanne gripping her arm.

"I'm fine," Alice said. "I've just realized..." She stopped there. "I'm not going to say."

"Say what?" Suzanne asked, in a voice that made her mother want to hit her. For years now Suzanne had been too persistent, too anxious for intimacy.

"What did I just say?" she asked. "*I'm not saying.*"

Andy asked her what was wrong.

"I don't want you," she said. "I want to talk to Meg."

She plucked the name out of the air. She needed somebody, and Meg wasn't completely random. She could remember hearing Meg's voice. Alice did not want her children to be part of this.

"Not Meg," Suzanne said.

"Yes, Meg. That's who I want. Get her to come."

32 NAVIGATION SKILLS

M eg came upon Kent in the corridor outside Alice's room. He was leaning against the wall with his feet crossed at the ankles, staring at nothing. The recessed lighting along the wall left his face in shadow, but she thought he wore a distracted and worried look.

"What are you doing out here?" Meg asked. She was surprised to see him at all. Alice had summoned her. She wouldn't want Kent.

"I came to tell Alice that I found the guy who attacked her. I thought she might like to know. When I showed her the picture of her sculpture, I think it all came back to her. She got very upset. After she calmed down I came out here to call the police, to tell them she remembered the guy, and it's good I did. They were about to let him go."

"So they've got him? The guy who hurt her?"

"It seems that way."

"And he's in jail?"

It came as a relief to her, like a soft pillow to sink into. She hadn't realized how tense she was. Her ex had been a cop, but she had never so appreciated the law.

Her attention turned back to Kent. "You're just going to stay out here?"

His eyes drifted away from her, as though he were looking for somewhere to rest them. "My kids are in there. I don't want to interfere."

"For heaven's sake, they're your kids. You can't stand out here like a scarecrow. Come in with me." She said it emphatically and pulled on his arm as she opened the door. Her dark eyes had narrowed on him, as if in anger. He followed her in, reluctantly.

As soon as she entered the room, Meg's attention switched to Alice. Some color and energy had leaked back into her slight frame. She was no longer the wax figure. The realization ran through Meg like a warming current, that Alice had survived the worst. Without hesitation she walked to the bed and took Alice in her arms. It felt like embracing a balloon doll: light as air. Meg squeezed, and Alice winced.

"Sorry," Meg said, letting her go. "I'm just so glad you've come back."

Alice gave no answer but seemed content to let Meg loosely hold her arm, petting it with her free hand while speaking quietly.

"What are you saying?" Suzanne asked. She and her brother Andy had taken spots in the middle of the room, not against the wall where Kent had found his place, but halfway between the bed and the door. They watched Meg with a horrified fascination. She was so uncalculated.

Meg smiled happily at Suzanne. "I don't know. Poor thing. You're safe now." She turned her gaze on Alice, leaning over her protectively. "That's what I've been saying, you're safe now."

Then Meg turned back to Suzanne. "Did you know they caught the guy?" she asked. "Your dad found him and now they have him locked up." She nodded toward Kent.

"Really?" Andy asked, suddenly activating his hands and face and looking almost shyly at his father. "You found him? How did you know where to look?" It struck Meg that Andy was like his father in the loose way he held his body. His face was his mother's.

"I didn't," Kent said. "I just looked everywhere. Luckily, I bumped into him."

"Yeah, some luck," Meg said. She was not going to let Kent disappear. "He knew where to look. And he traipsed all over the city searching for him."

"But how did you know who to look for?"

Kent froze. He had to be careful not to say too much. His children probably had no idea of Peter's link to the past. He didn't even know whether Meg had figured it out.

"When Meg went over to your mom's studio to make sure everything was all right, she found a statue still in the kiln. It was a man's head. So we thought it might be a bust of the last person your mom had seen. Just on the odd chance that he might be somebody recognizable, I took a picture and showed it to the men at the mission. They recognized him, all right. He had been at the mission, and he left just before your mom was attacked. I thought, *Maybe he's ended up in one of the homeless camps.* I went looking, and there he was."

"And that's your dad," Meg said, with her wide mouth smiling. "Mr. Detective."

Kent scrunched himself against the wall, embarrassed. He wished Meg would not do that. Though partly he warmed to her praise.

Meg turned back to Alice. "Did you want to tell me something?" she asked. "Suzanne said you had something on your mind."

Alice was caught short. She had forgotten that she had summoned Meg. Now the subject didn't seem urgent. She spoke, but in a tone so low Meg had to lean over to catch the words.

"Say that again, would you?"

"I didn't want Suzanne to know that I brought the guy home."

"She doesn't have to know," Meg said.

"I wanted to sculpt him." Her words were in the lowest register, and Meg could barely catch them. "Then he wanted to stay, and I said no. Next he wanted money, and I said no. That's when he hit me."

Spontaneously Meg seized Alice's hand and held it. "You remember, then," she said.

"I remember the first smack. I thought it was just the one, or I would have run. I don't remember anything after that."

She did in fact remember something, though it was dark and lacking detail, more like a swirling storm cloud than a series of events. The memories repelled her when she tried to approach them. They made her afraid.

Meg's eyes filled with tears, and those tears fell copiously as she leaned over Alice. She made no sound, but Alice felt the wet drops. Her immediate response was to be startled; perhaps no one had ever cried over her like that. Then she reached up a hand to hold Meg's. Now both of her hands were in Meg's.

Meg did not stop crying. This was her helplessness. She had invested so much in being above vulnerability, but it never went away.

Suzanne and Andy watched in fascination. Suzanne felt she should respond somehow, but she had no idea how. She had never seen their mother like this. Perhaps it was the aftershock of the blows. Perhaps it was Meg, who brought it out.

Meg saw them watching and took charge. "Come here," she said, firmly but quietly. "Your poor mother." Andy went to her first, for Suzanne was still of two minds about Meg. Meg put her hands on Andy and brought him to stand where she had been, next to Alice. Then she gestured more emphatically for Suzanne to come, bringing her in close as well. "Your poor mother," she said again, spanning them both with her arms. "Alice, these two were champs. Any time I showed up after work, they were already here. I'm telling you because you wouldn't know, and they probably won't say a thing."

Alice murmured something.

"Say that again, a little louder," Meg said.

"I appreciate you all," Alice said drily. "I'm glad to be alive."

Stepping back to look at them, Meg thought she had done what she could. What a family. The way they kept their distances, even in a hospital room, as though they were repelling magnets. You could pull them together, but they would slide away, back to their accustomed spots.

She glanced at Kent. He wasn't even looking at his children; he was gazing steadfastly at his shoes.

"Do you remember anything?" Andy asked his mother, really looking into her eyes for the first time since he had entered the room. "This guy who attacked you, was he looking for money?"

Alice closed her eyes, as though searching for strength. "Yes, it was money, in a way," Alice said. "He was a model. After I was done, he wanted me to pay him, and I said no. If I do that, there's no profit left for me. That's when he hit me. Without warning."

Andy found it horrible to think of that. "Where did you meet him, Mom?"

"Oh, at an art show. He had an incredible face, we got talking, and I asked if I could sculpt him."

Andy adopted a puzzled expression. "I thought he was homeless. He was at Dad's shelter. What was he doing at an art show?"

Alice's face had gone blank, as though she had been asked to solve a quadratic equation. Kent jumped in. "Oh, you would never believe he was homeless. He looked more like he belonged at the country club." Kent understood that Alice was attempting to wall off the past from their children. Whatever stories Alice had told them, she evidently had not told them about Peter.

"Anyway," Alice said, coming to life again, "I met him months ago. He wasn't at the mission then. He was pouring wine for one of the wineries, and I gave him my phone number, in case he wanted to model. He didn't call me until..." She almost said "yesterday," but realized she had been gone for weeks. "Whenever it was."

"That was really stupid, Mom," Suzanne said severely. "You like his face and you invite him to your house? Nobody is that stupid."

"Apparently I am."

"Did you have the hots for him? It sounds like maybe you did."

"No, no, no!" Alice shook her head, and then winced with pain from the movement. "He wasn't a stranger. I knew him from way back. And I just wanted him to model for me, nothing more."

Andy was following the conversation closely, his head shifting back and forth between Alice and Suzanne. The facts confused him, and he wanted to make sense of them. "When did you know him?" he asked.

Alice realized she had said too much and was silent. She closed her eyes. "This conversation is tiring to me. I think I need to rest."

"Don't change the subject, Mom," Suzanne said. "The guy nearly killed you, and you just told us that you've known him forever. Like when? How did you know him?"

Alice kept her eyes closed and was quiet. Kent saw with a small thrill of panic that Suzanne was not going to be put off. He went to Alice's rescue. "Your mom and I knew Peter way back when you were children. He was in the youth group at the church."

"Really?" Andy said. "This is crazy. It's like the plot of a crime show. What kind of kid was he?"

Kent wanted to answer the question, but he couldn't. Words stuck in his mouth. He could have said, "Just an ordinary kid," and closed off the subject, but Peter wasn't an ordinary kid. He was a kid who blew up a bomb in their home. The question activated all Kent's years of stored-up anguish. He couldn't speak.

"Did you know him, Meg?" Suzanne asked.

"No," she answered. "I've never met him." Meg stayed stuck near the door. She had been ready to leave, but she couldn't go in the middle of this.

"Come on, Mom," Suzanne said, sternly. "You can't stonewall. You knew this guy, you invited him home, he almost killed you. I've been sitting by your side every day for the last three weeks; I deserve to know."

Alice didn't answer, nor did she open her eyes.

"Dad?"

He hesitated, looking to all sides, anxiously seeking a way to keep the peace. "Your mom doesn't want to share this, and I think that's her right." His eyes were wide, seeking agreement.

"All right," Alice said, suddenly, opening her eyes and looking around like an angry hawk. "It's all going to come out at his trial, anyway. When you were both little, Peter and I had a fling. It was meaningless, but it caused your dad to leave. I hadn't seen or heard from Peter since that time, until I ran into him at the arts festival."

Andy swiveled toward Kent. "You said he was in the youth group."

"He was," Kent said. "He had a rocky patch with his family, and he moved in with us until they could get it ironed out." It was a relief to get it out in the open. He didn't anticipate how it would affect Suzanne, however.

She howled and made to hit her mother; her hand stopped awkwardly in the air, and she leaned over as though she had terrible cramps. "You had a little fling? With a kid? That's why you got divorced?"

"It was much more complicated than that."

"So do tell! I want to know how complicated it is to have sex with a teenager living in your home, and then tell me and my brother that Dad left us. That must be some complication." Suzanne began to sob.

Kent moved toward her to offer comfort, but she turned away from him angrily. "I can't believe this family!" she said. "What is wrong with you?"

Kent looked to Alice. She seemed imperturbable. Her eyes were closed again, like someone under a sunlamp.

Meg moved in. She seemed somehow taller than Kent had ever seen her as she took Suzanne in her arms, not saying a word, merely holding her while Suzanne sobbed.

"Kent," Meg said with a voice full of authority. "Talk to your children. This is the time."

He needed a few minutes to understand what she meant. When he did, he was almost elated. For so long he had kept his peace, smothering his desire to talk honestly to his children.

"When you think about it," he said into the air—he couldn't look at Suzanne or Andy—"you'll probably understand why you never learned about all this. You were just children, and though your mother and I never discussed it directly, we both wanted to keep you from bearing our burdens. I'll just speak for myself, they were almost too much for me to carry. I didn't want you to carry them too. And I didn't know how I could explain it without seeming to blame your mom. I realize now that

I was equally to blame for letting our marriage get to that point. You're probably old enough now to understand that."

He sighed deeply, and flipped a glance at Suzanne. She was still wrapped in Meg's arms, but she had stopped sobbing. She was listening. "It was a terrible time," he continued. "I don't know if I've fully recovered yet. And I suppose it's done you both a lot of damage. You had your life ripped apart for no reason. That said, I'm very proud of you both, and I know when you think this through you'll understand better."

"What will we understand?" Andy asked out of the silence. Meg noticed that he had his head down, studying his shoes, in exactly the same pose his dad had been in.

"You'll understand that we are all human beings, and we make mistakes that hurt us and hurt other people."

"I want to say," said Alice, opening her eyes, "that your dad was not at fault. He was just being himself. He loves his damn church and he can't help it. We just should never have been married."

"Okay," Meg said, taking control again. "Enough said. You should take some time to think it over. All of you. And then talk about it more, if you need to.

"It's pretty obvious," she continued, "that you love each other. Suzanne, would you mind giving your mom a hug, or something like that?"

Suzanne was now weeping silently and copiously, but she moved to her mom's bedside, lowered her head to her mom's, and kissed her. She stayed there, resting on the edge of the bed. Andy moved next to her and put his arm around her shoulder.

Kent was leaning against the wall again, his feet crossed. His face had reverted to sadness, watching his children very intently.

"You ready to go?" Meg said to him. "Let's go have a cup of coffee."

He snapped out of his distraction and nodded, whereupon Meg moved back to the bedside. "Are we done?" she asked Alice. "There wasn't anything else you wanted to tell me?"

Alice shook her head.

"Okay, lots of love. I'm gone, but I'll come again soon." She leaned over to give both Andy and Suzanne a kiss. They both accepted it.

Walking down the hallway Meg said to Kent, "We don't really need to do coffee. I just needed some excuse to get out of there."

Kent was taken aback. "Really? I'd love to have coffee, if you have time."

"Let's do it later. That's enough for one day, don't you think?"

Kent widened his eyes to show his surprise. "Okay," he said. "But I do hope we can sit down and talk. Soon."

"I have a lot going on," Meg said. "We'll get together sometime."

She wanted to think about that family before she said anything more to Kent. They were so odd. So disconnected. So emotionally cut off. All of them. She was glad that she could be of some help, but probably it was time to put some distance between herself and them. All of them. What had drawn her toward them in the first place? Because she couldn't deny that something had. Otherwise why would she keep coming back to Kent? Why would she visit Alice so often?

She didn't understand why she had been called. Suzanne had said that her mother had something to say and she would only say it to her. Well, Alice's experience was harrowing and terrible, but why just tell it to Meg? That was very strange, listening as though to a secret, with the children in the same room trying to hear.

And Kent just standing there, watching but saying and doing nothing. Of course, he was in a terrible place. He couldn't do much.

33 VOTE OF CONFIDENCE

" I'd like to make a motion," David Stearns said. "Is that okay?" He got the nod from Michael Tilden, the chair, and proceeded. "I move that it's the sense of this body that we have no confidence in the current leadership of the Sonoma Gospel Mission."

"Is there a second?" Michael asked out of the silence.

Don Markens hesitated and put up a hand, no higher than his shoulder. "I want to have this discussion," he said to no one in particular. "I'm not saying whether I'm for it."

Kent did not think that his face showed anything, but for an instant he closed his eyes, looking for rest. He was so tired of this.

"All right, David, we have your motion on the floor. Would you like to speak to it?"

David pushed his chair back and stood up. He was a tall man, so firm he seemed to be constructed of wooden boards. Kent reflected that David was never sneaky or devious. He said what he thought, and he followed his convictions without fear or favor. *He doesn't hate me*, Kent thought. *He doesn't even dislike me.*

"I believe I've made this argument as clearly as I could a number of times," David said. He had short, iron-gray hair, and today he wore blue jeans and a long-sleeved red-and-black checked shirt. "The important thing that I'd underline is this: the Sonoma Gospel Mission exists as the hands and feet of the Christian community of Sonoma County. It is meant to be a hand-and-glove operation. There should be perfect understanding and perfect harmony between our churches and the mission. I believe that for the most part we've had that.

"For the last few months we've lost that connection. We had the lawsuit, first of all, and you know what that did to our reputation. Right along we had no effective response to that—just a very loud, guilty-seeming silence, and a refusal to take any corrective action. Since then, nothing has changed at all. We just got lucky and the people involved dropped the suit. However, we still have the same people in charge who created the problem in the first place, and none of our pastors in the community know anything about the true story. When the suit was on, our support dried up completely. The next time it will be permanent. The trust isn't there. We've lost it.

"My concern is not just the lawsuit, either. We had a developer willing to buy our building for an outrageously high price, and we as the board never heard word one about it. Not one word. It just happened to leak out later, when it was too late. Now that developer has moved on to some other area, and we are left with an aging, decrepit building, riddled with plumbing problems and needing a new roof. As far as I've ever heard, we have no plans to replace it or renovate it.

"I won't say any more, though I certainly could. I'll just add this. At the moment our finances are okay, and we trust that our ministry with the needy of Sonoma County continues to be effective. It's easy to assume that we are doing fine. My case would be that we are not really doing fine, because our leadership has shown that it isn't capable of taking corrective action when troubles arise, or plotting out the future, or informing the board when opportunities arise. The leadership is just a closed book, and we have to guess what is going on. What little we know isn't encouraging, and what we don't know...we don't know.

"I could say a lot more, but you've all heard me on this subject before. My hope is that we can move ahead today and establish this ministry on a more solid foundation."

David slowly sat down and for a time that seemed to last an eternity, no one said a word. Eventually the chair asked gravely if anyone had anything to add, or any questions. No one did. He turned to Kent. "I don't hear you volunteering to defend yourself, Kent, but I think I speak for the board when I ask you to address the questions that David has raised."

Kent felt tempted to throw it in. He could tell them to run the program themselves, and then he could walk out of the meeting. He knew, however, that he wasn't going to do anything that dramatic. He wasn't that kind of man.

Looking around at the tableful of expectant faces, Kent didn't know what to say. He could explain everything all over again. He didn't have the energy to do that.

"Okay," he said, pasting a lopsided grin on his face. "Let me just say that you are my brothers and I'd like to think that you are my friends. I realize that I haven't always led the way you'd like me to, and I'd even admit I haven't always led the way I want me to. It's quite a hard job, and I was never really trained for it. I do my best. I do my best, I can honestly say."

He stopped there and looked at them. He couldn't get anything from their expressions. Most of them were looking at him, and not at the floor or the ceiling. That was probably good. But nobody was smiling except him, and he didn't know what he had to smile about.

"I'll just say this. I should have told you about the offer to buy the property. I know that and I guess I knew it at the time, although I just didn't want to think about it. I had a sense. I can't explain it, but I still have it. I have a sense that God picks up some tools, and whether they are broken or not, he makes beautiful things with those tools until he puts them down. I've come to the conclusion—not because I think this is something you can read in the Bible, but just by watching and listening at the mission for fourteen years—I've come to the conclusion that the mission is one of the tools that God has picked up. That includes you and it includes me. It includes all our staff, who I think are pretty good at what they do but they certainly aren't perfect. I think I can say that sooner than anybody here." Kent took a breath. "And here's the strangest thing: I think it includes the building. God gave it to us unexpectedly years ago. Some of you were here then. I wasn't. But that's what people have told me, and I've concluded that it's one of the tools God uses, and he hasn't put it down yet. I don't want to be the one to take it out of his hand. That may sound strange to you, that God could love a building. But if he can love me, why not a building?

"I will tell you frankly that I hope and pray God will tell us—you and me—when he's done with any one of his tools, but he hasn't done it yet. Including the building. It's old and it's beat up, and I could tell you about its problems. Nevertheless, countless men have been touched by the Spirit of God in that building. Those walls, they have the sweat and tears and smiles and hallelujahs of countless men. There's an atmosphere in the mission that I can't explain, but I know it matters. When men come in the building, they sense it.

"So unless I get a clearer message than I've got so far—and it could come, it could even come from you, because I do listen to you—I'm not going to forward to you any old plan or offer that comes along. I think we have better things to do. I think I have better things to do, and I think you have better things to do, and I'm not going to waste your time.

"That probably sounds arrogant, but I've thought about it a lot, and it's my conviction. If you think that means I should go somewhere else to do God's ministry, that's okay with me. If you think that I am still being used as one of God's tools, then keep me on and I'll keep on trying to do my best."

He stopped again and looked around. Kent still could get no sense of how his words were received, although it was extremely quiet in the room. They're thinking, he said to himself. *I hope that's good.*

"One other thing. I do want to say that though I know David has a point when he says we should have done something to communicate that we were taking our reputation with the community seriously—and I do take that reputation very seriously—I am not open to firing somebody who did nothing wrong just to save our reputation. I don't believe in that kind of human sacrifice, and I won't do it. We probably didn't handle that whole thing correctly, but God dug us out of our hole, and who can say for sure that he would have done it if we sacrificed Jake in order to show how serious we were?"

He sat down at that, thinking with some satisfaction that he had preached a pretty good sermon, especially when he hadn't had any preparation time. There was certainly no telling how the board would respond. They had a decision to make, and they would have to make it.

Michael Tilden asked if anyone had any questions for him that they needed answered. When no one said a word or even looked as though they might like to, Kent was dismissed from the room. He thought that since the motion technically wasn't about him, he could have insisted on staying, but what would be the point?

Once again he sat in his office and wondered whether his life was about to change dramatically. If they voted him down, he would resign immediately, clean out his desk, and walk out of the building free as a bird. In some ways it would be a liberation. However, not to kid himself, he did not want that.

Don Markens came to get him. As he led him back through the central office, Don said in a low voice, "You won. Easily. There were only two votes against you."

The atmosphere was awkward when he reentered the board room. He was glad that Don had told him the result, because otherwise he would have been sure he was out. Why was everybody so grim? Then he realized it was because David had been humiliated, and they feared he would take it badly.

Michael, who was a stiff, straight, formal man, always in a tie, announced the result. He did not mention the numbers, only that the motion had failed. He said they should proceed with their business, and he would like to call on Kent to make a report.

David raised his hand. His face was always solemn, but now it looked as though he was announcing a hanging. "Mr. Chairman, I don't want to interrupt, but I think it's best that I resign my position on the board."

There were a few quick objections, though not perhaps as many as David might have expected. At any rate, he shook his head at them all and insisted. He got to his feet to make his exit. "Mr. Chairman, I'll give you my written resignation at a later time, but I think it would be easier for everybody if I departed now." David picked up his file, nodded, turned toward Kent and nodded to him as well, and walked out of the room.

"I'll entertain a motion," the chair said, "that we communicate to David our deep appreciation for his service, wishing him well in whatever endeavors God leads him to."

After the meeting, when everybody had gone home, Kent told his secretary Marci what had happened.

"Really!" she exclaimed, and a brilliant smile broke over her face.

"I thought you liked David," Kent said.

"I never liked him," she said. "I always thought he had a slide rule up his behind."

Kent couldn't help laughing. "There's something to that, Marci," he said, "but you have to admit he was a hard worker and a good thinker. Better than most on the board. I think we'll miss him."

She made a dismissive sound. "Good riddance," she said.

* * *

When Kent reached the solitude of his house, he had a powerful wish to call someone. The best someone would be Meg, but he knew he couldn't do that. She had turned him down for coffee and put him off when he tried to say they should get together soon. He had to give it at least a week.

The more he thought of that visit to Alice's hospital room, the more she impressed him. She had been the boss in the room, he wanted to say, but that wasn't quite right. She didn't really boss anybody. She just knew how to convene them. She was fully in synch with everybody's emotions, and somehow she had conveyed to them all, separately and together, that they could be in synch too. It was hard to explain how she had done it, and he didn't think it was conscious. She just showed confidence that she knew what needed to happen.

The thing was, she could help him and his children. She could pull together the split pieces. He was just beginning to understand how much they were split apart.

Kent longed to talk to someone. So much had transpired in his life, and it was all locked up in his brain. He poured himself a glass of ice tea and went to sit on the porch. He thought more of Meg, with a hangdog mixture of misery and longing.

34   A CUP OF COFFEE

By Tuesday, Kent felt he had waited long enough. Feeling very nervous, he called Meg and asked if they could get some coffee. He was not at all sure of what response to expect.

"Sure," she said. "That would be nice. When were you thinking?"

"Any time, really," he said. "We could do it right now." He hoped his eagerness was not too obvious.

They arranged for him to come by her showroom. While she waited, Meg experimented with her shelves of product, shifting sachets and bottles, stepping back to look at them, considering how best they looked on display.

He appeared in the doorway, dressed in a casual shirt and olive-colored slacks. She knew at a glance that he had dressed especially with her in mind, and she was glad for that. He brushed her cheek with a kiss and asked how she was.

"Let's walk over to the Flying Goat," he said, and without further ado they set out. Meg's mood quickly switched to annoyance. Her high heels were not made for walking, as he should have noticed. It was only a few blocks, but not particularly scenic: through the mall and its parking garage, under the echoing freeway where the homeless would sleep when the rains came, and finally down Fourth Street with its small restaurants and antique stores and wine bars. Why not drive? And since he was leading her through this concrete junk pile, he owed her some leading conversation, something bright and distracting. Instead he hardly said a word, leaving it up to her to ask him about his kids and the mission and even whether he had seen the Giants game.

It was not much better when they got their coffees and sat on the leafy patio that bordered the sidewalk. Light filtered down through the sycamore trees, gray and green, and you could observe people passing on foot. The temperature was perfect: warm and light on the skin. Meg found herself annoyed by the lack of conversational skills. Previously, she thought, Kent had been able to hold up his end of the bargain, but today he seemed moody and withdrawn. He did not look at her, either. Why had he invited her, if he wasn't going to try?

She finally got tired of it and stopped talking. He did not pick up the hint. She asked him, "Cat got your tongue?"

He smiled at her, a very likeable, shy smile. "I'm sorry," he said. "I'm just distracted."

"What are you distracted by? Tell me about that. I'd like to know."

He sighed and lifted his shoulders. "Just distracted. I've got things to think about."

Then why did you bring me along? she thought, though she kept the thought to herself.

Just as she was thinking it, a homeless man ambled up to their table. He had hair everywhere, billowing out over his shirt in a red bush and cascading down his back in dark dreads. His clothes were a clown assembly: oversized, brightly colored, made from wool or unblended cotton from another era. As though that weren't enough, he wore broken glasses that tipped to one side. Meg thought he was almost a cartoon of a homeless man. She also thought, *Good grief, get me out of here.* She was not in a mood for beggars.

Kent stretched out his hand to shake. He introduced himself, and Meg, to the man. For a moment Meg thought, *Dear God, he knows this man,* but it was soon obvious that he didn't, because Kent asked the man's name—it was Reggie—and how long he had been in Santa Rosa and how he was getting on. She was stunned. He couldn't talk to her but he was talking to this homeless man.

At first Reggie was close-mouthed—he probably hadn't seen such behavior either—but he warmed up. He came from San Bernardino, he said, and he had been here about a week. Kent asked him if he had a place to stay. For a moment Reggie reverted to suspicion, but he relaxed when Kent told him there were beds and meals at the mission. Did Reggie know about the mission? "I work there," Kent said. "I've worked there for fourteen years."

Reggie didn't know about the mission. He was noncommittal. He changed the subject to talk about the dangers of sleeping by the creek.

When Kent asked Reggie what he was hoping to do in Santa Rosa, Reggie told him he had a cousin who did iron fabrication in Rohnert Park, and he had thought he might work with him. Unfortunately his cousin had disappeared; he couldn't find him.

"You look for him on the internet?" Kent asked.

"No, I went by the address I had and there's nothing there now. It's become a sandwich shop. They didn't know anything about him."

"But if he is still doing the same kind of work, you might find him on the internet. You haven't tried that?"

"How would I do that? I don't have a computer."

"You can use the computer at the library. The librarians are glad to help you if you ask. They'll practically do it for you, if you're not used to the internet. You know where the library is?"

Reggie didn't, so Kent gave him directions. "It's an easy walk from here. You could go there now."

Kent wasn't yet done: he established which side of the family Reggie's cousin came from, and when he had last seen him. To Meg it sounded like a very sketchy connection, more of an excuse for trying a new town than a genuine possibility.

About the time when Meg was ready to scream, Kent finished up. He made sure Reggie knew how to get to the mission and when he should get there; he wished him well and said he hoped he would see him again. After a handshake, Reggie wandered away and Kent sat down with a sigh.

"How old do you think Reggie is?" he asked.

"Hard to say. Maybe forty?"

Kent nodded.

"You think there's any hope for him?" Meg asked.

Kent tipped his head to one side, as though trying out the idea.

"There's always hope," he said softly. "It's hard to even guess how much without knowing about drugs and alcohol and mental illness."

"What's the most hopeful scenario?"

"If his addiction—I'm assuming he has one—hasn't gone on too long. If he doesn't have a record and doesn't need to be medicated." He shook his head slightly, as though trying to clear it. "He could have a lot of strikes against him. But I have seen God do amazing things in men worse off than him."

"You were amazingly nice to him."

Kent gave a little laugh. "I usually like those guys."

"You're well suited to your job," she said.

He gave another little laugh. "I wish I spent more of it talking to men like him, instead of my board." He stood. "I'm going to get another cup of coffee. Do you want something?"

At first she was going to say no, but then she reflected that it was a perfect day to sit outdoors. "Sure, maybe a tea. Hibiscus, if they have it? Or chamomile?"

He wandered off. While he was gone, Meg thought about how comfortable he had acted with Reggie. She was still irritated that he talked to Reggie and not to her, but her curiosity outweighed her exasperation. Was it that Kent liked the lack of pretense? Or was it that he liked being around someone who could never compete with him? Greg would see it that way: people who work with losers are losers themselves, he would say.

Greg's voice still echoed in her head after all these years. That was probably because she was raised to believe the same thing, although in a less extreme way. People get what they deserve. You work your way up the pecking order by sticking to those on their way up with you. If she were really truthful, she would admit that was why she had married Greg. His hard-charging, ultra-confident manner. Which had proved to be a total joke.

Kent returned bearing two paper cups. He set one in front of her. "It's chamomile," he said. "They didn't have hibiscus."

She said thank you and decided spontaneously to plunge in. She hadn't planned to do this today, but she knew she would have to do it sooner or later, and why not now?

"You were very angry," she said, "when I told you how I egged Alice on. We haven't spoken of that since, and maybe it would be better to leave things unsaid, but I wanted to tell you again that I'm sorry. I apparently played a part in breaking up your marriage, which is something I didn't mean to do, not even at the time. It doesn't excuse anything, but we were all a lot younger then. I wanted you to know that I'm genuinely sorry for that."

Kent listened with his eyes, but without reaction. He was surprised by his lack of response. Somehow his emotions had shifted course. That painful past seemed to have lost its urgency.

"I appreciate your bringing it up," he said. "I wouldn't want that to come between us. It's gone down the river, and it's not coming back. You're right; I was very angry when you told me, but I think I've moved on."

"What changed?" Meg wanted to know. "That's a big difference you're talking about."

"It is," he said. "I think it had something to do with seeing Alice in the hospital. And my kids, too. I realized it's all very different than it was when that awful stuff happened. I'm different. Alice is different. The kids have grown up. Time changes things."

His eyes had dropped away from her as he spoke, and now he leaned back in his chair and stared up into the sky. "Maybe what I'm saying is that I'm not frozen in the past. Anyway, thank you for bringing it up again. It helps me to realize that I really have moved on.

"You know, working with addicts, there aren't many secrets. Most of the men, when they come into the program, they've given up on secrets. I find the attitude refreshing. It's healthy, I think, to walk in the light. I'm glad to have things out in the open. Secrets are like wolves that come out at night and attack."

"I guess that's why you enjoyed talking to Reggie. He wasn't playing any games."

"Reggie?" he said, momentarily puzzled.

"The homeless man," Meg said. "Who came up to our table. You were very nice to him."

"Oh, right," Kent said. "I'd forgotten his name. That's not good. I need to remember things like that."

She smiled at him. That moment of radiance beaming from her eyes prompted him to come out with the matter he had been stewing on all morning. "Meg," he said, "I realize this is very sudden, but I want to tell you. I don't want to hide anything. This is just informational. It's not a question. It's like a warning label. I want to marry you."

Of course she had known that for some time. Nevertheless she felt a jolt of terror, like ice-cold water running through her gut. However, she stayed calm. "I take that as a compliment," she said.

"I find myself thinking about you all the time. I know, that's maybe just loneliness talking. Though who says loneliness doesn't get some say? What really made me think, though, was watching you relate to my kids.

I don't know why, exactly. Well, I sorta do. I saw that you pull things together. My life has been so broken apart ever since my divorce, and I think you could help me put the pieces back together. I admire that. I love that. I love your wisdom."

She kept smiling at him, and then, quickly, as though inspired by a sudden impulse, she put out her hand and took his into hers.

ACKNOWLEDGEMENTS

I depend on friends and relations to read my work in various stages and help me see what needs improving. I want to acknowledge, first of all, my wife Popie, who is my best reader and who read this book at least twice. My grown children, Katie, Chase and Silas, also read it, as did my daughter-in-law Helen. Haron Wachira, Harold Fickett, Robert Digitale, Paul Gullixson, Dean Anderson, Mike Fargo, Joyce Fargo, and Joyce Denham all helped me. I believe and hope it is a far better work because of their input! Tamara Beach was my copy editor and a joy to work with. Kiryl Lysenka designed the book you are reading, inside and out. For him and for all these people (and for anybody else I (cringe) have forgotten), I am extremely grateful!

I want also to acknowledge the men I've come to know at Redwood Gospel Mission in Santa Rosa, where I have served for several years as a volunteer. Some of them have become dear friends, and all of them have taught me a great deal.

Made in the USA
Middletown, DE
14 October 2022

12746262R00146